JAGUAR RAVENZ KING

Jaguar Ravenz King

by
J. L. Skirvin

]Elementá[

J. L. Skirvin

Jaguar Ravenz King

Published by]Elementá[– Sweden

www.elementa-selection.com

ISBN 978-91-87751-91-2

]Elementá[is a Wisehouse Imprint.

© Wisehouse 2015 – Sweden

www.wisehouse-publishing.com

CHAPTER 1

HAZY ORBS LIKE HEADS OF BALD BIRDS PERCHING ON SKINNY necks driftin silvery fog that settled over the foot of the bed occupying all space beyond posters to mantel, floorboards and ceiling to tapestried window.

Queen Latezia lay in the fringes of a dream upon the ancient mattress-of-heirs staring at meandering patterns on the ceiling wondering if the queens who'd lain here generations before had contemplated the meaning of overlapping plaster-maze-swirls ending abruptly at cornices' right-angle planes. Then in fits of rage against nature's mandated force she'd slam her fists against its massive thickness, her head kissed at the ears by new feather-down pillows, eyes open…shutting…opening again…watching three heads float in and out, back and forth slowly and silent between her knees. She inhaled thin warm mist; the only comforting indulgence allowed this side of prayer.

What day is this? And the hour? Is it tomorrow yet or today still? I hear no lark's trill outside the sill and see not the sun's shining ray, nor moon's glow.

Perfume's heady silage of rose petal and bergamot wrestles the faint scent of laundry soap causing her nose to itch. Her thoughts turned to Breretyn.

"Look at *me*, Lady Qiaona!" Latezia yanked her maidservant's arm so fiercely the woman's face emerged inches from her own. When Latezia's gaze focused on the dark round pearly marbles that are her lady-maiden's eyes she hissed between clenched teeth, "Where is my

5

husband, His Majesty, King Breretyn? Is he in the castle still?"

"He's here, Queen Latezia, in the chair by the mantle yonder. See his form through the steam there."

"He's here in the birthing-chamber-of-heirs?! Bring his face unto me!"

A look of horror crossed the servant's face and she drew back.

"Your Majesty! What are you asking of me?" came the raspy gasp.

"I don't mean for you to bring his head to me on a plate, Lady Qiaona! For Heaven's sake, I'm not pagan!"

Breretyn's low faintly-accented voice rose above the whisperings of the women as he rounded the bed to pat his queen's knee.Kneeling by her side the king grasped her free hand entwining her fingers with his.

"I only wish to witness the birth of my first child is all, is why I am here in this place, Latezia."

Queen Latezia gazed up at the face of her husband forgetting the present condition of herself in the moment as her thoughts warmed in his strength and beauty.

You are my heartbeat, Breretyn, and my oxygen, the vortex of all my thoughts. Be with me always on this earth.

"Listen to me, husband firstly, good king, Your Majesty! If you love me as you have me believe then you will leave me to my own work in this hour! Ride away on your horse to the hills with the vision of me as your bride in your remembering brain before the next seizure splits my belly like a ripe tomato and a child spews onto these sheets!Bring a buck to roast on the spit or a quail to poach in the cauldron! I promise I will have a child to put to your breast upon your return. Please go." Laboring muscles gripped her belly with an indescribable force unknown in common vocabulary but universally known to all mothers. "Now!"

Breretyn acquiesced to his wife's wish with barely a sigh and bent to kiss her brow. Bringing her hand to his lips he kissed the small round knuckles and sweet wrist of the woman he loves before releasing the limb to the sheet. There is truth in what she speaks, of course. The business in this room belongs to her but the king considers himself a modern husband capable of attending the birth of his own seed without qualm. It is a fact he's harbored in his heart since the moment Latezia conceived his child that his hands would grasp his infant's head as he marvels at its first breath. He stands a man who readily casts aside royal coats and pushes silk shirtsleeves far past his elbows to assist mares foaling colts, the cow's in the season of calving and sheep birthing lambkins and even still each birth is a wonder which never ceases to overwhelm his mind. Ever

But Breretyn's queen languishes in ebb and throe of labor not a horse, cow or sheep.

And besides, Queen Latezia talks back.

So the king rose from his knees and with a feathery sweep of his hand across the flaxen crown of her head, gave his queen her wish and left the midwives to the duty that lay ahead. In the space of time between two heartbeats, he vanished like a fume from the room. Latezia exhaled. Her royal face felt soft intermittent breathy-wisps against her cheek and felt gentle fingers caressing her forearm and she turned her head on the pillows. Her eyes open to see the face of the maidservant she loves as a sister.

Qiaona… loyal lovely Qiaona, you've dipped the crystal spindle-stopper into my perfume flacons again.

"Don't leave me, Qiaona! Clutch my hand thus until the infant is placed to my bosom. Promise me!" Latezia glared at the maidservant and then smiled at the young woman's sympathetic expression.

"Keep your eyes open and gaze only on me, Your Majesty. What you ask is already a promise. See how your hand stays clasped in mine? Calm yourself now as you prepare for the final greatest spasm."Qiaona pressed her face to Latezia's cheek and felt the muscles thereunder relax into a smile. And she glanced to the foot of the bed where Anabaa, midwife-to-the-royals waited and winked.

Is it time?

It is time

In a flash faster than a lightning bolt strikes Constance covered Latezia's nose with soft brushed cotton soaked in chloroform.

Ah, what is the air I breathe? Where is this place I float? I see two fair cherubs hovering above my head…such sweet anesthesia is this air…such plump pink infant-angels sweet…

Latezia succumbed to deep slumber.

"It is a boy child!" squealed Anabaa, Midwife to the Queen. "Oh, how perfect and robust is the babe! King Breretyn's heir is a prince!"

Lizbett and Constance huddled about the midwife holding forth the squalling infant. Qiaona, seeing its tiny arms flail and legs kicking through the swirling mist, exhaled.She laid her head on the bed next the sleeping queen and closed her eyes.

A prince

Water splashes in a basin. A drawer scrapes open along its wooden guides. Towels mound on the bureau. And a baby's wail softens to faint bleats in the warmth of its first bath. Lizbett and Constance chanted tenderly above the infant's head.

A shadow moves a notch across the sundial's arc.

Anabaa screamed.

"What is it, Lightfoot?" whispered the king.

The stallion's muscles stiffen beneath Breretyn's thighs. The beast's great head flinched not atop its regal neck and its large brown eyes glare wide and stoic.Neither nostril flares for scent floats not in air. Crickets' chirping ceases echo in the valley and no grasshoppers leap from the path. Frogs mute their croaks. Snakes hiding in thickets hold their warning rattles.Not a twig snaps in any tree. Even the tufted grasses' blades brush silently against one another in the afternoon breeze.

A magnificent eagle soars as a missile above the canyon's crest arcing heavenward into the sun's brilliance, wings seemingly spread even beyond their tips, its iron talons curled yet empty.

"It's just a bird, Lightfoot!" Breretyn chuckles low and reassuringly while nudging his mount in the belly. "Some lucky hare found its hole in the nick of time, is all. Come now, good horse, let's on to the lagoon where we shall drink and swim!"The king laughed lightly as he tugged the reins. Lightfoot whinnied and tossed his head in the direction of the waterfall, its ears prick at the excitement of what lay ahead for the afternoon hours.

At Half Moon Lagoon's edge Breretyn stripped his body of the royal clothes and slipped into the cool burbling water.Floating on his back at the farthest edge from the basin swelling with the fall's tumbled water he felt its great energy dissipating beneath his back.

I could be tempted to sleep this way forever if a watery mattress could be only be trusted, mused the king, his laughter lost to the fall's roar. And drowsiness began overtaking Breretyn so he withdrew from his swim and laid his body upon soft moss. He closed his eyes against sheer absolute blue of the sky and his body warmed under the high noon sun.

And Breretyn dreamed of the beginning of it all that day when first he saw Latezia shimmering in the street.

"A gold medallion for your stinking blacksmith's garb, Ebo!" tempted the prince as he held forth the glinting coin above the coals glowing in the forge. Ebo's head jerked sideways startled at Breretyn's deep voice, so lost was he to his work hammering Ploughhorse's new shoe upon the anvil. The blacksmith's eyes glimmered at the sight of the royal coin. But he stood his ground and only shook his head.

"What's the problem?" demanded Breretyn.

"My garments reek, Your Majesty. I've been hammering since the rooster crowed and they are damp."

"So? What's the problem?"

"And my boots are caked with mud."

"So, that's a problem?"

Kidskin riding gloves and royal jacket, cravat, silken shirt, and brass-spur boots fling aside in an offhand heap aside the coal bin. Suede pants caught on a tong by a side pocket dangle limply an inch above the rough floor.

"Strip to the bone and your rags are mine for the gold!" Breretyn stood proudly in naked royal fineness hands on hips before the heat emanating from the forge.

The prince waited.

"Oh, come now, don't worry, good Ebo, I'll have your favorite threads back before the sun dips in the west! In the meantime work bare if you must or for my offer of fair rent you will work in my clothes if nakedness causes you to hide your manliness in shyness!"

Ebo recognizes a deal when he hears one and meets a good challenge when one presents itself. But the man also enjoys a certain length of ceremony in undressing. Perhaps the play of disrobing lay in this fault understood as the shedding of hours' experience in the event for which he'd prepared himself in the first place; selecting a garment that suited an occasion to frolic or of work to come, then considering the success of the effort and outcome of the activity his clothing is removed from the body as graciously as it had been considerately draped.

Breretyn waited graciously and patiently, considering.

Both men stand naked warming before the forge now, its deep orange glow reflecting on their skin.

"We are men, Ebo! Bucks, both of us! Adonis' DNA surges through our marrow and in our muscles. You and I stand as men together, equals both in limb and mind."

Ebo contemplated this thought as he stretched forth his arm opening and closing his fist watching muscles bulge and roll over radius and ulna while studying the mass and height of his knuckles.

"How do I look?!"

Ebo turned at the soft command and his eyes widened at the vision standing before him. And he bowed.

"Filthy...shabby...stinking.You look just like me, Ebo, Your Majesty's blacksmith!"

"Perfect then, in other words!"

"Where are you off looking like me, if it is not too forward to ask?"

"I'm off to do a bit of wife shopping in the village, is all!"

"A wife hunt! But I thought King Neptlyn holds balls in the palace for that gathering together the kingdom's most beautiful maidens for you to peer upon and thus make your selection from an easy *glorious* parade of worthy availables!"

"That's just the problem, Ebo!" Breretyn interrupted."No man can select a true wife of kind nature and a gracious generous heart if neck to toe is sheathed in billows of silk and lace, face shadowed beneath deep-brimmed hat, cascades of ribbons and flowers flowing down her back! And what of her manners, Ebo? Who can discern the true heart of thought when conversation in court is veiled in company prose? And such games the eyes do play! Winking and batting of lashes… what invisible message lay between a wink and batted lid? Did you not spy your beloved Fairie among all others as a free man on the prowl then enjoy the time you took wooing her heart until she'd won yours? This way I can shop for my wife as a free man while hiding in plain sight!"

Good point

The blacksmith bowed even lower. Then rising slowly Ebo stood looking earnestly at Prince Breretyn before uttering a comment.

"There is only one problem."

"Problem! What problem?"

"No Ebo I know ever rode into town with a pretty peacock's feather in his hat!"

Ebo rubbed his thumb and forefinger together suggesting a raise in rent forthcoming.

"You drive a tough bargain, Ebo!"

Breretyn flung a second medallion into the air perilously close to the furnace and delighted in his blacksmith's leap as his outstretched hand snatched the coin in hot air. When Ebo regained his composure and turned about to Breretyn his gaze fell upon the prince sitting in-saddle upon old Ploughorse' back, muddy boots in stirrups, reins held in well-worn leather gloves, faded crumpled cap crowning royal head.

"Good luck finding your heart's desire in that getup, Your Majesty!" Ebo laughed.

Breretyn saluted his blacksmith, then nudging Ploughorse in the ribs, turned the animal toward the trail.

It didn't take long for rider on horse to reach the end of Belle Passe. The passageway is the prince's most cherished trail for it affords him the view of the waterfall and its silver mist rising from the basin below. And at the edge of the lagoon just before basin narrows into river a gentle crest allowed the royal traveler to gaze upon his father's kingdom. From the lookout's loft Breretyn scanned the village throbbing with life; avenues of houses, the market boulevards, factories and farms, across vineyard, corn field, and orchard to the pastures and horizon beyond and sky above all.

Villagers swarm in the mercantile trading wares and gossip. Children chase dogs and balls. Birds peck at crumbs in the cracks then rise to the sky to sleep in clouds.

"The streets are especially busy today, Ploughorse! The day is yet young and the maids come to market for cloth and flowers!"

Melons on flatbed carts ripen under the sun's early urging. Heaps of baskets and woven mats lay among kiosks displaying dangling chains and strands of beaded glasslike marbles glinting in the sunlight. Rows of shiny-bottomed frying pans hanging by their handles from nails on posts reflect sunlight like a wall of mirrors.Brilliant woven cloths hanging by wooden pegs sway in the wake of passers' footfall. Buckets bearing freshly cut flowers add kaleidoscopic radiance to the burnished cobblestone street adding fragrance in air. Wind chimes clink and tinkle in breezes while wives planning their meals paw barrels of vegetables and shelves laden fat with crusty brown loaves.

Breretyn rode past huddles of husbands gossiping of policy and commerce in principalities and municipalities to the north, south, east and west of the latitudes and longitudes above and below the fiftieth parallel left of the mountain range and right of the forest to the banks of the river either side of the falls and ocean. Changes in weather patterns are discussed and the general state of farmland soil-science is argued as to the advantages of fertilizing after fall's harvest or before the spring seeding…until,

A diminutive artist hunched on his stool before an easel, palette in hand, brush silently stroking fluid lines of a dancing maiden's gown upon the snowy canvas caused Breretyn to pause in his little travel. Hypnotized by the grace of the artist's movements and mesmerized by the subject matter the prince stares in wonderment anticipating the brush's next stroke.

The maid's billowing gown is sashed high above the waist. Blue ribbons dangling from her hat fly like a kite's streamers free in the air. Golden ringlets bounce on shiny pale shoulders. On little skipping feet appear tiny satiny slippers. Only the face remains blank in its oval.

"Fancy a toke of my cigar, hard-working man?" Breretyn spun about in his saddle at the kind voice and gazed into the upturned leather-skinned face of a tobacco merchant. The man's hand held forth a thick rolled stogie, embers glowing at its end. "It's my secret recipe! My own tobacco plants grown in the richest soil, leaves dried many hours over smoldering mesquite. Ah, scent of sweet smoke and jasmine…exquisite taste of orange peel… Heaven-in-a-Bundle, I call it!"

Breretyn smiled at the merchant seeing that his eyes gleam like black cabochon onyx.

He reached out his hand. But in that instant a shriek shattered conversations' tranquil tone in the street and the clattering of tin canisters bouncing over the cobblestones added insult to the scream. Unaccustomed to such calamity, Ploughorse reared on his hinds and pawed the air with his fore hooves, whinnying and tossing his head. In horror Breretyn glanced at the ground seeing the form of a maiden skidding to a stop face down on the pavement beneath his mount's raised hooves. And in a flash quicker than the sun casts a ray the artist leapt from his stool and pulled the maiden aside Ploughorse' heavy landing thus saving the maid's head from being

14

squashed like a melon beneath thehorse's massive hoof.

But it isn't the radiant laughing visage of his muse dancing in the street that meets the artist's startled eyes but an anguished face contorted in pain, mouth crying out and fearful eyes flooding with tears. Golden ringlets splayed in an arc away from her head. Her hat rolled at a stop against the wall of the tobacco merchant's shack, pale blue ribbons lay limply over his shoes. An empty sack lay rumpled in the street. It took Breretyn but a moment to discern the cause of the girl's accident. The sash of her gown had loosened during her skip-along and slipped from her waist gathering about her ankles thus binding her there and causing hard mean skid across the gravely pavement. The skin on her palms is scraped and bleeding. Dirt and bits of gravel embed in torn flesh. Her knees fare no better. A nasty red blotch bloomed through the fair skin on her chin. Pearly teeth, edges still straight across and sharp give evidence to the escape of trauma. No crimson shows on her lip.

From the corner of his eye, Breretyn spied a group of young boys chasing after the rolling canisters. When he looked into the maiden's eyes he saw two pale blue sapphires watery with tears. Skin pale as milk and smooth as eggs' shells lay across delicate bones. His heart lurched.

"I've lost Mamma's bobbins!" wailed the damsel catching a glance at the empty satchel lying in the street and reaching forth her hand to point at its pathetic limp form.

During the course of her lament the boys retrieved the runaway bobbins and stacked them in a pyramid at the girl's side. Breretyn counted six.

"How many bobbins did you have?"

"Six! I spent my own penny on one as her birthday present for the cashmere she's weaving on the spinning wheel today and now it's gone…lost with the others! It will be a whole month before I can buy her another." her voice trailed away in a wail. "And now my new gown is tattered! Mamma just finished it this morning for my walk into town! I felt so pretty in it and now I've spoiled her toil."Her face crumpled into a sob as she gathered the fabric delicately between her injured hands.

Lifting the maid from off the pavement Breretyn tossed the artist a gold medallion.

"Latch that painting onto my mount's saddlebags!"

"But the work is incomplete!" Then the artist's eyes widened at the sight of the coin in his hand. "This is a gold coin! It is not a coin common among our commerce in the streets as it has the image of King Neptlyn's face engraved on it!"

"Of course it is a coin from King Neptlyn's coffers!" Breretyn thought over a few facts that would not betray his disguise and then settled on this.

"It was given to me for an act of selflessness just as yours in saving this girl from certain death below my mount's hoof just now! It is yours to pass on to the next deserving soul who displays such an act of chivalry! Lay it your breast and keep it with you always. Never forget! It's …*karma*!"

Breretyn settled the damsel in patiently-waiting Ploughorse' old saddle and turned back to the artist.

"And besides, your portrait is simply not finished *today*!" With that he tossed a nickel into an empty paint can at the foot of the easel. "That's fair payment for incomplete work!"

The prince mounted Ploughorse and taking up the reins cradled the sobbing girl in his arms. But hehesitated a moment then turned to the tobacco merchant who had been solemnly watching the scene unfolding before his eyes, cigar in hand still smoldering between his fingers.

"Two silver coins for that box of your special stogies, kind sir! And here's a penny for the sack of sweets hanging from that nail for those boys playing hacky-sak ball in the street for they gathered up this maid's bobbins after her tragedy."

A shrill whistle between the lips brought the boys running to the smoke shack. Satisfied with the ensuing enthusiasm and the divvying up of the sweets among all, Breretyn pressed Ebo's muddy boots against Ploughorse' fat middle, and clucked. The work horse raised its head, snorted proudly, twitched an ear and turned away into the street.

"What is your name? And which way is your father's house so I might take you to him?" the prince whispered above the maid's head.

"Latezia."

The gathering onlookers swept aside as the hard-working pilgrim and the injured passenger rode away on the old mount clip-clopping through the mercantile on rusty horseshoes with a satchel of bobbins clanking against its haunch.

Latezia pointed feebly toward the west.

"My father's house is on Rockledge Strip on the river's right bank. He is a brick-maker and his factory is there. Go this way past the little stone church with the tall steeple to the end of the road and turn the corner at Cluckers Corner where the chicken farm is then go past Potters Furnace where the dishes are kilned and over Billygoat Hill where the cheeses age through Vineyard Valley where the grapes and fermenting barrels are and you'll see a meadow and the river flowing beyond."

"I know where the river is, Latezia," interrupted Breretyn at first chance.

And I know of your father, the brick-maker and of his factory by the river.

Latezia spread her arm-limbs like wide-spread bird's wings over the kind stranger's arms, palms upwardly dangling in the cooling breeze. She leaned her head into the notch of his shoulder and looked up at the angles of his chin, nose and cheekbones. Stubbly whiskers fill in the hollows and shadow his jawline.

Your eyelashes are dark and long and curled up at the tips. In the light of day your irises are the color of jade framing pupils black as kohl.

Latezia closed her eyes and inhaled.

Though your clothes are tired and in need of a washing in extra soap, they smell of diligent labor. I detect frankincense and myrrh beneath. Your hair is glossy and gleams like burnished mahogany under that raggedy cap. Who are you, gentleman-laborer and where did you come from?

Breretyn sensed her upward turn of face and glanced down at her. Her nose did not crinkle in disgust at the smell of him nor did she turn her face away to seek sweet breeze. He saw a smile play at the corners of her mouth. Thin eyelids raised and she looked up. The mist had lifted from her eyes and now he did see sapphire blue and silvery stars shining there.

And I see my reflection in your pupils, kind travelling man…and sense strength beyond compare between these shoulders.

Warming in the overhead sun the maiden's body slumped against Breretyn's chest and her body relaxed in slumber. He wondered at the dreams playing in her mind behind those sleeping eyes and if any of them should be of him, and mused that Latezia is indeed the most beautiful maiden in all kingdom and she is his subject after all. But he feels in his thoughts that she must become more. Could it be that his heart has found his wife without even shopping? Gazing down upon the loveliness that is Latezia serene in this repose, the prince stifled the desire to kiss the top of her golden head.

Can love happen this simply? Breretyn pondered with a slight jolt.

But I reek of Ebo's work and my skin itches inside his sweated shirt, the sun bakes my back and flies buzz about my ears and I don't even care. I play as a free man in an honest free man's disguise and I've found treasure beyond.

Breretyn stopped thinking of words and simply succumbed to an unfamiliar power overtaking his being.

Ploughhorse glided down street and road over hill and through valley across meadow to river beyond joyfully bearing his load wondering the whole of the way what he had done in his life that awarded him this magnificent vacation from monotonous trudging through furrows of dirt in a field with a plough harnessed to his back.

In a fairytale's magical minute the humble trio came to halt at the brick-maker's gate.

"What's this about?" shouted a man on the run down the walkway. Then seeing his battered daughter in a travel-worn stranger's arms, gasped in horror at her injuries and unlatched the lock. "What's happened to our Latezia?" Concern veiled anxiety and pain veiled fear in the father's countenance and onrushing speech.

"Show the way to a place where I may rest your daughter and I will explain the whole of it all," commanded the prince. The group sped through the foyer down the hallway through the kitchen where a braise in a brick oven scented the room making Breretyn's nose twitch…and into a round room with high windows letting in bright afternoon light across the rugs on the floor to the soft velvet sofa laden with plump pillows.

"Bring me a bowl of warm water, and soap and a cloth for I must clean these wounds before fester sets in!" In less than a heart's beat the father returned to the room with a bowl, soapy lather foaming at its rim floating on water still steaming. "Set the bowl at my side and let me work." Kneeling at Latezia's side the prince wrung the cloth in the bowl and then reached for her hand turning her palm up in his.

The father watched as the stranger tended to his daughter's traumatized tissues gently dabbing and wiping away memory of it all with each light stroke. Again and again Breretyn lathered the cloth in the bowl between his hands then moving from palms to knees told of Latezia's joy dancing in the street with a gift for her mother.

"If I could find a man in this village displaying such thoughtfulness and care as you show to my daughter I would happily have him for her husband."

For the only time in his life Breretyn blushed.

Latezia lurched forward from the pillows.

"Father! What's wrong? What's happening to you?"

Startled, Breretyn raised his gaze from his work to see the body of her father fallen to his knees on the floor, rolling his forehead side to side against the smooth polished floorboard showing between rug and sofa.

"Are you suffering a vascular accident?" uttered Breretyn. "Raise your head so that I might better see your face, good sir!"

But Latezia's father only prostrated himself further on the floor, face flat against the shiny floorboard, bowl and gentle traveling man pointing a shaking finger at Breretyn's hand.

The prince looked down at the hand to which the father pointed. The golden signet ring on his sovereign finger glinted brilliantly in the sunlight, cleaned as it became in the soapy water of the matted dirt in Ebo's grimy glove. The rented leather gloves lay cast away at the side of the bowl.

The ruse now up and the disguise failed, Breretyn returned the cloth to the water and removed Ebo's shabby cap from his head releasing waves of soft curls to fall from the crown of his head, over ears to rest upon royal shoulders. The prince took Latezia's suffering hands in his, blew a kiss across their wounds and whispered, "Forgive me this, my lady."

Breretyn pressed Latezia's fingertips to his lips and kissed them one by one before releasing her hands into her lap. Then rising from his knees he came to stand before Latezia's father.

"I am Prince Breretyn, son of King Neptlyn, as you righteously suspect. Come now, there is no need to humble yourself thus in your own house." Breretyn reached forth his hand. "Put your hand to mine, and rise up," urged the prince.

"I knew it!" whispered Latezia "I just *knew* it!"

Breretyn grasped the father's hands lifting the awed man to his feet.

What is it you know, daughter?

The father forgot his wondering the moment he gazed upon Latezia laying in faintly vapor, head deep in the pillows beneath the bay window, dazzling sunlight warming her shimmering ringlets and rouging her cream-pale skin.

A dinner of braise and wine shared at the brick-maker's table brought forthwarm confidence between the two men as Prince Breretyn, son of King Neptlyn explained why he was riding through town disguised as a blacksmith in rented clothes on the back of a lowly work horse for the purpose of shopping for a bride while hiding in plain sight.

～

So it came to pass at the castle King Neptlyn quickly and happily and with great joy and relief the state of the monarchy should continue shouted,

"Long reign the line of my ancestors through Breretyn and heir-

And warm shall remain the seat of our throne!

For it is the brick-maker's daughter,

Latezia, Most Serene,

To be made new wife and queen of my son,

Prince Breretyn!"

Standing before the palace's great high arched window overlooking the royal grounds housing shrub mazes, blooming bushes and flowering gardens in the white glow of a quiet full moon, King Neptlyn raised a goblet and let forth an announcement in a ringing voice,

"Long live the monarchy!"

Crossing his heart, he prayed for a grand-heir...or two

"Long live the noble line of our ancestors! Long live the lives of our loyal subjects!"

And the king tipped the goblet to his lips and drained it of the wine therein in a single swallow.

A great seizure gripped Neptlyn's heart toppling the king to the floor.

The goblet clattered as it bounced at his feet, hollow and dry.

His sovereign crown twirled like a mad spinning top across the stone floor coming to rest

at the foot of the throne.

Legions of seraphim bearing the king's soul fast to their breasts rose swiftly Heavenward...chanting...enchanting...

A vision drifted through Breretyn's dreams of an artist sitting on a stool hunched before his easel in the palace's antechamber, palette and brush in hand stroking sapphire-blue eyes, silvery stars at their corners, nose and sweet lips above gentle chin filling in the blank oval in the portrait of a maiden dancing daintily in satin slippers among diaphanous pink-blue hued clouds in a pale lavender sky.

Lightfoot snorted in Breretyn's ear. Twice

Breretyn roused to consciousness and opened his eyes to blurriness.

Two orbs hang in the sky above his head; one dazzling white and the other softly glowing.

The sun and the moon do beam so closely together? How so?

And he blinked his eyes several times to focus binocular then stared again.

"Only one hot orb does shine on us now, good Lightfoot!" His skin dried of the lagoon's bath and itching with radiation Breretyn dressed quickly to shade his royal self from sun's stealthy damage and mounted his steed. Gathering the reins in his hands and nudging brass spurs gently against its belly, the king shouted, "Onward to the palace, Lightfoot! I have become a father in this momentous hour!"

⌁

"What's happened, Anabaa? What do you see?" rushed Lady Qiaona's whispering words.

"I see a foot!"

"A *foot!* What do you mean…with heel and toes?"

"As I stand here waiting for the afterbirth I see a foot…now two! Purple they are, near black as night! It is a babe…small and black like a tiny bird…but whole with limbs…and head… birthing backward!"

"It's a…baby?" gasped Qiaona.

"Does the queen sleep or does she stir?"

"The queen lies peacefully. The alchemist's potion is working its magic still!"

Qiaona looked on at the trio of midwives gathered at the foot of the bed. Faces stricken with horror turn ashen.

"Lizbett! Bring the firstborn infant hence and place it on Queen Latezia's breast cradling it to her thus to shield her eyes from this tragedy should they quickly open. Hurry!"

As light travels Lizbett cuddled the perfect pink firstborn prince against its mother's bosom. Tiny lips curled in suckling as it found nourishment at her breast before settling itself into sweet slumber. Though Qiaona feels gentled at the sight her heart panics.

"Do what you must, Anabaa, but hurry! Then we will never speak of this event again for all memory of it will be banished from our remembering."

"I will run from here with this purple corpse wrapped in my apron but to where? Is there a secret passageway I might flee?"

When Qiaona looked up to answer only the tapestries swish silently together. Anabaa vanished as a ghost from the room. Lizbett busied herself gathering towels and basin from the bureau and Constance laid a duvet over the bed.

Light flooded the room.

～✑

Two heads lay sleeping upon the pillows. One of golden ringlets combed to soft round curls splayed in a fan about its orb lay next to the other, tiny and seemingly bald but with soft wispy pinfeathers about his ears and forehead. Breretyn halted at the sight of such ethereal loveliness in prime post meridian glow and sucked in his breath in wonderment. Then rounding the bed to his wife's side the king dropped to his knees and laid his head on the pillows next hers.

Tiz two heads I see, beautiful and sweetly dreaming…my queen and heir

And the king slept.

Latezia awakened to the weight of Breretyn's arm across her belly and the warm swaddled infant cradled by her side. A wayward silken tendril of her husband's royal locks tickled her cheek. His fragrance hinted of the river's cool water and she felt the sun's energy still warm in his skin.

Ah, tis two glorious heads I hold close to me in this hour. I knew it! In my dream I saw two but only one is tiny and precious. The other, *royal and greatly loved!*

How does a brick-maker's daughter awaken a king?

Latezia closed her hand over Breretyn's fingers squeezing her fingertips about his, lightly at first then sweetly urgent…now softly commanding…tenderly demanding…until a halt tripped his breath's rhythm and his fingers caught hers in a clasp.

Latezia

Breretyn opened an eye.

My queen teases me!

"Your heir is a son, Your Majesty!" Latezia's whisper feathered his ear. "Raise your eyelids and see for yourself the prince's sweet beauty!"

⁓

"Oh, God! Oh, God in Heaven! Help me! If you but hear only one prayer today, please let it be mine! Where do I run to…what am I to do?"

A candle's flame flickers in its sconce on a wall casting halo on black brick.Voices echo beyond the wall and the scent of beef roasting on a screeching spit over coals wafts in the air.

The kitchen

King Breretyn is back from his hunt so quickly? Anabaa dashed along the stone floor to the light on the wall clutching the tiny lifeless babe in her arms.

A door opened a crack letting light seep across the floor. Anabaa swooped into the room and shut the door. The foul scent of mildew hangs thick in the air. Water drips into a drain causing an eerie echo deep in the pipe. The dark round forms of buckets emerge in the corners amid piles of musty rags. Mops prop against the wall.

"Oh, God, I beg you, tell me what to do!"

"I heard your prayer the first time! The next breath you utter best be given to the child!"

Anabaa lurched then fell to her knees. She gazed upon the little dark face and tiny purple mouth of the being in her arms.

"Put your mouth over the nose and lips of the babe's and breathe the air in your lungs into him. *Now!*"

Anabaa bent her head over the child's face and feels its soft cool cheeks under her lips. The cartilage of its tiny nose pressed against her palate. She exhaled. The child's chest rose, then fell returning Anabaa's breath as puffs of wind against her cheek. So she exhaled again and again into the child pleading with God, the angels, the Holy Spirit and Son Jesus Christ and all the saints whose names she remembers as the thumb of her free hand kneaded its sternum and her fingers pulse the tiny nubby bones of its spine.

A chirping sound rose from the infant's lips.

Anabaa thrust up her head. And she stared.

The baby's chest shuddered as its nose sucked in air. Then came wails from its lungs, faintly at first but increasing in strength, robust and fierce. Heels kicked against Anabaa's stomach. Tiny bony fingers grasped at the strings of her cap pulling it from her head. Her long ebony curls tumbled onto the child.

Anabaa's shoulders shook as she cried in overwhelming relief. In thankfulness the midwife recited the apostles' names in alphabetical order.

"Oh, little black bird, my tiny purple bird, you live! You *live!*" And she rocked back and forth, back, forth, back on her knees with the squalling infant in her arms until a swelling in her breast and an itch in her nipple caused her thoughts to restore unto the needs of the child. Pushing her gown from her shoulder she pressed the infant's lips to her breast and felt the muscles of its lips enclose the nipple and suckle.

"Ah, child, your name for all time shall be Ravenz for you were born a little blue bird but freed now of that ugly black grip...free to soar away to your life...free...my sweet infant boy-bird Ravenz."

An icy chill settled on Anabaa's scalp then crept down her spine causing her jaws to clatter against each other. Goose bumps rose on her arms and she pulled her gown back over her shoulder. The room dimmed slowly to darkness. No water drips into a drain for there is neither sink nor tap. The mops fade away from the walls. The buckets no longer sit among rags for they'd melted into ashes that skitter and roll hesitatingly along the floor before being swept away in a silent wind. The scent of mildew vanished.

Anabaa pressed her palm against a floor she could no longer feel. Her eyes searched the wall for the doorway that no longer beckoned there.

Something surreal is happening! Is any of this real? What is this place my mind is in? Am I in my body still? What's happened to Anabaa, the midwife...mid...wife...mid...

Birth!

And she felt the bundle weigh heavily now on her arm.

Oh, no! Tis King Breretyn's spare heir I clutch in my arms! Queen Latezia lies sleeping in anesthesia unknowing of her firstborn's twin! I'll rush to the birth chamber and as she sleeps and place the child to her bosom so she'll gaze at them both when she awakens!

Then seeing luminescence glimmering beyond the threshold, Anabaa rose with the king's sleeping infant in her arms and dashed into dazzling sunlight.

Stunned by the brilliance of high afternoon sunshine and the vision of green lawns, shrubs, flowering gardens and the gravel walkway on which she stands, Anabaa squeezed shut her eyes and inhaled a long breath to keep a fainting spell at bay and to ease her quaking knees. The snipping of a gardener's sheers pruning a bush, the fragrance of newly-cut grass and rose bloom clippings gently brought her senses to order. She opened her eyes to see the gardener's basket abandoned in the shadow of the lilac hedge. In a single step and a motion of her hand Anabaa slid the lid from the basket, set aside the cuttings and laid the infant in its depth.

I am Anabaa, the midwife, of course!It is perfectly normal for me to have a basket… I'll slip into the servants' entrance and climb the back stairwell entering the far hallway that leads to the birthing-room-of-heirs.

A great clanging of bells, drumbeats and blowing of horns sounded across the lawns and gardens causing a commotion among the servants and gardeners in all corners of the palace and grounds. The royal dogs barked behind their gilded gate. A cat stalking a field mouse relaxed its haunches and meowed. Birds flapped their wings in blue haze overhead. Butterflies rose in masse from a mulberry bush and a dragonfly danced in the breeze. French doors to the royal balcony opened and King Breretyn strode to the hand railing.

Anabaa froze.

"Loyal subjects of my kingdom, I give you joyous news! My Queen Latezia has delivered unto me this day an heir! She has birthed me a son!" The king raised his arm in a grand arc saluting the crowds gathering beyond the iron gates. Then he drained his goblet of its wine and tossed the pewter vessel aside. A tinkling noise accompanied its short journey across the balcony floor. In the next instant King Breretyn raised an infant in the air before his head for all gathered inside and outside the gates to witness.

"Behold my firstborn son and heir, Prince Rhynn!" roared the king. Cheers and applause rose like sweet gentle thunder's roll across the palace landscape.

Oh, no! I'm too late! It's too late to return the babe for the queen has wakened and seen only one child and thus knows only one...Oh...no...no...no!

"Swing wide the gates, guards! Come! Enter! Today our kingdom will celebrate with feasting, dancing and drinking! The groaning board waits! Wine from our valley's vineyard spills over goblets' rims! The musicians are strumming their instruments!"

Iron wheels squeal in their brackets and hinges squawk in protest as massive gates rattle across cobblestones. A horde of bodies swarmed across the lawns toward the palace steps and portico. Butlers swept open the banquet room's French doors letting free the aroma of deeply roasted ox to float like thick fog in the air.

Anabaa vomited.

Tender grass shoots tickled her nostrils and her eyes closed, face upon the ground, body lost in the shadow of the lilac hedge succumbing all else to blackness.

"Is she dead?"

Anabaa's upturned ear heard far off voices echoing like trade winds through a mountain's corridor above her head.

"She smells dead."

"She doesn't look dead. The skin of her lid flickers."

"And her chest rises with breath."

The ear pressed against the earth hears distant retreating rumble but Anabaa's body feels caught in a swirling crosscurrent as a war of arms gather about her body pulling limbs at their sockets, lifting her shoulders, grasping her head turning her face so sun's fierce light shone through the thin skin of her eyelids. The scent of lilac, honeysuckle, rose and soap filled her nose. The steely grip of one's arm crosses her ribs and a cool palm clasps her forehead. Generous softness of belly and bosom now cradle her shoulders and head.

Anabaa moaned.

"We've been looking everywhere for you!" whispered Constance above Anabaa's head.

"Why are you here picking flowers in the king's garden and falling asleep in his hedges?" demanded Qiaona.

Anabaa's trembling voice passed through quivering lips, "A cloudy moon rises…" and she lifted a shaking finger pointing to the sun.

"What cloudy moon? The day is summer solstice! It is Earth's longest day and the sun shines high in Heaven's vault still! The moon is to be full tonight, glowing silver in its finest hours."

"The whole kingdom celebrates with dancing, feasting and drinking in the castle for today King Breretyn's heir is born!" chimed Lizbett fluttering her hands.

"You yourself attended the queen! Why did you run off in haste like that?" Qiaona's face hovered so closely to Anabaa's that the midwife felt puffs of breath against her cheek with each syllable uttered her way.

Constance rocked Anabaa back and forth, back…forth…back in her arms as a boat lists on an open sea.

Stop doing this, Constance…stop!

Anabaa retched.

Qiaona reared back.

"What is this sour swill you lie in? What illness consumes you to cause such queasiness?" Constance' faint breath tickled Anabaa's ear.

Anabaa pointed feebly toward the balcony, turned her face into the hedge's lengthening shadow and shuddered.

"What of the king's balcony? What happened above its hand railing to cause this awful fear in you?" Qiaona searched Anabaa's eyes.

Anabaa turned her face toward the mound of discarded blossoms and stared at the gardener's basket a long moment before turning back to see Qiaona's visage awash in honest concern.

Your simple mind is vacuous, Qiaona and your memory bankrupt… only joy at the birth of one heir consumes your single thought.

"There is truth in all you say, Qiaona. I am Queen Latezia's midwife and I attended the birth of her *first* infant son." Anabaa spoke in a flat low tone, slowly, firmly."And while I waited for the afterbirth to expel I saw a second babe emerge feet first, blue…almost black as night, even. Terrified, I ran from the room with the tiny corpse wrapped in my apron! I prayed the whole while I ran down the stone hallway until I came to the mop room there behind that great wall."

Anabaa pointed toward the castle's east side, flat but for a row of high arched windows opened wide to let in cool afternoon breeze and where gay tones' of dance music playing in the ballroom within floats over the gardens.

"What mop room? There is no doorway at all to the place you point! And what is this nonsense about a purple baby? The queen's baby is a healthy pink robust boy!"

"I thought the tiny infant dead but as I clutched it hard to my chest it nudged against my breast with every step thus causing its heart to flip in weak beats. I fell on my knees to the floor and put my mouth over its nose and mouth and blew the air in my lungs out into the babe. I blew and blew again until a chirp rose from its tiny blue lips and its fingers pulled the ribbon of my cap and it fell from my head. I cried tears as the babe began to wail and kick its legs! Then my breast swelled and when my nipple itched I placed its tiny lips to my bosom and it suckled there! I sang and prayed thankful words. I named the little black bird in my arms, Ravenz."

Anabaa closed her eyes and covered her face with her hands. Her body shook as if ice had taken hold of her bones so Qiaona grasped at her arms and rubbed them up and down with her hands furiously trying to warm cold flesh.

"And then a terrible memory swept over me that I had run from the room with the queen's twin hardly a moment burst from her womb. I searched for the doorway to the hall I ran down but I could no longer see the way I had come and found sunshine and lawns instead! In panic I stole the gardener's basket and placed the baby to the bottom of it. I was about to dash up the servants' stairwell to the birthing chamber and replace the infant to Queen Latezia's breast with the first child but then King Breretyn stood on the balcony there and held up his firstborn heir for the crowd gathered at the gates to see!"

Overcome at the memory, Anabaa's face crumpled to a sob. "Too late and sick with panic my knees turned to mush and I fell on this ground. After that I remember nothing."

"You babble, Anabaa! You have lost your mind!"

"No she hasn't," uttered Lizbett's flat reply. Startled, Qiaona and Constance looked up to see Lizbett kneeling over the basket, her face bent downward, eyes wide open and peering. "Come, see for yourselves. What she says is true. All of it…is true!"

And the others gathered at the basket and looked on the face of the infant asleep upon remnant rose petals fallen from their stems; innocent work of a gardener's pruning, and all memory of the day's event in the birthing chamber-of-heirs rushed into their minds flooding their beings with the anxiety of it all and what it all means now.

Qiaona, Anabaa, Constance and Lizbett huddle together tightly, arms bound about one another, heads upon each other's shoulders and rocking as one back and forth…back…forth seeking solace…seeking air…seeking an answer…seeking a way…until,

"What happened in the room after I fled?"

"Lizbett gathered the towels and basin from the bureau and Constance covered the queen with a silken duvet while I sponged her face and combed tangled ringlets into curls over the pillows. We swished aside the tapestries and light flooded the room! In that instant King Breretyn stood in the doorway beholding his Queen Latezia asleep with the babe at her side. Ah, so regally-beautiful and sun-bronzed stood he at the side of the bed gazing upon his fair wife with a look of tenderness I greatly envy." Qiaona's voice trailed away in a hum at the rhapsody of it all. "We departed the room silently then, and did not look back."

"Qiaona?"

"What is it, Anabaa?"

"If you are here stroking my arm then who is it attending the queen?"

"Why, her mother, of course! And her father sits by her side!"

The lyrical strains of a lullaby filled the air as Lizbett swayed on the grass before hedge, bush and flowering garden, singing in her girlish voice while holding the infant, Ravenz, wrapped in her shawl on her arm.

"What a miracle you are, sweet babe in the land,

Tiny and free bluebird to fly castle in King Breretyn's realm!

Over kingdom's gates will birdie be free to learn and be

As the tinker,

And bell ringer,

Bread-baker and candle-maker!"

"What are you doing, Lizbett?" shrieked Anabaa. "Someone might see!"

But Lizbett kept up her joyful singing,

"The king has his heir! And we; his spare!"

"Lizbett!" screamed Anabaa.

"You are a midwife and we are all *women*, are we not? It is perfectly natural for us to be in the company of babes." answered Constance in soft creamy voice.

Lizbett chants,

"You are the luckiest boy-babe in the land for you've *four* godmothers!"

Anabaa collapsed to the ground.

"Gather yourself, Lady Anabaa. Lizbett sings the truth." Constance's soothing voice gentled an anxious attitude. "The child was born to Queen Latezia *dead*, Anabaa, but in *your* arms he was given *life*! The outcome of this riddle is a mystery and in Ravenz'

34

journey only will the meaning of its reasoning unravel. Lady Qiaona accesses the castle every day for she is the queen's first maidservant. By way of her firstly, Lizbett, you, me and the child can pass freely through the gates. He will learn the speech, manner and way of the royals and lessons of the realm but will be a fee man of the world with the countenance of a prince in whose soul flows the blood of a king!"

Anabaa raised her head and gazed Heavenward. Her eyes softened to powdery blue and the crease between her brows vanished. Her lips quivered as if on the brink of a smile but instead she asked,

"Are the babe's eyes clear and do they focus? Does he watch as you sing, hearing with his ears respond peacefully, and comfort?"

"Ah, baby boy Ravenz sees me with both eyes twinkling green as emeralds, and his tiny lips smile at my silly song! He is so pretty, like a wee chick, pinfeathers curling about his ears and forehead."

And the midwife reached up her hands to Qiaona and Constance and each pulled Anabaa to her feet. They all joined in Lizbett's little dance about the blooming bushes and through King Breretyn's lilac hedge mazes, circling granite statues of ancestors gazing into each other's stony eyes across the reflection pool smooth as a lake, then under the trellis over a footbridge, around the bubbling fountain toward the opened gates.

"Let's take leave of this noisy celebrating place and take infant Ravenz to the world of King Breretyn's people!"

"I want to hold him now!"

"I get him next!"

"I get last dibs!" laughed Anabaa as they skipped over the gates' threshold and into the roadway beyond.

"Last dibs!" giggled Lizbett. "What request is that, '*last dibs*'?"

"Well, unless something mystical happened to any of the three of *you* I don't know about, I believe *I* am the only wet nurse among us! Our little birdie will need feeding eventually!"

Anabaa smiled.

CHAPTER 2

THE EAGLE WAITS

Gnarled talons curve as crescent moons, steel-tipped claws digging into the rough log beam extending below the castle's eve, exactly where it had landed an hour ago seeking refuge in the overhang's shadowy cover, such welcome relief from its aerial journey under sun's blaze circling above waterfall, along river bank, then soaring skyward from deep canyon's side to cross heather meadow around gentle forested knoll toward the stone castle that came to be the horseman's final destination.

The great fowl arrived first for far easier is the way of the firmament and easier too, does curiosity's satisfaction fill at tracking a beast's deliberate footfall picking its way along earth's knotty pathways.

Long since had the eagle recovered from its loss of the hare gone to hide in its hole for far more interesting to the bird than its failed dinner was the view of a man splashing naked in the lagoon as his horse pranced free of its reins circling thickets, kicking up its hinds and fore-hoovesin frolic. Perched on a limb in a brave tree's branches grown high above forest's canopy the eagle whiled away the noon hour watching with unblinking eyes as horse grazed and man slept.

The animal brushed its lips against the man's cheek causing him to rise from his dream and in the space of a heart's beat, mount the steed and turn away from his play.

What manner of beast is this and what of its way? What cause nudges urgency now as its hooves click upon the trail casting dust clouds up in its wake? Who is this rider leaning over flank, face close to pricked

*ear, four eyes in two faces pressing forward...gaze at the horizon...as
the steed gallops onward?*

Now only the strength of its grip kept the eagle from falling off
its perch, so startling is the sound of royal bells clanging, blaring of
horns and drumbeats resonating across the castle's vast lawns over
the high iron gates to the valley beyond. Though tumultuous the
noise and odd the event the great bird's eyes never left their focus on
the ebony-haired woman crouched over a gardener's basket in the
shadow of hedge and bush between flower garden and gravel
pathway. The small thing asleep in the basket intrigued the eagle far
greatly above drama unfolding on balcony and lawn, in ballroom
and on banquet table. For the object appears to the eagle's eye as a
newly hatched bird, head poking above its soiled sheltering wrap,
eyes closed tightly against sun's glare. Pink is its skin, and bald is its
tiny round head but for a hint of pinfeathers about its ears and
forehead.

*And what manner of mother is this to sleep on the grass at her nest's
side, with chick hidden beneath the thin cover of reed lid?*

And there appeared four mothers on the lawn huddling about
their nest, all bodies enclosed in each other's limbs, free of warring
and each unselfish until one scooped up the chick and twirled
herself about the bushes and flower gardens singing as she danced.
The eagle sat rigid, motionless on the log in camouflage of shadow
and eve, its gaze following the head of the chick as its silly young
mother drew closer. For a moment's fraction did the infant's tiny
face turn upward, open its shimmering marble-green eyes to meet
the blazing white gaze of the eagle's own.

The chick's lips parted as if to smile.

The eagle blinked.

Lizbett spun away in a waltz, the babe's face now turned to the
others.

Four women skip through hedge's maze, around bush and flowerbed over lawn, circling granite statues guarding reflecting pool then over footbridge, around fountain over gate's threshold and onto the roadway beyond, twittering in strange high tones the whole while cradling the chick to their bosoms.

The gardener's abandoned basket lay cast aside the gravel pathway in the wake of the women's hasty exit. Only a stack of cast off limbs retaining fading blooms lay in a scattered mess on the lawn. Forgotten shears long dropped to the grass glinted in the late afternoon sunlight. No human occupies ground or garden. No sentinel stands at the gate. The cat stalking the mouse bounded ahead of the crowd up the palace's steps disappearing into the foyer with thoughts of a fresh giblet...*a giblet!... a giblet!*The speedy mouse darted to refuge under a turning leaf. King Breretyn's royal dogs quieted their barking upon a butcher's toss of an ox's femoral bone.

In flight to the earth faster than a lightning bolt strikes the eagle came to rest on the basket's rim, eyes peering down upon rumpled soiled linen forlorn on a wilting-petal mattress covering cold darkening depth.

What manner of bird's nest is this and what of this odd shell lying on foliage's sweetest cushion?

And the eagle lifted its wings and soared away from this place over gates and open roadway circling high in sky over the heads of ebony Anabaa, ginger-locks Qiaona, ample Constance and tawny Lizbett. The bird flew in diligent guard of the four, its majestic wings' shadow moved as a black ghost upon the ground absorbed in shadows cast by great trees' limbs, the acute focus of its eyes never leaving the shiny head of the babe asleep on arms.

The wind uplifting my wings belongs to me as the earth bearing their footfall belongs to them. I am Eagle, royal in this sky kingdom as the jungle cat is king of the forest.

Cascading river water over the falls camouflage the crunch of the women's footsteps upon the pathway's fine gravel as the full moon's silvery glow shone through the shrubbery lighting the gateway's steps. The lamppost's blinking hazy-green beacon gently beckoned. The massive oak door quickly closed against the night quietly enclosing four women and an infant within the shelter's brick walls.

The eagle soared upward in the pale night sky free of mottled cloud and quilt of fog driven to flight by incessant gnawing happening in its belly. The bird swooped low over Half Moon Lagoon snatching a coppery-scaled top-feeder from its thin watery cover. As stealthily as the eagle had descended upon the unlucky fish it soared high in the heavens with dinner wrestling to stillness in its talons. And the great bird with incandescent eyes gazed down as it dined from its narrow perch on rocky ledge to peer through a window where a candle flame's flicker made dancing shadows on a wall within.

The silhouette of a woman's foot pressing a cradle's rocker slowly up and down, up…down…up…down and the babe's tiny fingers clutching its blanket…eyelids twitching in its dream entranced the majestic fowl where it sat hypnotized by the sight.

The flame burned to the end of its wick shuddering away into smoke. In darkness Anabaa looked up to the night sky into what appears to her eye two perfectly round stars, brilliantly white and closer to Earth than all others…*unblinking…unblinking*

Latezia turned her face from the high arched windows where her gaze had followed the full moon's glide along its nocturnal orbit until blackness filled all space beyond the pane. The serene mother's face lifted upon her daughter's movements on the pillow and the woman smiled at the girl-queen lying in silken linens on the ancient mattress-of-heirs.

"Come closer, Mamma." Latezia's outstretched hand beckoned her mother rise from the chair and sit by her side on the blankets. "We are alone here as I see no maidservant and Breretyn is gone to his guests."

Mother-and-grandmother-in-one leaned back on Down-fat pillows and silently swore she'd never felt such loft in cushioning in all her life nor felt such luxury as silk sheets smelling of lavender soap. And her hands locked in a handclasp entwining Latezia's fingers with her own. The woman looked to the ceiling and seeing swirls in the plaster wondered at the queens who laid here looking upward before birthing baby kings-to-be.

"He is beautiful, isn't he, Mamma?"

"Your infant son is a prince, Latezia! Of course he's perfectly beautiful! King Breretyn is off with the babe in his arms to stroll about the castle's gardens. Your father accompanies him, too!"

"His Majesty is happy then? With *me*, I mean?"

"Of course the king is deliriously happy with the mother of his heir!"

"He said not a word to me when he first looked at the infant boy I made for him but simply scooped the babe up in his arms and sped away from this room! My lungs vacated their air as I called after him! I called and called…calling his name, 'Breretyn! King! Your Majesty!' and yet he did not turn back, Mamma!"

Latezia's face crumpled and tears rimmed her eyes and a sting came to her nose.

"Oh, child, come now… come lean your head in my arms, sweet daughter and listen to your mother as I say to you these things. The symptom you suffer now is completely natural for only women who are true mothers can feel it. Your husband feels a spark in his heart upon the reception of the child in his hands the same as you felt the spark of his seed unite with your egg in your womb! What seems a joy lost from our body in the moment of birth becomes a bountiful gift in the arms of the father who's waited nearly one year to experience this joy! What pains forced this loss from our belly is simply great nature's first nudge along a mother's pathway-of-letting-goes, is all.Did you not see how the king looks at you with those green eyes of his softly glowing? You merely take his breath away!"

The mother silenced a moment as she stroked her daughter's head. Her fingers play with a platinum curl.

"What makes you ask such a question, Latezia?"

"Breretyn was here in the birthing chamber-of-heirs nearly all hours while I labored to deliver his child."

Latezia's mother reared forward from the pillow and glanced down in horror at her daughter.

"*Here?* The king was in this room as you struggled to bear his son? *Why?*"

"He wanted to witness its birth, Mamma! I just couldn't get my mind to accept His Majesty seeing me like that so I beseeched him to leave at the most crucial hour! I *commanded* the king to leave his queen! Has anyone ever commanded a *king* before, Mamma?"

"Not that I know of…but it's about time! And I'm glad it was you, daughter! No man should witness a wife in birthing distress." Her words fell on deaf ears as Latezia's face turned away to the window, eyes glazed, gaze distant…but searching.

A brick-maker's daughter

"What is it Latezia? What is this trouble that sobers your countenance?"

"After Breretyn departed the room I breathed deeply in grate-fulness and then I dreamed behind sleeping eyes that I saw two tiny winged cherubs floating above me. What's it all mean, Mamma? Did you dream thus in your final moment and awaken to see me in your arms?"

"All manner apparitions drift through a woman's mind as she works to bear her child! You have two eyes so it's reasonable you could see one cherub in each."

"But one babe floated closer…the other flew up and away. Can either eye see independently of each other? Has that happened to you?"

Latezia's mother sought answers in her mind but could recall no similar experience. But Latezia carried on with her tale.

"And when I awakened my eyes I saw only one babe at my bosom but Breretyn's head lay in slumber on the pillow by mine." Latezia paused as her mind reasoned for an answer. "That must be it then, the meaning of my dream, that the midwife put the babe to my breast while Breretyn was turned away."

"What? No midwife or maidservant present in the room when you awakened?"

I did not sleep in the final moment as I remember it all still to this day; seems as yesterday my baby girl Latezia was held up squalling and kicking before my eyes.

The mother kissed the top of her daughter's hand and rising from the bed went to stand at the window.

These modern ways baffle me so!

"The king carries the babe to the reflection pool where his ancestor's statues stand guard. Your father walks with King Breretyn as he has no father, of course. A prince is not king with his father still living."

"The royal child's lessons begin so soon, Mamma?"

"The king is proud of this day, Latezia. He's showing off his heir, is all! Let him to his babe, daughter. A man carrying an infant in his arms tenders him properly."

The woman paused in her observations to gaze upon the scene on the lawn below the chamber's sill.

"Ah, the king stands by King Neptlyn's statue now! I can see his eyes looking up to that marble face. The king's mouth speaks as he holds baby Rhynn forth…and his face is wet with rivers of tears flowing from his eyes! I see a glow above King Neptlyn's statue! I swear I see a halo forming, a beam emanating from the whole of it, even! Before my very eyes I see granite luminescing! I didn't know stone had such properties!"

"Mamma?"

"King Breretyn's face glows like white marble in rain!"

"*Mother!* Go back to the part of this wet face you speak of! My husband's eyes *cry*?"

"Hush, Latezia! Your father and the king are returning to the castle in haste!"

Even before mother-grandmother-mother-in-law-in-one turned away from the window did she and Latezia hear the king's voice, "Our son, Prince Rhynn is needy of a rinse and dry clean linen! And he squalls for his supper!"

Latezia watched her husband fumble with the child as her mother filled the basin with water still warm in its cauldron. Soiled cloth fell away to floor. In a heartbeat the baby's kicking heels splashed foam in Breretyn's face as the king lathered his infant's tiny head and round belly.

My husband is bathing my infant? How naturally he goes about this chore as a mother does.

"Grab a towel from the bureau's top drawer there, please, good father-in-law!"

Latezia watched as her father, the brick-maker fluff up a towel from the bowels of the drawer and spread it widely to receive the whimpering babe. Never had Latezia seen any man perform such work and her heart softened to mush as her eyes watered to their rims at the sight of her father and a king fussing thus over her child.

"Latezia," Breretyn strode to the side of her bed, "my end of things is complete here. The next order of business belongs only to you, my queen!"And without hesitation, shyness or apology for his next action King Breretyn, husband of Latezia, gently slipped the silken gown from his wife's shoulder and away from her breast, then placing the child in her arms encouraged his infant son's lips to suckling his mother's nipple.

The baby contented itself, eyes closing in drowsiness.

The king lay next to his queen upon the ancient mattress-of-heirs where he himself was brought from his mother's womb to first light and putting his head to the pillow next hers took Latezia's free hand in his and kissed the small bones of her knuckles one by one. Overcome by emotion and the whole wonder of the day, the king held her wrist to his lips...*gentlykissing ...lingering tender*

Latezia's father took his wife by the elbow and patting her arm 'til their hands clasped together, departed the chamber in silence and did not look back.

Oh, Mamma, should I become half as wise you.

CHAPTER 3

"IT'S TIME, ANABAA."

"I know, Qiaona. Just give me one more moment."

Qiaona wonders why Anabaa could possibly need another moment. The windows lay darkened beneath heavy shutters. All the furnishings are covered with layers of clean muslin. Journey's necessities stand tightly packed in bags like pickled fishes in jars. Jumpy Lizbett fiddled with fading silk ribbons dangling from the ends of her hat. Gracious Constance appeared as if silently praying for her lips moved in speech though no audible words escaped her mouth. A soft plump hand caressed her heart. Qiaona nuzzled baby Ravenz to her shoulder, her right hand gently cupping his head as his babe-voice cooed sweetly in her ear. Still, Anabaa stood rigid on the threshold as one overcome in bone-depth fear, eyes fixed and staring, features stony, hands gripping the door knob to the point where her knuckles showed white through the thin skin of her hands.

"It's not like this is the first time we've spent winter at court, Anabaa."

King Breretyn had been pressing Qiaona about moving into the castle for more than a week. Word in the mercantile told of the almanac hinting an at an early snowfall thus ushering winter over the land at any hour. Leaves had barely begun turning before shuddering to the ground. Nights had grown increasingly colder. Logs in the fireplace smolder till dawn.

And still Anabaa hesitates.

Lizbett did something next none of the others had seen the

young maid do ever before. The girl took initiative.Perhaps she is simply impatient to leave for the palace for even though its labyrinth structure lay confined within high gates and stone walls, the mecca of it all offers dizzying exploration of the myriad of artifacts sheltered in mazes of rooms, poster beds on high platforms bearing thick wide mattresses...ah, such feathery comfort to come...and food on tables tasting far beyond compare. But the entertainment! Beyond imagination! Dancing 'til midnight, musicians' strumming, swirling satin dresses, young knaves in coattails... royal dogs to run, kittens to pet, King Breretyn's ponies to ride along trails anywhere endless. And Christmas, of course! And Easter

Perhaps Lizbett has grown simply bored ofwaiting...waiting to follow directions given by others, waiting to walk in explorer's footpaths laid down before her, waiting while others call shots manipulating moments while persons like she, Lizbett waited. So agile Lizbett and youngest of all and who loves to skip and dance, hop and bobble overtook Anabaa's body in a single motion scooping up the midwife from where she stood paralyzed at the doorway and spinning about with the woman in her arms kicked the door closed with a bang! The brass knocker thudded against old oak. The latch clacked shut in its bracket securing the bolt. One shutter dared rattle but a trifle.

And that was that.

Stunned, Anabaa stood on the walkway and stared after Lizbett's willowy figure dancing ahead all others swinging a gardener's basket in one hand and a necessaries-bag in the other, though not her own. Lizbett's bag remains left at the cottage's gate. It matters not one whit to the girl if Anabaa totes it along for the king's tailors will measure her body forhis royal seamstress' to needle new dresses and his cobblers to mold her arches in soft white plaster then later sew satin slippers over her toes.

Ah,the hats! Oh, the hats; ribbons and feathers, bows upon rows of

bows! Oh, the hats, such hats!

"Toddle along at your will but I'm off to the castle, to court! To court I go a-skipping!" Lizbett's girlish voice sang out as she hopped over stepping stones and along the pathway.

She did not look back. Her ears being as young as her spirit soon picked up the soft echo of footfall shuffling along gravel as three ladies and a baby rushed up from behind.

Lizbett giggled.

"King Breretyn spent all last week putting the staff to preparing Mountainwing's thirteen rooms *just* for us! Imagine, Qiaona, waking to sunrise on high purple peaks!"

"Thirteen rooms are not just for *us*, Lizbett! Widows, the infirm…and the orphans will be sheltered there."

Anabaa quickly interrupted Qiaona's cold-splash.

"Your bag is too light, Lizbett! Did you pack *nothing*?!"

"My toothbrush and comb, of course…and some cotton stockings and my pink sleeping shift. And we can see bucks and doe come out from the forest to drink at river's bank, andred foxes and snow hares in chasing games there!" Lizbett held fast to her focus.

"I adored our East suite last winter best," sighed Constance.

"That's only because of Queen Latezia's maternity, and the king's desire that we hover near, is all." Qiaona picked her way around pebbles and damp clumps of fallen leaves turning to mounds of limp mush in the roadway.

"The queen has taken to her feet now with Prince Ryhnn clutched to her bosom and traipses up and down hallways in and out rooms gazing at portraits and sniffing bloom's fragrances in giant bouquets bunched in vases sitting before tall mirrors. It's better for us in the west wing's rooms what with baby Ravenz along."

A child's emerald-green eyes gaze long to the way from which he's been carried from threshold down steps through gateway now along road, head resting upon shoulder in an arm's secure grasp. His ears hear soft voices but his gaze catches two tiny orbs glowing white in the bush.

The bird-baby sees that I follow

Lifting its wings to the gust upwelling their tips the mighty eagle lofted skyward arcing over treetops along road's edge.

I am hovering, small chick and guard.

"Why is the babe quiet now? I hear no coos from his lips." Anabaa turned back at the child's sudden silence. "Oh, I see it! Squirrel darts there, is all, acorns puff its cheeks!"

"Lizbett, stop this chanting-dance of yours and put down the basket! See the great turrets piercing the sky above the castle gates there? Baby Ravenz sleeps now!" Qiaona whispered. "It's time for his cover!"

Anabaa froze in her tracks.

Too soon

As her eyes watched Qiaona lay fair sleeping Ravenz on the straw basket's feather mattress and cover over the whole of him with its lid Anabaa's heart raced its beats though her feet can move not. But Constance's lips close to her ears spoke these words,

"Come, Anabaa, This moment of arrival has come for the babe." Whispering breath tickled Anabaa's ear causing in her a shiver even in late September. "The way of our journey from here is a mystery to us now but this mad riddle we find ourselves in will reveal itself in the course of *Ravenz'* way."

Sweet gentle fat Constance, there is truth in those words you speak, but a lie at the heart of conspiracy clouds my reason. I can't breathe…breathe! Breathe! Sweet oxygen, don't fail my lungs now!

The scent of lawn and summer's last blooms lingering in hedges wafts into Anabaa's nostrils filing her nose and swelling her lungs.

Old iron wheels clattered upon cobblestones and hinges complain loudly in rusty brackets as guards swung wide the gates and bid the four women enter King Breretyn's castle grounds.

Ebony Anabaa, ginger-locks Qioana, ample Constance and tawny Lizbett skipped up palace steps, glided under high portico across majestic threshold ushering light footfall through foyer to hallway beyond.

Anabaa whispers,

"The three of you take our things and the basket to the west's Mountainwing rooms while I pay Queen Latezia a visit. I have not seen her since the birth and I will be a distraction. Qiaona, she sees you three every day."

Anabaa glanced about where she stood alone in the foyer deserted there in ultimate silence surrounded by marble and stone in all its forms gracing the space above her head and beneath her feet and all walls about her sides. Gleaming silver urns overburdened with branches bearing berries shine on bureaus lining a hallway. Rising mid-morning sunlight beaming through a high window lit the floor to snow-white glow and Anabaa floated across it entranced. When her eyes looked into the parlor from whence the light filtered she saw the dark silhouette of an artist sitting on a high stool hunched before an easel, palette in hand, brush swiftly stroking lines on a vast white canvas. Mesmerized by his movements Anabaa stood silently under the grand archway.

Queen Latezia's face turned to the figure shadowing the way.

"We have a guest, Parqai. Rest your brushes and move about a moment. Take nourishment from the fruit platter on the table under the window's ledge."

One serene sweetly-accented voice nudged the spellbound midwife to turn her head at its sound and her gaze fell upon the regal countenance of young woman posing on a crimson velvet chaise. She sits gowned in ermine and satin, strands of jewels bathing young white neck, a tiara of pearls and twinkling diamonds grace her head. Thick platinum ringlets fall to her shoulders. Chandeliers of sapphires dangled from her earlobes. In her arms lay an infant sheathed in embroidered silk robes. Seed pearls adorn the little cap covering his head. A ribbon loosened itself from the tie beneath the child's chin and tiny fingers grasped it free of the other pulling the cap from its curly-haired head. The babe's head turned away from its mother and in that instant emerald-green eyes lock with Anabaa's own.

An icy chill gripped Anabaa's back.

Vertebrae rattled the length of its rack.

"Welcome and come forth!" Latezia extended hand, warmth in her voice beckoned Anabaa closer. "What is your name…and what is the cause of your visit to His Majesty's castle?"

Anabaa dropped to the floor in deep curtsy, forehead nearly touching the tops of Queen Latezia's soft kidskin shoes white-pale pink the color of seashells. The shoes smell new. The queen smells of powder.

"I am Anabaa, the midwife. I assisted the birth of your infant son, Prince Rhynn, three months-ago-to-the-day."

"Of course! *Now* I remember your face! Your hair flows free of that skull cap today! I did not recognize you at first because of that but now I see! Forgive me, but at the time I was quite lost in the chore of birthing." Latezia laughed easily and low. "Come closer, Anabaa! Look at the babe King Breretyn and I made! See for yourself how he's grown in beauty and how quietly he lies now in babe-sweetness!"

The silk cap now fallen away to the floor exposed soft blond curls playing about the heir's ears and onto his forehead. Anabaa's breath caught in her throat as her eyes stared into tiny glimmering green gems. Riveted where she knelt, the midwife stared at the child in Latezia's arms and sees.

Ravenz! An identical twin! Identical...the first is the same as the second is the same as the first!

The child's cupids' bow lips moved not a twitch nor did his eyelids blink.

"Oh, Queen Latezia!" gushed Anabaa. "Your infant son is...*beautiful*...truly a marvel...*perfectly identical* in *every* way!"

Tears welled in Anabaa's eyes then and her lips tremble in rapture at two babes' mirror likeness. Her shoulders shake in their sockets as incomprehensible relief warms her quivering bones.

"Identical? What do you mean, *identical*, Anabaa?"

Anabaa's heart banged against the bony confines of her ribcage like a rock knocks about the bottom of a dry bucket. But she calmed herself by clasping her hands together as if in prayer and pressed them to her bosom. Looking deeply into Latezia's warm star sapphire-blue eyes, she spoke in a soft gentle tone.

"The heir is identical to King Breretyn and identical to *you*, of course, Queen Latizia! See Prince Rhynn's platinum-golden curls turning into ringlets, *just* like yours!" whispered Anabaa pausing for emphasis while regaining her composure. "And his eyes are pure *Breretyn!* His Majesty's eyes are green, like jade as I vaguely remember...it's been three months to the day...of course..." her voice trailed away in a hum. "The babe owns the king's jaw but his cheeks and forehead are all *you*, Queen Latezia!"

"You are right, good midwife! Silly me. Why would not a child resemble its true parents thusly? Exact duplication of a few of their parts showing forth in a babe is Replication's greatest receipt for the hour two procreators' spend..."Queen Latezia's eyes grew dreamy halting her lips' breathy reply.

Anabaa exhaled but did not look up to meet the queen's unblinking warm gaze but stayed on the visage of baby Prince Rhynn, so magnetic the pull of his eyes to her own.

What secret does your exaggerated expression of joyful relief camouflage? I scent milk in your bosom veiled under that lace...a babe's lips have been there.

"The portrait is complete, Queen Latezia. I'll turn the easel about for your eyes to behold, if that should be your wish, Your Majesty." The artist stood bowing, eyes downcast and hands clasped behind his back, just aside Anabaa waiting patiently for the queen's command.

"Oh, please turn it about, Parqai! I've been sitting here for hours and am simply dying to see it!"

Anabaa rose slipping aside the chaise to stand near the wall clearing the queen's view.

A gasp rushed from the queen's lips as she lurched forward on the chaise clutching up Prince Rhynn to her bosom pressing him there with her palms. Anabaa turned at the sound of gown and robe softly rustling as Queen Latezia rose and saw the woman's widened eyes staring. Nothing else moved at all in her face.

"Does the piece... *please* Her Majesty?"The diminutive artist asked in a hesitant timid tone.

"It's the most *breathtaking* painting I've ever seen in my whole life! How did you *know*, Parqai, of the dream I had of two cherubs with those same tiny wings flying so delicately behind my closed eyes, *exactly* as you have depicted them here! I awakened from the birth to find my infant prince and King Breretyn asleep at my side!" Latezia moved closer to the canvas with her child to stand in awe of the scene before her eyes. "How did you see this amazing thing,

Parquai?"

Anabaa stepped out from the shadow of massive fern fronds overhanging its pottery box on the ledge above her head.

What is this ridiculous story of a dream...two cherubs flying...birthing and waking

And then she saw what Queen Latezia sees. Barely visible to the naked eye and nearly lost to transparency in a sky painted the sheerest lavender hue hover two fair sweet-faced identical cherubs above the queen's head. Neither babe flew forward, upward nor away but linger tenderly there. For a fleeting moment Anabaa saw tiny diaphanous wings oscillating ever so slightly as cupids' bow lips blew feathery kisses over Latezia's cheeks. Anabaa stood transfixed, hypnotized.

Dreaming...birthing...waking...one infant...and king...Oh, no! I'm too late...too late

The floor began to heave upward and spin slowly away beneath Anabaa's feet. She raised her hands to her face shielding the sight from her eyes and to steady the sway. But her ears remain opened to the sound of the artist's low soft voice.

"I did not see these little beings at all in the beginning, Your Majesty. But when this lady happened into the room and fell to her knees to adore Prince Rhynn did the cherubs appear flying above where you sat there." Parqai pointed a bony finger to the empty space in the air above the crimson velvet chaise that only moments ago held Queen Latezia and her infant son.

Anabaa turned her face to the spot where the artist pointed only to see the babe's head above its mother's shoulder facing back, its sparkling emerald-green eyes turning jade-green cool then icy white-blue, obsidian-black pupils glinting at their centers. The reflection of herself emerging in the eyes' round deep pools stare back.

Anabaa fainted away in a hard fall to the floor.

What mischief does this absurd behavior conceal, woman?

~~~

"Is she dead?"

"She doesn't smell dead."

"She looks dead!"

Anabaa's senses rose to consciousness upon hearing voices swirling about her ears like water tumbling over rapids. Though her body felt elevated and moving forward in bumpy flight it lay in tight bondage; iron-strong arms holding her fast against a frame hard as brickwork and fingertips as steely talons digging into soft places between ribs and over bony kneecap. Her head dangles on its neck exposing her face outward.Behind closed thin-skinned lids light beckons from beyond.

"Something laid an egg on her head!"

"It's a goose egg, Lizbett!" King Breretyn's unmistakable deep soft voice rose above Anabaa's head, above all others.

"A goose? How could Anabaa let a goose do such a thing!"

"She fainted flat away to the floor! Her head hit the tile hardly, is all! And now she has a great bruise rising." Anabaa felt a change in the course of their direction; a sway to the right and light behind her closed eyelids shading from gray to white.

Thirteen rooms…Mountainwing's row…west… purple peaks…deer…foxes and hares

"In here! We'll set her down here!"

Something hard rose up from the ground to meet Anabaa's spine and her head stopped its bobbing as her neck went limp into her chest. Soft nubby fabric feeling like wide-wale corduroy invited her fingertips to play innap's ridges. A cushion happened beneath the midwife's feet and she worried of ankles and hems.

"Ice! Oh, good speed, Bazil! And such fine chips in this bundle! Hold it thus to the injury." King Breretyn's voice drifted away like fleeting wispy winds as a deep icy shudder raced from Anabaa's crown down spine clattering vertebrae through belly to femurs rattling tibias and fibulas in its wake. Ankles to toes felt nothing but air.

Summer...September...October...winter

Someone gently enclosed Anabaa's limp cold hand between palms radiating warmth like molten rock. She opened an eye, then two. Shadowy figures hover in haze until Anabaa blinked once, then again. Qiaona's image came into focus at the foot of the sofa clutching an infant in her arms.

Ravenz? Prince Rhynn? Which one of the two of them is him...?... Anabaa turned her face from Qiaona to see it is Queen Latezia's warm hands clasping her own. *Oh, Latezia...Latezia*

"Two! I *brought*...one...back! *You have*....two...*babies*...back!" Anabaa's mind processed sentences but her lips only spewed a stammering stream of meaningless words.

"Two back? She's come to! She'sback, Latezia! How many fingers am I holding up?" Breretyn waved two fingers before Anabaa's eyes.

"Two, Your Majesty. I see two."

Queen Latezia held Anabaa's hand to her cheek then kissed the top of her hand. "You are back!" spoke the queen in hushed tones. Anabaa saw the tiara glittering on the queen's head though her snowy ermine shawl had been cast off. Golden ringlets rest on white creamy shoulders. The scent of powder rises as invisible fog in the close space between them and Anabaa thinks of the queen's pretty new shoes.

And she remembered Ravenz' tiny green eyes.

"I…two…majesty…heirs…"

"Air? Open the window a crack, Parqai! Let the breezes in! Lay still now Anabaa, so the injury can…" interrupted Queen Latezia.

"How could you run off to play with wild geese like that?! You fell on your head and a Jersey laid an egg there, Anabaa! You could have been killed! But don't you worry! King Breretyn has shown Bazil how to hatch it under an ice bundle he holds over it here!" Lizbett pantomimed the insult and ensuing treatment pointing to prominent places on her own head. "Jerseys are the worst meanest gooses of *all* geeseness, Anabbaa!"

A tear welled in Anabaa's right eye as both orbs rolled back in their sockets under semi-closing lids.

Ah, sweet precious dumb Lizbett, I love how you love me like that.

"Shush! Shush, Lizbett. Don't scold Anabaa so. 'Tiz an *injury*, is all. She needs quiet voices and rest. It will all be over soon." Constance wrapped her plump warm arms about waif Lizbett's shoulders attempting to draw the girl from the room.

King Breretyn rose from his knees.

"There is a chair reserved for you in my new university, Lizbett, just as soon as the last brick is mortared."

"Really, Your Majesty?!" Lizbett gasped. Then her voice turned somber and low. "But…but I've never been *anywhere* outside this old city and the universe is…well… *big* beyond mountain and river. It's all new…*to me*. Who would go out with me, I mean…and what's a chair reserve?"

Shuffling of shoes' soles on marble tile caused Anabaa to open her eyes. She focused on the image of King Breretyn's signet ring glimmering on his royal hand cupping Lizbett's head then tilting her chin upward to meet his unwavering jade-green gaze and the lovely kind way his lips move when he spoke to his simple subject.

57

But a gusty coo coming forth the lungs of the babe Qiaona held in her arms shattered the spell.

Constance and Lizbett vanished in a fume as Breretyn turned to the infant reaching out wee hands for his father. Anabaa sees two twinkling green gems in the face of the cherub, lips parting as if in a little laugh. Softly-flowing embroidered silk robes swirl about the child's bare toes as the king scooped his son from Qiaona's embrace.

I see now… You are baby Prince Rhynn…firstborn and heir.

The infant prince waved a pudgy palm in the air over King Breretyn's shoulder.

A confession tripped on your tongue just then and now dozes on your lips, woman.

And the baby turned to the face of his father and did not look back.

Anabaa closed her eyes and exhaled slowly feeling lungs compress beneath her heavy bosom like shriveling balloons forcing the last whiffs of their air through her nostrils. She waited until the lungs screamed in her thorax for oxygen before inhaling new air smelling faintly of essential oil and lawn. When at last Anabaa opened her eyes it was to Bazil's thick wrist hovering above her brow and Queen Latezia's tender star sapphire-blue gaze.

You possess a gentle soul …serene and kind… Anabaa felt courage surge through her veins in the flush of her tongue's forthcoming confession.

"Latezia…first…two…black…bird…I…back…"

The queen pressed her fingertips to Anabaa's lips silencing hesitant babble. Anabaa lost focus as the hypnotizing scent of an elixir's pure extrait of jasmine, freesia and patchouli wafted from the queen's hands.

Ah, sweet perfume…heavenly-potent is thy anesthesia.

"Please don't speak, Anabaa," whispered Latezia. "You served me dutifully through my laboring days and birthing hour. I will remain the same here with you.Close your eyes unto sleep and dream now 'til wellness comes into you."

Anabaa felt fur tickling her cheek and caressing her earlobes as her bones turned to smoldering kindle beneath ermines' gracious skins.

This story is not for my telling but for Ravenz

Anabaa slept.

◦◦◦

"Oh, thank heavens! I was hoping I would find you here! The baby must starve and fuss so! I simply couldn't leave Anabaa's side and it took forever for her to wake up! My breasts are so full I'm about to spew as a fountain! Iswear I must have enough in these things for two... *times* two!" Latezia floated across the parlor's glassy marble but then halted midway in her flight at the sight of her king standing before Parqai's work; mute and seemingly paralyzed so entranced is Breretyn by the artist's masterpiece.

Latezia glided to a stop at Breretyn's side softly brushing his elbow so as to not fracture the moment or startle the king to fear. And she saw them again just as she'd remembered the moment Parqai turned the canvas; two identical winged-infant angels hovering in the heavens' translucent pink-lavender skies, wings oscillating, charming tiny lips in fair plump faces blowing air-kisses falling as snowflakes on pearlescent shoulders, tiara glittering, Prince Rhynn's eyes twinkling.

"Itisdreamy, isn't it, Breretyn? What does it mean...that an artist's recognition of a vision forming is captured in his brushes and portrayed so...I *wonder*." Baby Rhynn turned his head at his mother's whisperings and upon seeing her face sprung forth his little arms opening and shutting his hands fiercely demanding. "Ah, little heir, you are such a sweet good boy! Come, come to mamma and fill your belly full now."Latezia lifted the child away from its father's arms and turned toward the crimson velvet chaise.

"Be still, queen," rushed a whispered command. Breretyn's hand enclosed about the nape of Latezia's neck. Warm fingertips lightly caress the ridge of her clavicle, thumb softly nudging atlas and axis...gently...patiently...riveting Latezia to the place she quit her step.

"Why are women's gowns engineered thusly entrapping all necessary parts so stubbornly?" In the hush of Breretyn's whisper royal satin slid from Latezia's shoulders to billow at her feet freeing her bounty unto the king's eager child. Little Prince Rhynn contented himself at her nipple, his sweet hand lost to her cleavage. "The savages inhabiting rainforest and savannah have the whole of life right, Latezia. Naked do they run in their ways free to grow and to give holding nothing back wasting not a minute more."

Lataezia stared into her king's eyes seeing her reflection and that of his heir's tiny curly-haired head captured in their large warm pupils.

There is a reason you and you only are king, Breretyn for you see things and know far more.

"Come, sit now." The king's hands caught at his wife's waist, his lips brushing her forehead. "Our child dines peacefully."

But Latezia could not move a step so overcome was she in this moment. The only motion her being could conquer was that of allowing her heart's command. She raised her face to Breretyn and leaning forward to his lips placed a kiss there, lingering...longing.

"I love you, husband, King Breretyn, Your Majesty, sir."

"Oh, look! Anabaa's come back!"

Constance, Lizbett and Qiaona gather about Anabaa. Their eyes search the woman's forehead for telltale signs of trauma as their expressions sought to discern the state of her wellness.

"Bazil hatched the egg! It's completely gone! Did it hurt when the egg cracked, Anabaa? What happened to the gosling?" demanded Lizbett.

"Come closer and sit. Let's have a look," soothed Constance.

"I'm good and well! But my breasts swell to their brims with baby Ravenz' supper! He must be fussing about his neglected belly! Has he been quiet in sleep or does he squall?"

"See for yourself how calm little Ravenz is and how peacefully he watches all this!" Qiaona muscled her way between Latezia and Constance hovering-over. "He's been asleep the whole while in his basket and just awakened as you entered here. He doesn't know a thing has changed in the course of the day at all!" But the babe Ravenz, seeing the source of his nourishment sitting serenely amid pillows and chintz sprang forth his chubby arms, hands opening and shutting…fiercely demanding.

And the child contented his hunger at Anabaa's breast, its sweet fist lost in cleavage.

Anabaa looked up into three kind faces to see the images of her face and Ravenz' tiny curly-haired head reflecting back to her in their eye's large warm pupils.

The way of all this will be alright with Ravenz, Rhynn and King

Steely gnarled talons gripping the branch loosened a bit, but the eagle's stellar-white eyes never blinked so fixed had their gaze been on the closed straw basket before and on the curly-feathered head of the chick now. In the depths of great cedars' darkening shelter the bird relaxed its wings about itself, enclosing a majestic body in its own feathery shell of security.

Little boy-chick, I hover...I soar...I dive for you, brave little boy-chick laying there.

CHAPTER 4

"IF YOU VALUE THE PRETTY SKIN YOU STAND IN YOU'D BEST stop this twirling, Lizbett!"

"But the taffeta shimmers so magically in this light, seamstress Penelope! It's impossible for my feet not to move even the tiniest bit on this crazy little stool!" Lizbett pleaded her case to the seamstress' cap-covered ears.

The seamstress did not look up or halt in her pinning of free edges together, sleeve or hem. She shuffled herself about on the burnished wooden floor moving up or down as the gown's pattern demanded and Lizbett's fidgeting allowed.

"These new steel pins are especially slender and extra sharp! If I am to finish this dress before winter solstice's masquerade ball and before your skin becomes scabby and scarred you'd best stifle yourself unto stillness!"

"King Breretyn is giving a masquerade ball? Where are we to find fancy masks in the height of winter here behind the castle's gates? The river is frozen over and no boats bring new goods. How am I to hide my eyes in the course of the yule dance?" Lizbett's voice quivered close to the edge of a childish whine.

"All these things arrived from the Orient on the ships with the king's fabric bolts just this summertime past! Such pretty masks, too; pearl encrusted with lace and ribbons streaming down and feathers and crystals adorning the eyes' holes! And the colors! There is a mask to match every shade of gown! Just you wait and see, Lizbett! You'll be the prettiest maiden dancing in Champagne Hall at Christmastime! But if I'm to get these armholes right you must stand *still*!"

"Is it permissible for me to sneeze? I feel an itching creeping across my inferior nasal conchae and it's tickling my nasal turbinate unmercifully!"

The seamstress reared back and looked at Lizbett's eyes. "What strange language is this on your tongue, maid?"

Ah choo! Lizbett inhaled. *Ahh chooo!*

"Sneezing! It is breath's own language expelling from the diaphragm." Lizbett brushed her fingertips along the bridge of her nose then pressed delicately at her eyes' tear ducts.

"No, before the sneezing part, the words you spoke of conch shell and tickle... Where did you hear such words, maid Lizbett?" Penelope stopped her work, slender steel pins glinting like daggers bobb up and down between her teeth. Her hands cupped Lizbett's fragile white shoulders as if to steady a teetering porcelain figurine on a pedestal during an earthquake.

"In King Breretyn's new university, of course! He reserved a chair just for me in a theatre there so I can hear stories told to me for an hour! There are giant pictures of a body's insides hanging on walls; all painted such colors! Rouges...hues of blues...shades of orange, purple, pink and yellow, all outlined in black kohl! Muscles and tendons that work for walking and laughing glued on bones. There is a real skeleton hanging by a hook in its head from an iron frame in the corner of the theatre! It has all its ribcage bones and vertebrae in a string of knots down the way of its back here. And the skull has real teeth anchored in the mandible! Both its feet have metatarsal bones and the hands display phalanges." Lizbett pantomimed yesterday's lecture pointing out phases of it in vocabulary she remembers on her own body.

But the conversation is too full of exotic vocabulary for seamstress Penelope's mind to process, she being in the middle of an incomplete gown's pinning, an hour's worth of needle-sewing looming and at least two hours of beading afterword yet…so with a faint sigh the woman proceeded onward in her labor about the armholes making little grunting noises as she pushed long sharp steel slivers through iridescent taffeta attaching a sleeve.

What use is this university…and for a girl to know such things, I wonder? An hour listening to such storytelling but the words…great and wondrous words my ears have never heard! Is all this truth or is it merely silly legend to entertain a young girl's mind? I want to hear words like that. I wonder if I could slip along for an hour of storytelling?

"Lizbett?"

"Oh, I'm sorry. Did I move or did I forget to move?" Lizbett glanced down at Penelope.

"Do you skip out to the university by yourself? Do you think I could go along just once to hear the stories? If it's just for an hour I could work into the night with an extra candle burning and then take the beads and a needle in my satchel to work on the small garments. I wouldn't make any noise."

"Bako accompanies me the whole way by King Breretyn's command!"

'Who's Bako?"

"Bako is Ebo-the-blacksmith's son. Ebo is the husband of Fairie and father of Farayya, Fairie's daughter who is Bako's little sister. She comes along too and is practicing drawing her letters and numbers. Farayya already knows how to read two short words and she's only four! Bako talks endlessly of polynomials, real coefficients and complex zeros occurring in the conjugate pair theorem." Lizbett paused in her answer upon catching her reflection in taffeta radiance in an old oval bronze-edged mirror leaning against the closet wall.

"This Christmas gown is very beautiful, seamstress Penelope, and I like cherry-red terribly much! It would be prettier still, like a blossom even, with some snowy white fluff outlining the shoulders and bosom here, you know, like Queen Latezia's mink trim." Lizbett's voice sighed like a dream humming. "But white seed pearls will do just as finely, and some lace gathered along with snowy ribbons perhaps." And then she remembered Penelope's wistful wish and replied, "Of course, Penelope, please come along with Bako, Farayya and me to the university and listen to an hour's worth of storytelling and picture-looking. King Breretyn encourages it, of course!"

"Perhaps after Christmastime when the galas and feasts are done and the winter months grow tired and empty of activities. I still have all the orphans' costumes to finish yetand the ball's solstice hour draws quickly nigh."

"The babies are going to the ball, too?! In *masquerade* costume?"

"They aren't *all* babies, Lizbett. Two are toddling and three are as big as five and six. And King Breretyn and Queen Latezia have arranged with their wardens that a small ballroom is to be decorated with a great manner of toys; rocking horses, dolls and drums for all the children wintering here. There will be sweet treats and trinkets stuffed in woolen stockings hanging from the mantles and musicians playing nursery carols on fifes and lutes! The little ones shall dance about in glee of it all, their pretty faces hidden behind kitty-cat, bunny-rabbit and cocker spaniel masks! It is to be a surprise till the very last minute! So, hush yourself about it, Lizbett! Don't forget! Not *one* word!"

Lizbett's ears closed to the last words falling from Penelope's lips for her mind was racing ahead to thoughts of baby Ravenz' first Christmas in the castle mingling in disguise among all others seeing for himself his King and Queen in this realm and everyone in their kingdommattering equally importantly.

And you shall see Prince Rhynn; firstborn and heir, little Ravenz, second-born-by-a-minute and identical to the first-brother and heir

～

"Anabaa!" Lizbett whispered as loudly as possible without waking the others. "Are you sleeping or just lying in wakeful dreaming?"

The lump in the eiderdown shifted slightly and a head reared from a bank of pillows.

"What is it, Lizbett? Are you ill?"

"No! Even better! I'm only going to share this news with you and then you can make plans about the matter once you hear it all."

"What are you babbling about, Lizbett? The hour is late and the temperature dips. It's too cold to be thinking thus in the dark."

"No, it's not! Listen to me, Anabaa. Open your eyes so I know you listen!"

"For heaven's sake, spit out this crazy news that can't wait 'til morning!" Anabaa spoke on the brink of hissing.

"There is to be a masquerade ball on winter solstice night just at the twilight hour before the big ball begins in Champagne Hall!"

"So? It's called the mingling hour, a reception with crystal flutes filled to the brim with pink champagne bubbles teasing the nose with sparkling-tickles 'til all guests are light hearted and laughing in well-meaning spirits. What's so secret about what you are telling me that can't wait?"

"It's not a holiday dance for *us*, Anabaa! It's a party for the orphans and all children wintering in court! A separate smaller ballroom is to be decorated all in toys and such, with dancing music and musicians even, sweets in stockings, for Christmastime! But the best part is this!" Lizbett leaned closer to Anabaa's ear and put her hand to Anabaa's cheek to steady the woman's gaze to her own and back again for insurance. When Lizbett was certain she controlled Anabaa's unblinking attention she continued,

"The little ball is to be a *masquerade* party, Anabaa! Tiny masks for baby faces are already put aside for charming costumes yet to be sewed! Seamstress Penelope told me of all this herself when I was being fitted for my gown! And then she made me swear not to breathe a word about it as it is to be a surprise for the orphans and all wee children wintering here! Do you know what this means, Anabaa? Think about what this can mean for Ravenz!"

Lizbett knew to stop talking once Anabaa's eyes grew wide upon hearing such a secret into causing dramatizing expressions to play across the midwife's face.

"Well, that's it, my news I mean, *all* of it. Good night, Anabaa, sleep well." Lizbett turned away to her pillow and yawned.

Anabaa lay back upon the pillow and listened to the low gray noise of fine sleet kissing the windowpane numbing the ambient dissonance of Lizbett, Qiaona and Constance in deep slumber breathing.

CHRISTMASTIDE BALL

"Ah, what teasing animal's pretty face is this I spy in my vanity's mirrors?" Latezia stared at the reflection of her king dressed in jacket of glittering brocade and pants of black velvet. Wide satin ribbons tied back his supreme wavy curls like a colt's tail falling to rest between royal shoulders. But the mask's identity is a mystery to the queen and she ponders a short list of critters she remembers.

Beaver? Hare? Fox? Might you be whiskered sea lion? Bear? Are you merely a beautiful vision lurking in silver paint hiding behind these mirrors and if I should turn my eyes away from this apparition would you still wait there in this magical place, my husband and king?

"No guesses, Latezia?" laughed Breretyn over her shoulder. "My disguise is better than even I imagined. Nicoli was right when he suggested I select this muskrat mask to hide my Breretyn-face!"

"Nicoli is a bright butler, Your Majesty, and he serves you well!

No one will ever guess it's their king's eyes blazing thusly behind that robust rodent's clever nose!" giggled Latezia as she dipped a long crystal stopper into a perfume's vessel. Halting in her movement from bottle to earlobe to hold the instrument a trifle beneath her nose, Latezia sniffed the oil's opulent scent and wondered to herself at the course of an alchemist's thoughts along the way of a perfume's recipe to arrive at just this perfect scent. Lost in the moment of this thought Latezia sat with closed eyelids inhaling the result of a plant's blooms opening in that crucial dawn hour evaporated of its night dew and of a laborer she would never know toiling to collect such petals to press extracting precious attar thus condensing this elixir for the secret places a woman knows.

"And what is my beautiful queen to be this winter solstice night?" whispered Breretyn into Latezia's ear causing a flutter in the muscles of her neck. *Where did you go away to just then, my beauty and was I with you in the way of your little dreaming journey?* Breretyn watched Latezia's slender white fingers holding the stopper above her décolletage dragging it there tender as a whisper across soft vanilla puffs. The king leaned forward and placing a kiss on her ear inhaled the scent of Stephan's genius wafting there.

My garden's flowers; lilac blooms from my hedges, petals of roses from my lawn's bushes and freesia in beds, jasmine and orange peel, oil from the junipers…my wedding gift is your choice for this winter hour–

Latezia reached for the glittering mask dangling from its brass hook and held it over her eyes. Dazzled by the crystals radiating a rainbow of colors refracted through tiny faceted prisms pasted on the mask's white damask even she is overcome by the beauty of the piece. She simply stares at the transformation reflecting back to her recognizing only the pale soft blue of her eyes.

"Let me tie the ribbons." Breretyn's low voice edged the spell. Latezia held the mask against her cheekbones as her king tied the white satin streamers in knots behind her head. "Now stand, queen, so I may have a proper look in order to unravel the mystery of your disguise."

Latezia rose and turned to face her muskrat-face husband. King Breretyn studied the fabric's gleaming whiteness, the pointy designs outlining the edges of her mask above the forehead and cheeks and the soft round pearls resting across the lower process crossing her cheeks and over her nose. Within the geometric designs lay circles, triangles and cone shapes interlacing and all twinkling.

Star? Suns? Fire? Snow! My wife is a,

"Snowflake! You are a snowflake in winter's solstice snowfall! Stunning!" And Breretyn saw Latezia's lips part in a grand smile as her eyes sparkle as playfully as the crystals sparkling on her mask.

"Ah, your guess is close, good king! My aim was be Snow Queen! But a snowflake is the loveliest of all ideas!I quite think I shall rather love being a snowflake instead! Come, muskrat and melt some little snow away!" Latezia twirled away from her vanity in a quick-step waltz about the chamber over the threshold into the hallway taunting Breretyn to chase her as the wind swirls flurries to drifts.

"Oh, my snowflake queen teases her muskrat king! I think I shall quite like melting a little snowball between my paws!" It only took three long strides to grasp hold the giant bows adorning the back of Latezia's gown and catching her fast to him. Breretyn held his wife in an arm-clasp until her panting subsided to soft even breaths. "Offer me a challenge, my lady, and I win!" whispered King Breretyn silencing his tone as he caught his reflection in the liquid blue pools of Latezia's eyes.

Damn...So do you, my queen, Latezia win me.

~⌒

"Are you certain Qiaona is dressing Prince Rhynn in the nursery? And she is alone there?" whispered Constance as she watched

Anabaa's nimble fingers dress baby Ravenz in fleece. "You are positive this is an *exact* match of the prince's costume? And the masks are identical?"

"Enough, Constance! Of course, I'm certain! I'm beyond certain of all of it! Qiaona is Queen Latezia's first maidservant and her hands are the *first* to pick up Prince Rhynn in the morning tending to his needs before taking him to his mother and the *last* to cradle him into dreaming in his night hours!" Ravenz giggled and grasped for his toes as Anabaa slipped tiny buttons through tight tinier holes. "Even Lizbett eyed the seamstress fashioning these costumes and watched as the mask was selected from the bins so that there would be no mistake! Qiaona herself confirmed this identity once the queen made her selection for the prince's costume known! So hush yourself, Constance and finish with your own dressing! We must have our composure under complete control!"

"I'm always in complete control of my composure, Anabaa." Constance uttered softly. "You, of all people should know that by this stage in the game we've laid for ourselves."

Anabaa looked up.

"I'm sorry, Constance. Forgive my frayed nerve. I meant no meanness toward you." Anabaa looked upon shimmering Constance standing dressed inspectacular green brocade appearing as a Christmas tree and decorated all over just as festively in colored beads and glittering sequins. Her gentle face lay stoic behind a handsome mask of cranberry-red velvet trimmed all around in miniature holly vines. Red and green feathers plumed above the eyeholes gracing her brow.

Anabaa stared

"You look astonishing, Constance," Anabaa sighed in soft voice. "You are right, of course. If I could just grow to be half as gracious as you...please have patience with me. I struggle in this nightmare game not of our choosing."

"The four of us are caught up in this game so together we shall come to see the light at the end of it! Every day our play in this is a mystery because the unknown of it is vast, vacant and dark, is all."

"How much longer 'til Ravenz is dressed?" interjected Lizbett as she flitted through dance steps behind the women huddling before the bureau watching her reflection in the mirror. "I'm simply dying to see how this little panda mask looks on his itty bitty face!"

The eagle sat under the eave regal and camouflaged in dusk's subtle shadows watching the strange happenings unfolding in the chick's chamber.

What strange game is this that humans take on the role of animals to hide their identities in silly play…and the chick is to be a panda-babe this night? But I see your eyes through the holes there, green and clearly shining and they see me.

Ravenz turned his gaze from two small white orbs incandescing in the face of the shadowy form sitting beyond the windowpane and parted his lips as if to form a word. The eagle parted its beak, its eyes never blinking.

The babe Ravenz said one word. The sound rang from his lips as a complete word to Anabaa's ears clearly and without question as to its intent and meaning.

"Abaa!" Ravenz clapped his chubby hands together. "Abaa!" The child turned his gaze again to the eagle and flapped his arms up and down in the air, lips parting in giggles.

I hover over you panda-chick, always will I be near. The eagle's wings lifted in its slow silent aerial journey along Mountainwing's westside high arched windows.

The significance of the babe's word this night would not be lost amid the hours of childish play. Anabaa picked up the child and holding him close to her lips whispered in his ear,

"I am Abaa!"

~⌒

"Just so I know in what disguise is our young heir to be hiding in plain sight this night?"

"A panda's mask will shield his baby gem eyes and his body is clothed all in fleece! He'll be the only one in such a mask as only one was in the bin!"

"In that case, my snowflake queen, I shall veer down this service way to catch a glimpse of my prince in my Christmastime kingdom as you try to fool the revelers in Champagne Hall! Until I return, pretend well, Latezia, my burning heart's balm."

~⌒

"Wait! Take the servants' way!" whispered Constance. "It circumvents Champagne Hall and is hardly used at all at this hour as pushers of linen-filled laundry carts and soiled dish tray-carriers jam the hallway after the ball. We will be able to slip into the children's room without chance of running into Queen Latezia or King Breretyn! If the sand in my hourglass flows correctly she should be arriving in Champagne Hall this very minute!"

Children's laughter and squeals following harlequin-clad musicians' lutes' strumming, drumbeats, bugles' blowing and bells' jingling enchanted ebony Anabaa, ample Constance and tawny girlish Lizbett as they sought to catch up with widows and wardens ushering orphans and cousins, babes, two of toddling age and three of five-and-six dressed to the nines and masked in sweet animal-faces sashaying through the castle's great hallway and through the high archway into incredible fantasyland that is Christmastide in King Breretyn's realm.

~⌒

"Ah, little Prince Rhynn, so handsome are you in baby panda disguise!" giggled Qiaona as she studied their reflection in the chamber's wall mirror. "So let's be off to the ball! It is your very first masquerade party, your baby royal highness, heir Rhynn!" Qiaona started to spin away from the mirror but halted at the sight of her own visage unadorned of its disguise.

My mask! Where did I set down my mask?

Her gaze swept across the top of the duvet to the rumpled pillows and then to the rugs on either side of the night nurse's bed.

Oh no! I've lost my mask! This can't be happening! I'm to be in Champagne Hall within the minute! I'm to lead the receiving line with the prince for all the guests are waiting to see his little majesty dressed so royally awaiting his parents' grand entrance!

Qiaona grasped Prince Rhynn against the soft velvet of her gown. Its white marabou trim tickled his nose causing his small fingers to rise upward to his mask as his face crumpled into a sneeze. Qiaona held her breath thinking the child about to tear the mask from his eyes but Rhynn only giggled.

Stop this dizzying spin and focus! Breathe…breathe…now open your eyes and look

When her eyes did open it was into the prince's royal cradle that her gaze fell upon the mask lying amidst the crumpled eiderdown and pillows where it had fallen from her grasp as she'd picked up King Breretyn's firstborn and heir.

"Oh, what great relief for I spy my mask! Wait here, gentleman child while I tie on my ornamental disguise!" Qiaona's nimble fingers snatched the mask from the crib's depths and racing the hourglass' diminishing sands to the mirror tightened the satin ribbons back of her head with one swift flick of her wrists.

A ribbon snapped free of its fastener.

The mask fell at an angle across Qiaona's nose dangling by its remaining ribbon caught in a curl over her ear.

Oh, no! How can this happen? I'm late! I'll be too late! Needle and thread…where is…where do I find a needle…no wait…I'll just tie this streamer through aneyehole and make a pretty flat knot…who will ever know…no one will even notice a pretty flat knot hiding amongst all this glittering loveliness!

And so her work was done and the mask fit snug on her face, its streamer weaved over itself at the back of her head. Qioana smiled at the eyes in the mirror looking back.

The last sand grain drained itself through the hourglass neck and lay above all others in gentle dune sloped at its base.

∼◦

"Ah ha! It is my young prince I see in the arms of his guardian angles!" An unmistakable subtle-accented voice floated like a vapor over the heads of Anabaa, Constance and Lizbett.

The women froze their footfall along the stonewalled corridor then turned slowly to meet the gaze of one royal muskrat-masked king dressed in regal shimmering jacket and black velvet pants. Stunned with surprise and deafened by their heart's thundering pulse not one heard King Breretyn's praise of their gowns' beauty and the clever trick of their masks' camouflaging their identities as he scooped the child, Ravenz from Anabaa's arms and strode away with the panda-masked baby-lad clasped to his shoulder.

What's happening to me and where am I going carried in these strange arms?

Dumbstruck with horror the trio slumped to a huddle on the granite floor and shuddered together in waves of shivers.

Ravenz looked back over the king's shoulder to see three women fallen to the floor in a heap.

Abaa!

Ravenz turned his face to the windows then to follow two small orbs glowing in an eagle's sky-king face, its body dark and shadowy in flight gliding by windows only to disappear from view as King Breretyn crossed under the high archway and into the children's fantasyland ball.

～～

Oh, no! I'm too late here with you for the dancing has begun! Qiaona swayed between the waltzing guests searching the eyes behind a dazzling kaleidoscope of silks, velvets, taffetas, feathers and beads. *Oh, I remember her gown now. White I think, with crystals adorning a pointy silk mask.*

"I see your Mummy, Prince Rhynn! She dances in sparkling snowflake grandeur! Why, the queen is practically an entire snowfall as she twirls in her dancing slippers, little one! Come let's glide through this crowd and surprise Mummy and her guests with your royal panda-masked cuteness!" And in that moment Qiaona's arms were freed of their burden for Queen Latezia and her court's ladies adored Prince Rhynn in a soft chorus of hums and chants as they gazed upon King Breretyn's heir.

I see a panda-boy in my eyes' two fovea…the panda-chick rides high on the king's shoulder in the celebrating chamber of laughing children and the panda-other is in the clutch of the queen beneath twinkling chandeliers and holly boughs. Curious and strange are the golden curls falling identically over foreheads and tickling ears, eyes shining green as earth's emerald gems…green as its summer grass…green as its trees in timbers' line…golden and green. The panda-child the queen holds in her arms laughs and his hands clap and reach forth but the king's panda-chick-eyes remain open and staring outwardly and his lips stay closed nor do his hands open or his arms clasp. I follow both.

Qiaona rushed from Champagne Hall up the great hallway

toward the children's ball enchanted by the musician's playing gay nursery carols on fifes and lutes and shrieks of childish laughter hypnotizing her into a slow gliding trance upon the glistening marble floor. And her ears heard the sound then, coming from somewhere beyond a wall like a faint wailing or wind gathering strength as it swirls down mountainside through corridors then swoops across rooftops. Mesmerized by the lyrical tones and curious beyond measure Qiaona passed by the high archway entrance to the children's ball and floated onward in this daze until the hazy vision of a huddled mass of three bodies swaying as a boat lists upon the seas in a gale filled her focus.

The queen's maidservant stood over the clinging huddling mass of green silk, cherry-red taffeta and gold velvet and wondered at the strange beautiful masks covering their eyes and what the meaning of this act is.

The king swept up his spare and Queen Latezia sways with his true heir! What if the two should meet and compare? Who can tell a Ravenz from a Rhynn, prince and heir? Neither the king norqueen-mother can know who is and why two!

And the feminine wailings wafted to Qiaona's opening ears and she hears their words swirling to her mind as storming winds blow and then she knew.

"Constance, Lizbett and Anabaa, collect one another and stand! It's me, Qiaona! Lift your faces upward to meet my gaze!"

The wailing chant stopped as three women raised their masked faces to lock eyes with Qiaona's own.

"Where is Ravenz? Queen Latezia has Prince Rhynn in her arms as we speak! She dances with him as he delights her guests this hour. But tell me, where is Ravenz?"

The huddled mass disentangled their arms and legs and rose upward to the faint rustling of gowns falling about their feet as rolling fog quietly settles.

"The king intercepted us in the corridor here and plucked Ravenz from Anabaa's arms and vanished away from us in that instant! He called him his little panda-faced prince and went straightaway with him to the children's room to play with the toys and eat treats!"

"So? There is truth in his words."

Anabaa's eyes drew large at Qiaona's tone and the whites shone as hard-boiled eggs in a face as ashen as a bisque breakfast plate.

"But the time of this discovery will be of Ravenz' choosing, not by this simple accident in holiday's deceitful play. Listen to me now and follow my plan exactly. Lizbett, go with Anabaa to the children's hall. Ravenz recognizes you well. Constance will accompany me to the ballroom and the two of us shall be at the queen's elbow should she be looking for relief. Once Anabaa and I have the babes secured in *our* arms Lizbett and Constance must relay each other's news to us others. Anabaa and I shall sway away from one another under the disguise of the dance and neither the king nor queen shall see two pandas together. The very moment an opportunity arises for Anabaa to retreat to Mountainwing with Ravenz I'll appear on the horizon of King Breretyn's and Queen Latezia's vision and remain on that line with Prince Rhynn in my arms until they bid me leave with the prince for his chamber's crib."

And with those hush-uttered words now absorbed to silence in the stone-wall corridor Anabaa and Lizbett stood under the high ballroom doorway entranced by the scene unfolding before their eyes. Musician's dressed in brilliant jingle bell-trimmed costumes blew fifes and bugles and strummed lutes as King Breretyn lead the children hand-in-hand in a line-dance all about the room snaking his way with them following between low little tables groaning with biscuit-trays and deep punch bowls then circling back again before high mantle bearing long fatly stuffed woolen stockings, their toes brushing the hearth, around painted rocking horses and porcelain dolls, toy trains and plush teddy bears.

Where is Ravenz?

In panic Anabaa pushed Lizbett into the ballroom hissing, "Search the walls that way for the panda while I search this way! We shall meet again along the way of four walls!" And in that moment her heart filled with relief at sight of hobbling widow Becca cradling a panda child against her frail shoulder.

"Dame Becca! It's me, Anabaa, the queen's midwife. Let me relieve you of your precious burden so you may enjoy the children's amusement more!"

"It has been an honor holding the king's prince but my hip still hurts from the bruise I suffered in that little spill and I can't dance as I wish with his child weighing heavy on my arm."

"You are brave to hold him this long, Dame Becca. Rest yourself against the pillow on the chaise there and be calm this night."

Twirling away from Dame Becca now cushioned in pillows Anabaa brought her lips to the child's earlobe concealed behind his panda-masked face and whispered,

"Ravenz"

Ravenz looked into Anabaa's eyes and wrapping his fingers tightly about her thumb whispered, "Abaa."

In a heartbeat King Breretyn danced before Anabaa's sight and rejoicing at the sight of his prince in her arms commanded her join the line.

"We're off to winter solstice's dance in Champagne Hall so all in the palace can witness Christmastime's charm in these children!"

As Anabaa stepped into the dance at the end of the line she looked back catching sight of Lizbett's cherry-red taffeta gown's hem vanishing around the corner in the direction of Champagne Hall.

⁓

"Queen Latezia?" Qiaona curtseyed demurely before joining the dance. "I'm ready to relieve you of the prince a moment while you partake of refreshments, if you should agree, of course."

"Oh, thank the angels! I'm steaming in this costume, Qiaona and the pearls dangling from my mask tickle my cheekbones. My eyes water and I have been on the brink of a sneeze this entire hour but with Prince Rhynn in my arms I'm tortured to distraction. Please, take him now while I seek cool air at the balcony."

Qiaona's arms clutched the king's child to her bosom and stared after Queen Latezia's immense white bows gracing the back of her shimmering white dress disappear like a ghost lost to darkness beyond slowly-closing French doors.

Constance' words waft to Qiaona's ear uttered between lips as light kisses float on summers' breeze.

"Lizbett passed me this news; the king is line dancing with the children to this place as we speak! Anabaa carries Ravenz and waltzes at the end of the line. Remain here in the shadows of all dancers until the time is right to join in the line. Where is the queen?"

Gracious Constance

"Latezia is outside on the balcony yonder seeking fresh air. It is Christmastime, after all and solace is ours this night."

And the plan successfully came to end in the way two babes never crossed either one's path nor did the king or queen learn of the other twin's existence of one each in one another's arms.

⁓

"You may leave for your own room, Qiaona. Zayanna is following us here. The king and I shall watch the prince while he sleeps."

Qiaona bowed her head, retreating from the room to vanish into the hallway. King Breretyn stood at the crib's side, his hand on its smooth polished rail gently rocking the ancient structure in an ancient artisan's crafted frame carved of a tree's branches old as time and wondered at the caretakers' hands who'd touched this very rail rocking himself this way and his father and grandfather and all fathers in the line of his ancestors.

"It was a glorious ball, Breretyn, just as I imagined in my dreams." Latezia's whispered words brushed against Breretyn's ear as faint white sleet brushed against windows' panes. "It was a quaint lovely vision seeing you enter Champagne Hall like that leading the little ones in by their hands clasped one to another together…like that…little feet dancing like that." Breretyn did not look away from the face of his young heir twitching in his baby dream nor did he turn to his queen as she pressed on his arm in the subtle way a woman does when she seeks acknowledgment. And even when she turned her face upward to his silently questioning his mood he did not look back.

"My son did not know me tonight, Latezia." The bony knuckles of Breretyn's hand rocking the crib turned white beneath the thin covering of skin and his golden signet ring faded to steel-gray in the shadow of the high curving silk canopy draping his child's head asleep on the pillows. "My Rhynn did not call me Poppi nor did my boy look at me but turned his eyes to the windows gazing only outward into darkness. I searched the view beyond the windows to discern his interest there but saw nothing. Even when I hoisted him to my shoulder which delights him to distraction he did not respond in his usual glee but rode there with his tongue tied silent between closed lips."

Latezia did not breathe nor turn her gaze from the king's solemn face for fear of breaking his fragile sad trance. With a serene turn of her ankles still bound in satin sippers' ribbon bows she moved to

King Brereyn's back and reaching up her hands to his head, gently picked at string's knots binding the mask across his royal face. With an angel's touch her fingertips unraveled the tangles freeing the strings to stream over her king's shoulders.

The mask fell away to the floor.

"The muskrat has departed your spirit, Breretyn and Your Majesty's true visage is returned to you."

The babe in the crib opened his eyes upon hearing its mother's words weaving quietly in the airspace above his head and reaching up his chubby arms, kicked up his heels under the eiderdown and hollered,

"Poppi!"

And when Latezia next looked into her king's eyes it was to great joy and a glad tear that repaid her simple gesture.

"Forgive me, son. I've terrified you this night in my thoughtless hideous disguise. What was great frolic to me ruined the whole of it for you. But you are gentled to me now in attitude by way of your baby memory, and all thought of this night is gone from you."

"Poppi!" squealed the prince. "Up, Poppi, up!" Breretyn scooped up his heir from the mattress and clutched the child to his breast. Pudgy ball-fists pummel the king's shoulders.

"Up, Poppi!"

The king rejoiced as he hoisted his heir in the air above his head.

"My little prince, my Rhynn, you see Poppi this Eve, my little heir-boy!"

But it is to Latezia's eyes Breretyn gazes into longest now as he sways back and forth, back and forth with Rynn in his arms. The child giggled and clapped together his hands.

Latezia, my gracious queen, you have returned myself to me restoring me to my son.

"Time for our own revelry, my lady!" whispered the king as he pressed Prince Rhynn into the awaiting warm lap of the babe's night-nurse, Zayanna.

"Last beneath the duvet is a rascally muskrat!" taunted Latezia as she raced ahead her husband-king through the hallway.

"After you, then! A muskrat, no matter how rascally can melt snow between its paws till it warms to sweet-water puddle, my snowflake!"

Ah, you remember well, my Majesty, King B! 'Tiz Christmas! Lucky, lucky me this wintery solstice night!

Latezia flung her mask in the air only to see it catch on a poster's spindle by an eyehole. White satin ribbons stream downward to rest in swirls upon tangled sheet.

Far longer than a moment Breretyn lay with his ear to Latezia's heart listening to the ebb and flow of her life echo through vena cava to ventricle flooding auricle then throbbing through pulmonic artery to lung rising and falling, rising and falling with air as hemoglobin transporting oxygen surges onward through aorta to artery and vein…in chambers, echoing…

There is no finer mattress than my bride's belly and Heaven's pillow is her bosom.

"Tiz good to be the king," whispered Breretyn.

"To be his queen, even better," purred Latezia.

Ah, my queen wins…wins me. It's good to be me for I win…

CHAPTER 5

EARTH TURNING ON AXIS GLIDING ALONG ORBIT FACED SUN'S rising temperature in springtime's awakening. Snow melting into slush became drink to seeds thawing in spring's warming soil. Birds shook free their wingtips to soar and animals roused from their dreams to explore.

And during sleepy winter's yawning into young spring baby bones grow longer when new cartilaginous cells multiplying in epiphyseal plates push large old cells toward diaphysis to be replaced by osteocytes. Osteoblasts riotously multiplying in periosteal crazily divide themselves into osteocytes in the quiet business of thickening a child's long bones.

Prince Rhynn wakened in this phenomenon feeling his toes pressing against the far flat hard edge of the crib. His heels sunk into the soft mattress now curling up at his sides under the weight of his body. The boy raised his arms upward and seeing both hands extend in the air beyond the crib's height, grasped its railing. In a subconscious discovery and application of the theory of leverage Rhynn hoisted his head and body from pillow and mattress to stand wobbly-legged against old burnished wood.Green baby-eyes gazed about the realm of his chamber in wonderment.

A master wood-carver's rocking horse waiting on its matted yarn rug before the high arched window stands majestically silhouetted in dawn's gentle blooming light. Loved-to-well-worn sawdust-stuffed forest animals slump wide-eyed and belly-up against the closest wall. Brightly painted wooden blocks engraved on all sides sit piled in pyramids aside a bureau. An article of clothing partially trapped in the clutch of a middle drawer dangles lifeless over its latch-pulls.

Crowded next to the crib is a pewter lamp claiming sole ownership of the nightstand's top.

Rhynn gazed upon walls at pictures of animals grazing pastures laying matted in frames hanging thereupon and then through windowpane to royal greyhounds playing chasing games through hedge mazes beyond. Rabbits sought cover in flowering foliage. Birds swooped from clouded sky to fountain's rim to peck at imaginary insects hovering in mist.

Zayanna lay bundled beneath a thick duvet lightly snoring. Her hand rests demurely upon the pillow aside her cheek. Rhynn watches his night nurse's eyelids twitch in dreaming. Her lips curl up at their ends in a gentle smile. Favorite worn slippers wait patiently at the side of the bed for feet's awaking and a cotton robe lay in wait of limbs' rousing.

The prince stood transfixed in a state of study watching morning unravel itself from the fringe of night. But the soaked garment about his loins grew miserably colder in its miserable bulk causing the child to shake and twist his straight child-hips thus releasing the diaper from the grip of his belly to fall with a thud upon the mattress at his feet. Rhynn looked down at the discarded heap of disgusting fiber feeling coolness waft over his skin at the loss of the cumbersome burden.A sense of profound freedom came into the boy and he contemplated the nightstand.

As a cat leaps unto a windowsill Rhynn lifted a sturdy leg planting a chubby foot on the stand's top. The second foot swiftly followed the first. The night nurse snorted in her sleep heaving her body in a turn under the duvet. Bedsprings squawked in protest but soon quieted themselves under her settling weight.Zayanna's face lay turned away to the wall, the duvet crowded in a drift under her chin. Her shoulder rose and fell to the rhythm of her breathing.

Rhynn slid from nightstand to floor in slumber's noisy camouflage and spying thethreshold over which his nurses carried him since infancy the curious prince dashed across the floor through the doorway into the great palace world beyond propelled forward by his newfound steam.

Long open hallways tease him to running and shadowy alcoves tease him to hiding. Stone-topped tables offer imaginary caves under urns bearing forestry bouquets and wide silver mirrors hanging on walls in-between reflect child unto child and back again unto child as child giggled and clapped at the sight of himself giggling and slapping silver mirrors' glass.

All persons in the castle slept.

Rhynn stopped in his play suddenly overcome by the true feeling of aloneness. No mouse ran along baseboard. No cat lay in wait. No sentry or butler darted from posture to sabotage the thrill of his flight through King Breretyn's immense stone realm.

Rhynn's thoughts turn to his mummy and he yearns for her now. He thinks ofPoppi and the shoulder he adores and desired a lift to its height. The little naked prince turned on his heels and broke into dashing back the way he'd run away from it all seeking the way back to all that he knows.

Doors appear in every wall down every hall. Sounds of sleep sound the same behind each until,

A door lays opened a crack emitting quiet rising sunlight across the hallway's glassy marble floor. Mummy-perfume scented the air tickling tiny nostrils of the child in search of its mother so he pushed the door further to reveal magnificent royal furnishings within. Tapestry-canopied bed stood upon vast high platform. Painted white vanity shoulders mirrors-of-three-sides framed in fanciful hand-wrought iron painted white and feathery gilded.Sheer morning sunlight reflecting through engraved lead crystal vessels cast brilliant rainbows across walls and pointy-topped stopper-dippers lidded them all. Powder bowls house plump furry puff-balls beneath glittering jeweled covers and engraved patina-silver wrap about hairbrush and comb.

This kingdom is magic as is its air to the child hypnotized by the spell of it all.

Rhynn entered the chamber tiptoeing across angular rugs of soft deeply-furred skins snowy-white and leopard-spotted feeling old heat subtly warming his arches as ancient pulses throb to the beat of his toes. The child halted before vanity gazing in wonderment at feminine wealth displayed thereupon.

A large clear glassy orb attracted his eye above all others. Reaching forth his hand Rhynn grasped the crystal ball lofting it before his baby-boy face. Young East-rising light beaming through windows refract through aqua trapped with no hint of escape from this globe. So the prince turned the orb in his hands 'round and 'round and seeing small luminescent speckles scattering within stood entranced watching them falling through liquid space back to the place they'd rested before.

King Breretyn watched his son in this discovery-play from the pillow his head lay on shrouded beneath canopied bed high on its perch. He'd sensed Rhynn's entrance the instant the child stood at his chamber's doorway considering it all. And it brought to his mind a memory of himself at this age when his own child-mind filled with realization that growth's forward urgings cannot be held back.

Little Breretyn tiptoes this very trail across bear skins and wolves' hides to stand barefooted and naked-bottomed before armoire and vanity, velvet-clothed chaises and royal master-bed considering it all. But it was into his parents' four large silently-staring glassy eyes his curious gaze falls and they cause a lurch in his heart and a thunder roll in his stomach. A cloud crosses his vision as understanding dawns in his reason that his actions had been watched for indefinite time. Newfound fear crushes triumphant euphoria for now he stands embarrassed as a fool trespasser caught red-handed committing a crime yet to be known.

But darkness turns to sunlight upon Queen Myrinna's gentle tone and King Neptlyn's soft chortle.

"Well, well, lookie here! Our little prince is growing up!"

So Breretyn watches his firstborn now as the child beholds Parqai's shimmering speckles floating about as snowflakes through water in the artisan's snow-globe. But as Rhynn turns the orb over and fingers the hidden music box's brass key at its bottom does the king close his eyes and feign sleep. Curiously now as the seed of his loin is curiously exploring, Breretyn's desire is to learn more so he closed his eyes for the way of his heir's journey overrides his desire to openly watch.

The key did not turn on its axis nor did the music box's tinkling's ring forth from the globe. Only the quiet echo of object sliding across tabletop floats upon airwaves to wakeful Latezia's and Breretyn's listening ears.Little feet padded lightly onto each tread of the stool's leather-topped steps and child-heat emanating from his body filled the space between bed's edge and his mummy's closed angel-eyes.

Rhynn stood on the stepping stool aside the mattress bearing his parents' bodies in repose and looked upon their sleeping faces laying side-by-side on plump feather pillows facing his eyes.

Latezia's golden ringlets splayed over the pillow as a halo about her head. Her soft white arm reached beyond the silken duvet, its palm open as invitation bidding her child come hither unto her dreaming. King Breretyn's long arm lay languidly across his queen's belly. His strong bare shoulder so high and wide in consciousness' uprightness now lay prone and relaxed in slumber. Their eyelids did not quiver nor did lashes flit. Lips did not smile nor did any brow lift.

Rhynn leaned against the mattress and contemplated the flat space between his mother's body and the thick edge upon which he leaned. Latezia heard breaths drawn into her babe-boy's lungs through tiny nostrils and feels little lung's air expunge as feathery tickles against her cheek. But still she waits.

And in that moment Rhynn's patiently-waiting parents' curiosity is greatly rewarded for as quietly-gently as a kitten curls itself to comfort in the warmth of a waiting lap did their young prince gently-softly raise the duvet and silently-quickly slide his cold naked-bottomed-barefoot being unto the warmth of his parents' bosoms. His little head nestled into the pillow and his eyes closed. Both heard it then; the even deep baby-breaths that come to a child sleeping in security's peace.

Latezia's arm curved about her child cupping his round baby cheek in her palm. Breretyn's arm enveloped mother and son enclosing Latezia's fingertips with his own.

∼◦

Zayanna opened an eye.

Rising sun's beams shone confidently through windowpanes flooding the room with natural light. All in the chamber appear to her eye as the night gone before; rocking horse and toys lay abandoned in piles and crib aside nightstand cradle prince and heir. Limp cotton robe awaits her body's fill as cold slippers warm to her toes.

It's time, good little Prince Rhynn for warm bath and fresh cloth for Qiaona comes soon

Zayanna screamed.

∼◦

"Our little Ravenz has sprouted wings!" cried Lizbett as she flew about the suite chasing the runaway toddler over rug before chintz-covered chaises around poster beds on platforms between bureaus in and out of deep closets across chamber's burnished plank floor over threshold through doorway into Mountainwing's stone hallway beyond.

The whole way of the chase little Ravenz giggled and flapped his arms as he darted under tables bearing urns of leafy camouflage then squeal in delight as his cave is discovered only to run off into alcoves taking cover in shadows as he watches from a corner while his nurse calls his name until his baby-voice chanted,

"Look here! Over here! Here...no, here! Under here! Up here!"

And away Ravenz' little feetrush escaping Lizbett's grasp, giggling while little arms flail the air the whole way of the hallway beckoning his runaway dash.

~~~

"Kidnap! Kidnap! The prince has been kidnapped!" shrieked Zayanna as she sped from the horror of seeing Rhynn's empty crib save for a soaked diaper laying foul in its depth. Panic gripped her heart strangling its beats to arrhythmia. Air rushed from her lungs suffocating them of breath and her eyes grew dry in open-state stare at the door opened forth from its jamb.

"Kidnap! The king's heir has been kidnapped!" screamed the night nurse's trembling shrill voice as tears flooded her eyes causing a blur in her vision and quivering in both lips.

"Who has been kidnapped?" gentled King Breretyn's quiet voice in an effort to calm stricken Zayanna.

Upon hearing the king's words uttered quietly as a ghost's then seeing his tall form emerge through brilliant white light before her watery-hazed gaze she fell prone to the floor facedown upon cold marble, palms slapping and grasping trying to clasp at what she knew not.

"The king's prince has been kidnapped from his bed as I slept! Baby Rhynn is gone! Only cold sheets and diaper remain deserted in his crib!" And then a great wail rose from Zayanna's throat and she rolled over onto her back, face up, mouth open but voice stilled, eyes closed, skin ashen as in death.

From the loft of his perch on his father's shoulder, Rhynn giggled and clapped his little hands thinking Zayanna's theatre a charade for his entertainment. "Zanna! Good Zanna!" hooted the prince. "Wake up, Zanna!"

"Oh, great Heavens! What's happened out here? What happened to Zayanna?"

Latezia rushed through hallway from bedchamber upon hearing the commotion echoing off granite and marble. The queen fell to her knees gathering Zayanna's head in her arms. "What happened to Rhynn's night nurse, Breretyn? Why is she prone in this state upon cold marble with her face growing so pale and colder?"

In some far off place Zayanna hears tones chiming as words' phrased. The perfumed air her nose breathes smells of melting snow and a pillowy bosom cushions her head.

"This woman believes our Rhynn kidnapped from his mattress for when she looked into the crib all that remains there are cold blankets and soiled linen."

"Kidnapped! Our Prince Rhynn? Your heir only pussyfooted into our bedchamber of his own accord!"

And then Latezia hushed her words as her mind gained an understanding of the morning's event and its consequence affecting the king's firstborn and the child's nurse."

The brick-maker's daughter considers commanding her king in a way such as to make recovery *his* gift.

"Set down your heir by Zayanna's face, Your Majesty so when

her eyes come to focus it will be on your Rhynn's face her eyes see. She will become comforted and restored to reason at the sight of the prince."

As a swift eagle dives to the earth King Breretyn set his son on the floor at Zayanna's side then stood back waiting for the nurse to open her eyes and for calmness to settle her soul.

"Zanna!" Rhynn called to his nurse. And this time Zayanna opened her eyes and seeing the prince's sweet contented face so safe and close to her own she lurched up from Latezia's cradling arms to rejoice with happy sobs and joyful tears.

The king held forth his hand to the humble nurse. His golden signet ring glows warming in the new day's dawning.

"Our son controls his own muscles now as happens in the way of a child's growing up. He merely slipped from his bed on his own accord as a jaguar leaves the shelter of its lair to prowl freely through his jungle kingdom at night. This is Prince Rhynn's house after all, and his realm to roam about and explore. So, come now good nurse and rise up. Free yourself of this fearful worry. Your loyalty to the prince is greatly admired."

Zayanna released the child of her arms' clasp and rose to slump against the king's chest. In that moment Latezia caught the sight of little Rhynn's bare bottom fleeing the hallway carried away in fast fashion by speedy feet up the stairwell.

"Qiaona and Constance will draw you a bubbling bath, Zayanna, and fragrance you afterward with my powders." Latezia rose from her knees and gathering up silk skirts in her hands giggled, "I'm off to catch a little jaguar by his tail!"

And so it begins

Breretyn's gaze followed the flight of his queen down hallway 'round corner and he closed his eyes to the vision playing out in his mind.

Up stairwells down corridors through doorways into chambers...soft motherly voice calling out to her child while chiming little rhyme lines

"Mummy! Come catch Jagger's tail, Mummy!" The shrieks and laughter of a child's voice echo off wall and ceiling, from under tabletop and behind potted plant, around corner and doorjamb to bottom of staircase across vast marble foyer over threshold down stonesteps into sunlight around foaming fountain into hedge mazes and flowering shrubs gracing majestic castle's east side.

And around yards and through palace again the chasing games went on and on charming mother and enchanting child along the whole of the journey to an end they know not.

~

"Come catch Ravenz! Up here! Under *here*! Over here!" The shrieks andlaughter of a child's voice echo off wall and ceiling, from under tabletop and behind potted plant, around corner and doorjamb to bottom of staircase over threshold across porch under portico around fruiting trees and shrubs bearing berries lining gentle Mountainwing's west side. "No, *here*! *Closer* still!"

An eagle soared in the atmosphere winging its flight in grand circles over palace rooftop and lawns of fruited trees, shrubs and hedges, bubbling fountain and high iron gates guarded by sentries in brilliant waistcoats and plumed hats looking like soft upside-down nests. And the whole while of its flight the eagle followed queen-mother chasing fair curly-haired prince and maid-guardian chasing fair curly-haired boy-chick in their dashes about all...its eyes never blinking...its keen gaze unceasing.

~

Latezia slowed her footrace in Mountainwing's corridor not so familiar for its long hallway lay lined with doorways leading to guest suites not otherwise visited by one such as a queen.

"Jaguar? Rhynn?" called the queen's voice gently at first then rising a pitch as panic overtakes her for the quick-footed prince has vanished from view and his giggling voice muted in this strange side of the castle.

Queen Latezia stopped cold in her tracks at the sound of a child's voice echoing in walls down halls behind doors from within closets.

"I'm here, Mummy...no here...up here...under here...catch Jagger's tail, Mummy...catch Ravenz! Oh, Mummy! Look here...look there...come closer...Jagger is near! Ravenz flies *here*...no Mummy, down here! Ravenz flies near."

I'm losing my mind in all this haste and my heart pounds like thunder in its ribcage. Stop gasping for air, lungs, quit my lips' quivering!

Latezia closed her eyes listening.

Silence

The queen hears the sound then, far off at first then increasing in loudness; bare child arches softly slapping the shiny stone floor.

The eagle swooped low to perch on a beam beneath roof's shadowy overhang. Its eyes fix on the travel of the curly-haired boy-chick crossing threshold to run down hallway.

Queen Latezia opened her eyes to behold a little prince sloppily clad in mismatched pants-on-backward and shirt-inside-out-dangling-haphazard...for one button pushed through a hole not corresponding in line.

"Jaguar?"

The eagle did not flutter a feather nor part its beak. It drew in no air for it dared not squawk.

Ravenz halted in his flight at the sight of the regal lady

occupying the pathway between wall and wall. He clutched at a button with thumb and finger while latching a pinkie through a spare hole below crumpling up fabric in all the wrong places over britches on backwards hanging down shins above bare foot and one foot socked.

"Ravenz," muttered the child.

"Raven? So, you are a bird now flying off to hide in a cloud?'

But before Latezia could blink an eye or inhale, Lizbett dashed up behind Ravenz flushed pink in the face and quite out of breath.

"Oh!" Lizbett's eyes grew astonished so surprised is she at the sight of the queen touring Mountainwing's hallway. And then she dipped in a deep regal bow, a curtsey so elegant even Latezia feels envy. And with a sweep of Lizbett's white hand in a grand arc the girl said eloquently,

"Your Majesty, Queen Latezia."

Lizbett rose and stood demurely with eyes downcast awaiting the queen's response.

"Why does the prince look this way in his clothes?"

"He took to the wardrobe bins just freshly brought up from the laundry rooms below! The orphans are dressing themselves so he joined in the effort, too! It is a wondrous day when a little child wishes to learn the way of dressing himself!" are the only words Lizbett can gather to say for there is truth in the speech for, "Isn't it grand how he's grown? I'll have his clothes correct in a wink!"

Lizbett scooped away Ravenz in the fold of her arms just as a door opened and dowagers Becca and Josephine poked out their heads to see what on earth the commotion going on the hallway is all about. Upon spying their queen standing so royally and this closely to their humble suite's doorway both immediately bowed, stammering,

95

"Queen Latezia, Gracious Majesty! What joy and beauty you bring to Mountainwing's west suites!"

"Mummy! Look up, Mummy! Jagger is *way up*...on Poppi!"

On Poppi? Latezia turned around at the child-voice calling behind her and sees indeed her Prince Rhynn on King Breretyn's shoulders.

Here? Now there? You are Jaguar now? The bird, Raven was just here...now you are up there!

"Our curious son darted out from the alcove there into the light beaming through yonder window just as I rounded the corner and now it seems I've one more trophy to add to my wall; that being the tail of one little runaway jaguar!"

⁓

"The queen is in the hall, Anabaa! She's seen Ravenz and thinks he's Rhynn! She ponders at his wardrobe and the mess he's in about it all and I explained he's learning to dress himself! Tiz the truth, really it is except he's Ravenz but..."

"Hush yourself, Lizbett! Take Ravenz into the deep chamber and quiet him there with play while I distract the queen."

When Lizbett sought to utter a response Anabaa slipped from sight. No knob turning in its socket squealed. No door thudded closed in its jamb. Not even a drapery floated away from a sill in the wake of one rushing out or of door swiftly closing. Lizbett quietly picked up the delighted proud child and held him before mirrors in this parlor and that chamber all through the suite complimenting the labors of his little fingers struggling so courageously to button his shirt, pull up his britches and sock his foot. They chant at their reflections while Ravenz clapped his hands the whole time Anabaa stood faintly dumbfounded and mute watching the king bearing his firstborn heir upon his shoulders stride down hallway over threshold to foot-sprint across porch beneath portico over spring-sprouting lawns to explore the fruiting orchard beyond as doddering widows Becca and Josephine clucked compliments unto their tranquil-yet-dismayed golden queen.

~~⌒⌐

"Have you packed *anything* yet, Lizbett? Seriously, girl, you travel far too lightly as your bag seems airy considering your wintering needs."

"Both my big bags are packed and rest in the hallway, Qiaona! That's my little hand satchel you're clutching in your palms!"

"You have *two* bags? And a *hand satchel*? How are we to haul your load along with our own back to Falls House and care for Ravenz along the way of our long walk on the roadway?"

"Look out beyond the fruit trees toward tree-line's edge and tell if you do not see Bako's wagon waiting in the shadows. It is his father's team he's borrowed to carry out this chivalrous deed on our behalf."

"Bako! Who's Bako?" demanded Anabaa on the fringe of seizure.

"Bako is Ebo the blacksmith's son, son of Fairie, good and beautiful wife of Ebo and mother of sweet Farayya, Bako's faire little sister."

"How do you know this boy, Bako and what of Ravenz should he come to suspect?" interrupted Anabaa in a low but hysterical voice.

"King Breretyn commanded Bako to escort me to the university is all and he knows of a way through Belle Passe by Half Moon Lagoon where the Falls tumble before the river narrows along where our pathway is. We won't be suspected of anything for he does not even know of little Rhynn's face for he told me himself he's never set foot in any East wing of the royal's prime residence. So, how could he tell one boy from the others here, you know, apart from the orphans and toddlers growing taller and three of five and six turning six and seven?"

"Enough, Lizbett! Hush yourself! I see the wagon you speak of waiting far away there. It is a large wagon and four horses patiently wait!" Anabaa silenced her voice as her eyes opened widely. "He's taking the *whole* of this crowd into the village by way of himself driving?'

"Of course! How else could I camouflage this game we hide while escaping in plain sight under the veil of the orphans and children and their wardens, too! This little trip is a gift of his father, Ebo, King Breretyn's blacksmith and Ebo honors his son, Bako, escorting Bako's…well…*his inamorata* to her home near the village thusly." Lizbett's complexion turned from peachy-cream to raspberry-pink and her eyelids drooped dreamily as her voice trailed off in a whispery hush.

Qiaona and Anabaa stared.

"Come, ladies. Our Lizbett suffers sweet blooming-love, is all and great love to all of us that Ebo allows Bako this gesture on Lizbett's behalf." Gracious Constance nudged Qiaona and Anabaa toward the doorway.

Lizbett's willowy silhouette faded into suns' white brilliance as she dashed ahead of the others across porch under portico through yards of peach, apple and cherry-bearing trees toward the wagon waiting beyond.Constance sighed at the sight of it all with thankfulness bloating her heart.

"Queen Latezia honors feeble Dowagers Becca and Josephine with rooms in Southwing where magnolia trees bloom fragrant beyond windowsills there. Birds nesting in the branches are of comfort to womanly souls of an age. We are last to leave Mountainwing and the sun growing so warm in its arc dried the roadway and, well, it is late spring after all, and I yearn for our little Falls House."

Grasshoppers testing their wings flexed their legs in grand leaps from bush to blade. Armies of butterflies descend upon riotous-blooming wild flowers as magpies harp in branches above. Crickets enthusiastically out-chirp frogs earnestly croaking simply for the sake of it being a warm promising spring. Rabbits dart across the roadway dodging the plodding hooves of Ebo's lent team. Squirrels dart up trees' trunks to watch just because.

The whole while of the wagon trip's way an eagle circled in the sky languidly arcing high through a cloud before swooping downward to riverbank then lofting over treetops as its fovea, either one or the other never leaving sight of ebony Anabaa, ginger-locks Qiaona, ample Constance and girlish Lizbett huddling together the boy-chick and orphans, two toddlers and three at five-pushing-six and six-turning-seven. The eagle did not hesitate in its vigilant flight until the horses stopped pulling the wagon at Falls House's gateway.

Four women and fair curly-haired boy-chick dash past lamppost, its allure-blinking green beacon gently beckoning feet fly up steps over threshold through doorway into shelter as ever-watchful eagle perched silently in deep eaves' shadow.

CHAPTER 6

So on went the globe's years spinning away Spring's months unto Summer into Fall then to Winter as in a gentle slow dance to the plan-of-boundary-mandate scripted of a Hand in heavens above gifted to great Earth below.

And so did the years increase in the ages of two boys; Prince Rhynn of a stone castle and free-boy Ravenz of a brick house. They grew strong in stature and wise in mind, each curious and brave. King Breretyn's firstborn and heir busied himself learning the atlas of mansion passageways turning into corridors and grounds' mazes leading to pathways through iron gateways along roadways crossing Belle Passe to swim Half Moon Lagoon and view villages and kingdom beyond lying between riverbank and mountaintop, tree line and valley in high noon's light.

Queen Latezia's second-born bird-child busied himself learning the atlas of side streets to mercantile past marketplace and pasture around vineyard in valley through forest pathways along roadways crossing Belle Passe to swim Half Moon Lagoon or fish river's bank under full moon's glow.

Each boy is a prince in his realm gaining wealth in this knowledge gaining contentment in his soul.

As odd it seems never do two identical boys come face to face as they traverse the ways of each other's footsteps during the course of days' hours and nights' eras of this natural-circling-about-way as one and the other ravels his existence during winters in court and across kingdom in summers.

So goes the mystery of the two boys appearing to the eyes of all merchants in shops and free boys in streets, to all sentries guarding gates and butlers posturing at doorways, servants plumping pillows in chambers and cooks wielding spoons in the kitchens, to royals King Breretyn and Poppi and Her Majesty, the Queen Latezia and Mummy as one boy, Prince Rhynn, or,

There you are, Jaguar! "I'm Ravenz." *Oh, a bird!* "I'm Jaguar lurking!" *I just saw you hovering there, little bird but now you stalk here, jungle cat!* "I'm Ravenz" causing confusion tangling minds...except, of course, the eyes and reminiscences of Anabaa, Qiaona, Constance and Lizbett.

⁓

Ebo felt the boy's presence in the doorway even before he raised his eyes from the anvil to see a shadow darkening the rough plank-board flooring.

"Out and about early today, young prince?" Ebo continued hammering the hot steel into shape.

"I'm Ravenz."

"Cloud hopper...terra prowler...so what brings you by my old blacksmithing shack this time of morning? Had your breakfast yet?" Ebo laughed as he pointed to carafe of milk half consumed, sitting on a bench against the wall. "Feel free to help yourself if the kitchen was closed to you earlier. Those cooks run a tough ship! 'No one eats before the rooster crows!' they cackle through keyholes! I looked through one once and nearly got my eye scorched by all the steam rising from the pots boiling over onto the stovetops and all. So, I don't recommend peeking through keyholes!"

"Thank you for the swig of milk, Mister Ebo, sir." Ravenz watched Ebo shape a horseshoe, tapping here and there around the curve with his clubbed mallet until only he was happy with the result. When this moment happened for Ebo the man picked up the shoe and held it to the light admiring the gleam in the shine, the angle of the curves, and particular thickness overall proclaiming it a very adequate shoe indeed for the likes of the prince's young stallion, Pretzyl.

"The grooms are preparing to bring Pretzyl by later this morning to be fitted with his new shoes! The king has plans to put Pretzyl into training for hunting season coming."

"I've seen the grooms in the stables already today." Ravenz paused while seeking a place to sit straddling a sawhorse nearby the glowing forge's welcome warmth. "Horses sure do need a lot of fussing! Hay and oat buckets everywhere, saddles and bridles hanging on walls, blankets lay over railings, brushes and picks in pots, lots of stuff for horses down in the stables way back there and now four new shiny shoes for the Pretzyl colt in this place!"

"Well, stick around awhile and you'll learn how they are attached to the hooves, if your stomach isn't growling too much, that is!" Ebo laughed and winked at the boy before setting aside the last horseshoe with the others. Then with a turn of his arm to the bench picked up the carafe and drained the vessel of its content. Patting his stomach Ebo let forth a hearty belch. "Ah, great stuff! Milk makes men of us, raven-boy, and men of young jaguar-cats and princes, too!" Ravenz thought through the wisdom of the blacksmith's words upon watching Ebo's muscles bulging under the skin in his forearms below his rolled-up shirt sleeves.

"I'm late for breakfast, Mister Ebo, sir."

"Well, off with you then, prince! Remember, the doors lock up again right quick as those cooks sure do run a tight ship! Remember, no peeking!"

Ravenz heard Ebo's voice trail to silence as his feet flew along the dirt pathway past arena around stable over grazing knoll through fence's gate across lawns up stone steps down corridor through doorway to kitchen table only to slide to a stop on wooden bench's end before plate bearing high loads of steaming ham and poached eggs.

And a carafe of fresh milk waited just upside and to the right of a hefty fork's tip.

⌒

Breretyn felt his son's presence in the trophy room even before his eyes caught sight of the child's shadow darkening a length of zebra skin lying across marble floor. Reveling in the exquisite stealth that is solitary to children in this particular age of discovery, the king waited silently where he sat in his great high-back chair facing massive mantle supporting regal heads bearing crowns of antlers. The eyes of these majestic beasts glowed brilliant and clear even at this year, even so long after life's breath had been snuffed from their beings at the hands of King Neptlyn and his king-father before him and on backward in the line of royal ancestors.

What are you saying to me, wilderness beast, and what do you see in my eyes? Do you hear my heart beating and wonder of my intent? Would you have eaten me would that you found me first for you have fed many who found you?

Rhynn sneezed.

The king turned in his chair at the sound and seeing his firstborn standing on the threshold waved his hand to enter. But the young prince flinches not a muscle as his eyes stare up into the beasty eyes in the heads looking down at him from their mounts on the wall. The boy stood still as a statue frozen to the floor contemplating fang teeth and incisors in jaws still appearing to quiver in hunger and thirst. His ears hear low growls, or so he imagined...*or is the sound purrs or rumbles in bellies...do nostrils flare inhaling my scent...*

"Poppi!" whispered Prince Rhynn.

"Ah, you've discovered my lair and the lair of your grandfather and all fathers before him! Come, enter and sit by me, my son. Tis alright in this place as all spirits are as one in peace now that they rest silently where they lay mounted so high."

"Where is the rest of them; their legs and tails and all the animal parts? What happened to them that it's only the heads I see sticking out on those planks?"

"Ah, young prince, they've been hunted is all, and all that remains of them are these regal heads for they were the greatest of their kind and thus the greatest for our kind. In the days of my father and his fathers before him the meat of these beasts fed men's bellies and the bones were boiled for the broth that healed sickness in harsh winter's unforgiving cold. The skins of their backs lay warming the cold stone floors in the rooms of this castle and in our subjects' houses in the villages. Hides hang on walls keeping icy drafts out and fires' heat in. Fur lines our coats and coverings for heads lending kind gentle warmth over our shivering thin skin throbbing beneath. It is the natural cycle of great nature's nurturing way; that the taken lives of these beasts furthers our lives so all might survive and thrive; life unto life."

"But why keep the heads up there…like that…eyes looking out at what is yours and not the woods that is theirs?"

The king looked at his son as he pondered the child's question for a certain deep wisdom lay at the root of his query. For one as young as his heir to contemplate this thing rattled Breretyn so he sobered in his thoughts stilling a quick thoughtless response.

After a time of private deliberation the king offered up this;

"The heads are preserved here for our remembrance of and the gratefulness we have for the beasts' sacrifice that Nature lead us unto. All these things grew fat and strong in their realm that we may grow strong and fat in ours. In this way you and I looking up at them looking down at us will never forget that life builds on life, life after life."

Without pause or fearful trembling Prince Rhynn came to stand by his father's side. Taking the hand of the king in his own and after pressing his small fingertips into the deep engravings in the gleaming signet ring roundabout King Breretyn's sovereign finger asked straightforwardly,

"How much longer must Jaguar wait till he's big and strong enough to go with you to find such a big animal to feed all the people?"

"Ebo, the blacksmith is fitting new shoes on Pretzyl's hooves this very minute! Come, prowling-cat! Let's be off to the shed and see what we shall see! The hunting hours are upon us. The men in the villages will gather at forest's edge in fortnight's time.I will begin your special instruction this day so you will be ready to ride with me into the woods on that day, but only if you have tended to your breakfast of steamed ham and poached eggs, of course!"

~⌒

Latezia feels the presence of the one she thinks to be her young jaguar-prince's spirit emanating from the king's private room even before she pushed wide the door further to peek about its interior tosearch where her little jungle cat might crouch. She sees it then; a slight shadow darkening the striped zebra skin cast there by light beaming through high window. Her child stood alone having slipped away from his governess so stealthily and here he stands now, poised proudly, head raised and eyes fixed on a beast's face staring back at him from its mount on the wall above the fireplace's grand mantle.

This royal child bears the structure of his father's bones. I can see the king's pose in the back of him even now. I know he is my Breretyn's son when his jade-green eyes look into mine and his lips curve at their ends like that. And the way his little hands come into mine do I feel the same

strength in his fingers and warmth in his palms. He will grow greatly and wise as Breretyn and Neptlyn before Breretyn and all kings in this royal line bearing the blood of ancestors gone before. And what of this child escaping his governess for did not my king say this is his heir's house to explore and realm to discover? This time is upon me and I must not interfere in the way of his learning these things. So I'll wait here as mother and comforter, as listener and question answerer...

Ravenz sensed her presence on the threshold of this strange and wondrous room even before he'd turn around and drop to a bow.He'd smelled the woman's magical perfume in an earlier time when he was very young and just discovering his feet's value upon his escape from Mountainwing's west chambers down hallway in a runaway chasing game as Lizbett followed close at his heels. But he'd been stopped cold in his tracks at the sight of the royal beauty occupying all space between wall and wall, floor to near ceiling or so he imagined from his lowly stature of only three feet in height.

And she had stood before him then as she stands now; regal, silent and solitary, scented the same way in perfume so sublime as to anesthetize him to a near faint at her feet as he'd seen Lizbett swoop to the floor and then sweep her arm in a grand arc saluting, 'Your Majesty, Queen Latezia.' Even now as she did then Ravenz knows the queen only stares at him where she stands waiting for him to turn on his heel, look into her star sapphire blue eyes and drop to bended knee.

The boy turned slowly about in the spot where he stands upon warm striped zebra skin under a sun's ray shining across this room. And everything Ravenz remembered in his toddling-child time came true before his jade eyes that here stands the same exquisite woman known to Lizbett as The Queen.

But this time Latezia's gentle face beamed kind radiance. Her eyes twinkle like clear diamonds and laughter dances behind her smile. Her lips part as if to commence speech so Ravenz quickly dropped to his knee and bowed his head low. Ravenz' eyes see only the furry hairs in a skinned zebra's white and black stripes. His boyish hand brushed over their prickly texture as a child strokes a pet.

"Your Majesty, Queen Latezia!"

Latezia stared. *What's this? I'm Mummy! I'm not Mummy? Has Mummy gone...from you?*

The child rose slowly and stood erect with eyes downcast as he'd remembered Lizbett's pose waiting for the queen's response that day in the hallway in an earlier time.

"My, my! Oh, my goodness! You honor me with such a gracious salutation this morning, Rhynn!"

Latezia's child lifted his head at her words and without blinking looked deeply into her eyes.

"I am Ravenz."

"Oh, I see! You are a bird now...an *imaginary* friend... I see. Well, you've alighted in the right place to play this game for in His Majesty's room are such fabulous beasts once majestic in *their* prime, all kings in their forest realm."

"These forest beasts are King Breretyn's imaginary friends?"

"Oh, no, dear raven-bird, these are not *imaginary* friends at all but were very real creatures to His Majesty, King Neptlyn, your grandfather and father, Breretyn, now king."

"I have a real friend, too. He's an eagle, a king in the skies. I can see his white eyes looking down at me from the clouds like the king sees these dark eyes looking down at him here from up there on the walls."

The boy waved his hand in a grand sweep around the room, and up to beams' crisscrossing rafters from which hang large iron circles holding a thousand candles each and again to the mantle-place.

"Eagle's eyes watch me in daytime and they glow out in the night to me like two little white moons. Eagle hovers above me just as these beasts sit above King."

Latezia moved not a muscle from where she stood rooted to the floor under the doorway's arch. She considered this room His Majesty's private place where he came to contemplate his father, Neptlyn, and all grandsires before him having sat in these chairs pondering memories only they knew of and not shared with their queens. The threshold is the line she stops her footfall when advancing this place. The trophy chamber smells of cigars' smoke and leather, of old steel and feathered arrow. Even when the great armchair vacated of the king Latezia still hears forest rustlings and low rumblings swirling within. Soft breezes waft here while summers' heat eclipse winters' deep freeze.

Or is it all just logs smoldering in the fireplace there and drafts sweeping down chimney chute?

"You are very beautiful, Queen Latezia."

Latezia startled unaware she'd been staring...aware of her senses stirring on the edge of this place. Her eyes focus only on Ravenz now as his young form took control of her binocular.

Since when did you grow so big, infant boy? Even now I see the man you are to become in your jade-green eyes and I hear your man-voice in my ears. When did you grow away from Mummy that today you see a queen for one day you'll become king and... I am a brick-maker's daughter.

Latezia closed her eyes in this thought and when they opened again it was into an empty space they peer. No child stands before her on a zebra's striped skin warming marble floor before fireplace and mantle. Only tranquil solitude meets her gaze as sunlight beams softly through high windows causing hazy shadows to fall against wall, upon floor, over armchair and hearth.

"Rhynn?" Latezia stepped away from the doorway and searched the corridor both right and left, her eyes widely open. She gathered her skirts in her hands and her feet sped as in flight above marble floor laying between granite walls past tables bearing urns of floral foliage and intoshadowy alcoves then twirling before high mirrors hanging on walls reflecting all back and forth an back again that of a beautiful mother chasing her running-along child.

"Rhynn? Where did you fly off to just then, little raven?"

"I'm here, Mummy! No, *here*! Look back here!"

Rhynn!

Latezia spun around at the sound of her young prince's call echoing up hallway from stairwell's vault. And in that moment she saw her child let go his Poppi's royal hand as he dashed forward to clasp outreaching arms about the queen's quaking being caught up now in an urgent child-hug.

Mother and son stood locked together in this way swaying side to side as two souls who've been separated by mountain and sea and a year's worth of months gone from their eyes. Latezia smelled horse and saddle on the body of her son and the scent of smoke came up from his hair. Then taking his hand in hers pressed his fingertips to her lips smelling reins and bridle there.

"You should see Pretzyl's shiny shoes, Mummy! Ebo attached them already this morning! And Poppi says I'm to become a grand beast hunter! Poppi gave me my first lesson just today."

Latezia looked up into Breretyn's twinkling emerald eyes and understood all words Rhynn spoke of is true.

"Our Prince Rhynn is a young mighty jaguar possessing patience and stealth, stout heart and the promise of great strength to come in his growing-up muscles," declared the proud king.

When the queen looked back at her son standing now before window in high noon's brilliant sun she saw what she'd seen in the king's trophy room seemingly a moment before; the man-to-be blooming in the child's face before her, his eyes of clear green softly shimmering and their gaze on her being unwavering.

"You are so pretty, Mummy."

                         ◦

Sun's sweet post meridian rays beamed quietly now through the parlor's arched bay windows lending other-worldly dimension to Parqai's majestic portrait not otherwise noticed in any other hours' light. Latezia stands in this place entranced by images Breretyn's artist transformed onto a barren canvas those being a royal infant cradled in the arms of his queen mother as two angel-cherubs hover on clouds' feathery fringes above.

Two baby heads I saw floating in my birthing hour's dream...one drawing closer, the other retreating...And I look at these faces this day and I see what Parqai saw then.My child bears two souls that I know now to be truth; today I saw in my prince a man retreating his child-being, then a boy-child still rushing unto his mother closer andreaching. Even as I gaze on Parqai's painting I behold this truth in my vision for I see in the identical cherub faces the eyes sparkle differently; one set glows softly jade-green, the other's twinkle emerald-gem glimmer.

A silage of myrrh, frankincense and bergamot wafts into the room and Latezia knows King Breretyn enters this realm bathed of the day's earlier scent of hunter-on-horse straddling leather saddle on a galloping stallion's back, reins in hand, face pressed against neck...now only morning's dim memory.

And she knows in an instant of his advance unto her being as his palms now warm her bare shoulders, his fingertips playing gently along clavicles' bone and thumbs softly unyielding on atlas and axis.

Latezia leaned back against his warmth, her head settling into the hollow of his shoulder and she closed her eyes lost in reminiscence of a past summer day in the mercantile.

A young girl skips down the cobblestone street swinging a satchel of tin bobbins…and a gypsy stranger gathers the girl up in his arms, hurt and bleeding, and sets her on his horse. 'Tell me the way to the house of your father'… She leans back her head into the hollow of his shoulder and sees his eyes are soft jade-green. Who are you, kind green-eyed traveling stranger? 'Forgive me this…I am who you righteously suspect.'

"I see you in him, Latezia." Breretyn whispered above her head. "When I am with him you are with me. When we rode into the forest today he turned back his head my way and looked at me soberly a moment as if hearing I'd called his name, but then he smiled at me with the same smile I see in you and it halted my thoughts and all my actions paralyzed…so stunned was I by this boy-beauty in him.

"But my father, King Neptlyn, lives in him too, for he sits in the saddle as the king did and he communicates with animals in the very same way. In last month's ride he rode on my Lightfoot with me sitting behind guiding the steed over heather plain to Half Moon Lagoon and a snake hissed in the pathway startling Lightfoot to rear up in fear. But our prince sat calmly and only spoke in near-silent voice but heard above all chaos, 'Eagle is coming for the snake, Your Majesty.' And Lightfoot settled himself and waited patiently upon the path for then an eagle did swoop down from the heavens and snatch up the snake in its talons and was gone in that instant from our view."

I am Ravenz…imaginary friend…Eagle is my friend

"Our son will be a great hunter as my father was for he sees which beast to let be from the beast he will take by way of which beast's eyes glow out to him from those glowing not."

Eagle's white eyes watch me in daytime and glow out to me like two moons in the night

"Artist Parqai saw these things in our babe for he painted the cherubs thusly… identical…but yet quite not."

In her greatest dream which is not a dream at all Latezia knows of this place she floats in is Breretyn's arms. And behind her closed eyes she sees…

Two fair cherubs hovering above her head

Such plump pink infant-angels…wings sweetly fluttering

Coming closer

CHAPTER 7

"Ah, come on, Ravenz, just one more game," whined Kyrro. "The sun sits high in the sky still and Papa won't need me for at least an hour and you know we can't win being a player down and you're our best tackler and ball carrier!"

"I've already played one more game than I meant to and besides, you are the team's best ball catcher! Lift your knees higher when you dodge your opponent. That makes you tougher to tackle, Kyrro! I have to catch fish in the river right now because today is Qiaona's birthday and Constance wants to smoke her a celebration supper on the Alder wood plank Ebo gave me!"

Ravenz hears Kyrro's useless protest dissipate to shrieks and hollers as new harpastum match commences on the plot of trampled weeds edging the mercantile. Ravenz did not look back as he tossed the ball over his shoulder laughing softly as he heard feet shuffling across hard packed clay. He is to the count of four before he heard the muted sound of the sphere land in Kyrro's arms.

He knows it makes no difference if he stays and plays along; the outcome is always the same. No one remembers to keep the score because no one remembers to count. Body slams against body. Grunts and moans would be exhaled. Vocabulary follows. Sometimes if a player is lucky he'd grapple an opponent long enough to bring his belly to the ground, strip the ball from his grip then toss it off to a speedy teammate only to watch the ensuing action from the vantage point of his knees as one heroic teammate cradling the ball valiantly against his sternum makes a dash across center-line into home territory to the roar of the crowd. How a game comes to end is always a mystery. Even now Ravenz can't be certain how it is that he'd chosen this moment to call a quit to the latest event.

The only certain thought Ravenz holds in his mind at this moment is of the Alder plank soaking in slow-flowing shallows caught in the rocks at Half Moon Lagoon's narrow neck before flowing out into wide river along endless banks. At the farthest end of the basin lay Half Moon Lagoon, the place where Lizbett brought him as a small boy and patiently urged him to take a step closer the tiny lapping waves tickling slimy rocks. He had looked at Lizbett standing waist-deep in the water, her arms outstretched and sun dazzling her tawny hair. White skin under her eyes turned blush as if rose petals. Her teeth shone white as snowballs framed by crimson lips and her voice called to him as breezes rustling spring leaves. Her palms turned to cups scooping water up and then opened them flat to sweep it all away back. Back and forth her hands scooped and swept until he dipped a toe into the lagoon's frothy edge.

But it wasn't to the muddy bottom he sank but into the strength of Lizbett's sweet arms his little body floated. His face had pressed against her shoulder as his arms clung to her neck. He smelled bath soap in her hair and was comforted. They stood locked together like this the whole afternoon simply standing in one spot swaying back and forth in each other's clutch feeling water soak through pant-legs and skirt cooling sun-burning skin. And Ravenz remembered the silence of that time for Lizbett's voice hushed the moment he'd entered her embrace. It was after she emerged from the water and set his feet upon dry grassy ground did he hear the roar of the falls tumbling into Half Moon Lagoon's basin as it cascaded over the rocky ledge so far across the way where they stood and so high above their heads. White vapor rose from the great splash like ghosts amassed in space between water and air.

It all had been a magical day full of magical hours encouraging a magical first-happening occurring in a magical watery world below magical firmament above. And he'd learned to float on his back, eyes clenched shut against sun's glare, the thin skin of his face growing hot under the rays. Then one day he turned over and floated on his belly as his arms ploughed the water as Lizbett's had done. And he found himself moving closer to shore so he turned about and paddled back to Lizbett only to giggle as he splashed his hands down and kicked his heels up.

"You are swimming, Ravenz! What a big boy you are and so brave to paddle this far out in the lagoon! Good boy, Ravenz!"

And Lizbett had clapped her hands together and he'd seen a million water droplets spraying out from her arms like diamonds glinting in the sunlight. That night at his bedside as he knelt upon rag rug and right before his lips uttered, "Amen" he thankedGod-the-Father-God-the-Son-God-the-Holy-Spirit for Angel Lizbett.

The pebble Ravenz had been kicking along the roadway with each step since leaving Kyrro at the playing field skittered along twenty feet beyond before taking a bounce against a rut, hopping up in the air only to disappear from sight over the side of the road. All sound hushed in that moment before Ravenz heard the pebble clattering against rocks before plunking into the river.

I'm at the lagoon already, mused Ravenz as he glanced down to where the pebble had dropped, ripples still fanning out from the impact. The waters flowing here run gently but are deep and the fish he'd caught in this place were fat and their flesh very white and tasting sweetly-flavored almost like young spring air smells. Looking down from where he stood he saw his Alder plank lay fully soaked through where he'd trapped it in the rocks hours before. Ravenz patted his pocket where a bundle of string hid a lead sinker and sharp hook at its core.

It took only a moment for Ravenz to find a swollen gray worm shrouding from daylight between a cold rock and damp earth. It took only half a moment to drop hook, sinker and string-line into the dark watery depth that played just beyond the toes of his burlap plimsolls. His hands griped the ends of a smooth twig holding the end of the line, tied as it is in a knot after a few tight wraps about its middle. Setting himself down on the ground at the base of a sapling Ravenz drew up his knees to his chin then rested his head against the young trunk and closed his eyes. In the distance the great falls roar as a solitary eagle perched in the branches above his head cried an invocation unto the proceedings going on below river's glassy surface.

Ravenz' thoughts turned to Lizbett standing patiently in the gauzy white wedding dress Constance, Qiaona and Anabaa had taken turns pinning, sewing and beading in the evening hours. He remembered how silent Falls House became as the days wore on into a week as crates piled in the corner of her bedchamber stacked one more higher at the end of each day until Bako came by with his carriage and carried them all away. He'd stolen a peek through Anabaa's sheer curtain and seen Bako holding both Lizbett's hands in his own as his eyes stared into her face so close before placing a kiss on her forehead then turned away to his carriage. Lizbett stood at the path's end under the lamppost watching him retreat father down the roadway. The blinking beacon cast an intermittent green and white sheen across her creamy-porcelain features.

Green…white…green…white…green…

The church inside looked like the outside. Flowers billowed at the ends of the pews and filled the chancel. The entire way of the nave lay paved in petals flying up in a sweet wake behind Lizbett's slow steps toward the altar drawing closer and closer to Bako. A choir chanted in Latin and thick white candles were lit. The gossamer veil covering her face was lifted away and Bako kissed Lizbett's face once and then many times before the villagers gathered inside the church-garden. Ravenz remembered silence and then a burst of cheers.

That night after the wondrous wedding feast ended he'd returned to Falls House to discover his all his belongings had been moved from Anabaa's room into Lizbett's bedchamber and his patchwork eiderdown from his cramped boxy crib now covered her bed.

"It's your own private chamber now, Ravenz."

Snuggling into the dip in the mattress imprinted there by the weight of Lizbett's body Ravenz felt her presence still and smelling her perfume lingering faintly on the pillow he fell asleep in this otherly embrace.

He had been only four-and-a-half.

Ravenz opened his eyes and yawned. Fish nibbling at the bait caused subtle tugs on the stick to nudge his grip.

And now I'm eleven.

In one swift motion as in a jerk Ravenz yanked on the line setting the hook deeply into the lip of the surprised fish. The line grew taught and threatened to unravel and split apart but still Ravenz held fast to the twig even as the fish swam around in circles or tried several times to dart upstream or down. He saw the white bones of his pointy knuckles show through his thin skin. At times the line fell slack as the fish rested. Or maybe it simply wanted to finish nibbling a prime worm. Slowly now Ravenz began rolling the twig in his hands thus spooling the string around twig thus shortening its depth. He felt the weight of the fish pulling down hard on the string and knew it to be a very thick fish which pleased him greatly.

The success of catching such a splendid fish so quickly left time in the afternoon for reflective daydreaming and Ravenz considered spending every minute of the hour ahead watching the cloud formations waft and shift in the blue troposphere above. Besides, his fish would remain fresh where it dangled from hook and line only four feet below the river's surface. Ravenz smiled with satisfaction as he locked the twig-dangling-string and baited-hook-captured-fish under the bends of his knees then locked his hands together behind his head. Leaning back against the bank's cool moss-carpeted earth his thoughts turned to the supper Constance has planned for Qiaona's birthday.

Ravenz fished the river since he turned eight since the day he'd stumbled into Ebo's blacksmith shack and caught him snipping lengths of wires he unwound from spools lining a plank shelf along the far wall. He watched as the blacksmith gripped each wire piece with pliers turning it into a gently-shaped U. Ebo turned his pliers deftly in his fingers then held up the piece in his hand to reveal a small loop at one end. The other end of the U was cut shorter at an angle and filed to a sharp point. The little object was held over the forge's fire with tweezers for a moment before being dipped into a cup of cold water then hammered lightly on the anvil to temper its hardness. Ebo set his project aside and started the process over with a new length of wire. If Ravenz had not sneezed he doubted Ebo would have even noticed the boy standing inside the doorway watching his hands work.

But Ebo did know, of course, of the prince's presence in the doorway for he said, "Bless you, Jaguar, little terra-prowler! You are becoming stealthier by the day and hour!"

"I'm Ravenz." He wiped his nose on his sleeve. The smoke and dust made Ravenz' nose itch and eyes water.

"Ah, a cloud-hopper today is you?" Ebo laughed. "Still, either way you choose to be you are as silent as an eagle gliding in circles above the earth, eyes following every movement in grasses and pathways below or stealthy as the jungle cat stalking every movement in the grasses and on pathways happening before his prowl." By this time Ebo had accumulated a collection of three wire items on his little workbench. Even though they appeared in the same family of item each had slightly differing characteristics. Size was the main difference. The loops at the ends ranged from small, medium and large. And the width of the U ranged from narrow to near-closed circle in diameter. Stoutness and length of wire mattered. But the pointy ends were the same for all; very sharp and silvery-gleaming in the light that shone through the small window above Ebo's forge and anvil. Ebo abruptly stopped the whole process, hung up his pliers, tongs and tweezers and set aside the file in a box. Dumping the water from the cup over the flame in the forge he turned to Ravenz and spoke in a cheerful tone over sizzling hisses and through smoke.

"You caught me fashioning fish hooks for your Christmas present! How about I just give them to you now while river's water still flows free of winter's ice and I can show you how to tie the sinker and hook to the line and select an appetizing bait to lure a good-eating fish? Let's drop a line right now and see what comes of our labor!"

So the boy and the blacksmith had jaunted away for the afternoon down the path out the back way past stables and arena around orchard trees through the gate in a far fence then onto the roadway leading to Belle Passe and great falls' Half Moon Lagoon to its narrow neck stopping before widening into the river flowing gently endlessly onward. They had come to this very place where the water ran deep and cold at the bottom and where fish slept in crevasses in embankments and then wakened to fatten themselves on crawlers bloating on the muddy dark river bottom.

"Overturned rocks in shady places reveal the plumpest bait and the sleepiest…easier to capture!"

Ravenz opened his eyes and gazed at the sky and the clouds bunching in massive soft puffs hanging by invisible threads above his head.

What holds you up, cloud and what's in your belly? Where do you vanish away to in an hour or does the sky eat you all up? Why is the sky so blue when the only things it eats are giant white clouds?

And then he remembered the sky turning dark and sour as lightning flashed and thunder rolled spewing great belches of rain and knew then the sky had gorged too much on fat clouds.

Ravenz thinks of Anabaa and the soft lap on which he'd sat cradled in her arms as he suckled sweet water at her breast until the day he sat upright on her knees in a chair pushed so close to the table it pressed against his chest. It was the first time he remembered seeing a plate piled high with fragrant objects that disappeared into the mouths of Qiaona, Lizbett, Anabaa and Constance. His eyes watched as their jaws moved up and down-side to side behind muscles in cheeks working in odd ways not seen during speech. An errant pea escaped Anabaa's fork and rolled across the plate to its rim. He reached out to the pea and picked it up in his fingers then followed their lead placing the steamed orb in his mouth.

This event signaled the end of suckling and the beginning of chewing. He sat in a small high chair of his own before a small plate of his own eating morsels put there just for him the same as the others.

"And now *I* have captured food for *their* plates!" spoke Ravenz aloud in the quietness of the place where he sat upright now with twig still secured between knee and calf bearing Qioana's secret birthday dinner surprise.

"That's the duty of our station here; to care of our loyal subjects, Rhynn!"

An animal whinnied on the roadway above the riverbank spinning the boy about. Startled at the sudden deep boom of voice and horse but managing to grasp the twig with both hands before it could slink from his view below the gray surface, he looked to the source on the roadway. The vision meeting his eyes is one of a king on a stallion so regally poised in such stillness as to appear in a master painting. Ravenz saw King Breretyn's eyes shimmering green as the leaves in the afternoon sunlight and his wavy hair shone soft brown as branches. The golden steed on which he sits mounted snorted once again then lifted its majestic head and opened its mouth to commence chewing on small clumps of new leaves dangling from branches' smallest limbs.

Ravenz stared then found his tongue.

"I am Ravenz."

What? No jaguar? You are playing at being a bird now?

"Of course…a keen-eyed eagle can spot a fine fish in its solitary flight so high above the unsuspecting…"

"Eagle dives swift and low and snatches the top feeder snatching a fly."

"Well, don't be too sad if your talon-hook snagged a blade of river grass or is caught in the rocks. Fishing teaches great patience which serves eagles and young boys well."

"I wait patiently, Your Majesty." Ravenz felt the weight of the fish pulling on his line but he did not wind the twig upward in his hands but let it hang slack in that moment at the side of his leg. "Ebo told me all about patience the first day we dropped a line here."

"Ebo knows a lot of things and it's wise that you listen to his words when he decides to speak to you. As for me I'm off for a swim in the lagoon as I've been at the brick-maker's factory since dawn loading and hauling materials for my university's observatory. It is nearly complete. The optics engineers are assembling the telescope as I tell you this news. Then you can see constellations hang in the celestial vault through *two* lenses as your eagle scans the terrestrial plain through each eye's *two* fovea.But now my body is gritty with clay dust.I can't go home to my queen with mortar caked in my ears!"

And with those words the steed and King Breretyn turned away from Ravenz' gaze and ambled onward to the place in the heather where horse grazed happily on low grasses and king disrobed. Ravenz can see the man's nakedness even from this distance gliding through Half Moon Lagoon's clear water with powerful smooth strokes of his arms. He watches as the king turned his face to the side and breathed in air and how he turned his face into the water as his limbs propelled his body forward across the lagoon. In one swift move the king dropped his head beneath the surface and swung his straight legs skyward joined together at the knees and crossed at the ankles before disappearing beneath the glossy surface in a deep dive.

Ravenz stares.

No splash applauded the action. Not even a ripple followed the king's descent into the depths. It was as if the event had not happened at all so tranquil lay the water in the lagoon in its reflection of silvery clouds and deep green trees lining the basin. Dark shadows mirroring a flock of low-flying birds is the only movement unfolding in this suddenly surreal scene. Only billowing white mist of the fall's cascade added drama to the otherwise paralyzing state of Half Moon Lagoon. The boy leaned forward as his searching eyes scanned the vast watery surface. Ravenz' lungs ached in their demand for oxygen as he'd not breathed since the vision of such grace going down captured his eye.

But in that instant the king's body erupted from the depths, wet face turned to the sky glistening in the late golden sunlight and mouth open wide in a great smile as his long arms flew out at his sides spraying water droplets glittering like diamonds in an arc about his head.

Overwhelmed with unfamiliar relief the boy dropped back to the place where he'd patiently waited an hour long gone and thankfully inhaled the scent of damp earth, moss, river water and fish.

Ravenz pulled Qiaona's plump supper from the river and tied the string about its tail. The soaked Alder board slapping softly between two gray rocks played a gentle accompaniment to the yearning his heart felt as he daydreamed of swimming with Lizbett.

～❍

Clatter and clang happened in Rhynn's saddlebag-satchel as pick, tongs, pan, sieve and tin-lidded cup jostled in turn against Pretzyl's plodding hip. What might have been noise in any otherwise time seemed as musical dissonant tones to the young prince's ears in afternoon's summer silence. It was as if the universe had emptied itself of chirping crickets, buzzing flies and snapping-winged grasshoppers. No birds twittered current events from treetops and no snakes rattled or hissed warnings in grasses. Not even a rabbit grazes shoots by the trail and no squirrels dart off with stolen-property-stuffed cheeks. It is as if the day had forgotten to begin except for the sun's rising rushing a lazy moon into deep hiding.

Rhynn sought Ebo's help sharpening his arrows' points after breakfast but the shack stood vacant of heat, smoke, hammering and Ebo. The blacksmith had long before put down the fire in the forge. Every tool hung cold from its stout hook in the wall. A rusty water vessel canted against the anvil at an obtuse angle and the rough plank floor rests swept clean of coal dust and shavings. Not even a trace of litter bothered the bin and no scent of sweat permeated the shack's still air.Rhynn stood for a long moment in the doorway's threshold listening to the sound of nothing.

Absence has its own sound, mused the prince. It is the rhythm of one's spirit pulsing; the hum of a man's soul thinking and thunder of his being at toil that resonates silently in the vacuum of his absence.

This is Ebo's place and this place owns Ebo but where is Ebo?

So Rhynn replaced the arrows in his quiver and buckled bag over crossbow behind saddle and cloth, mounted Pretzyl then nudged horse onto trail heading off in the direction of stable past arena, around cherry trees, apple, peach and apricot orchard through gate in the west fence and onto roadway leading to Belle Pass and falls beyond. The lure of the mercantile pulled at his desire for his mouth watered to eat berry tarts from widows' baskets and besides, he liked stopping by the cigar merchant's shack best because sugarcane stalks oozing sweet crystals lay in a gunnysack hidden among fragrant stogies packed in teak boxes. One could be had for a halfpence.

And Rhynn fell into a daydream of his encounters in the mercantile cobblestone quarters.

It was a day in springtime past during a game of harpastum in the ragweed field next to the entrance gates opening onto the wide street of merchant shops that Rhynn suddenly hungered for cakes as long had the lectures of numbers and letters ended and endless had become the string of games until Rhynn tossed the sphere into the air above his head to land at will unto the hollers coming at him from behind.

*Just one more game…*shouted a boy named Kyrro calling him the name of a bird named raven…*You know we can't win without you…* and he'd shouted back, "My name is Rhynn!"*But his voice had gone lost to the shrieks of new game commencing and theprince did not look back.*

Pretzyl whinnied.

"I hunger for a nibble now so to market we go, Pretzyl! Artist Parqai will be there painting a scene at his easel while little girls giggle picking dozing butterflies off flower blooms' petals. Mothers buying silk cloths and vegetables will be chattering together as fathers stand in huddles next to the cigar-maker's shack discussing the weather and blowing smoke rings in the air. Tinkers annoy birds hammering copper onto steel pans and fat wax candles hang by their wicks from a rope like fringes on the candle-makers' tents. " Pretzyl plodded onward, head bobbing in rhythm to the clank and clink of the tools clattering about in a satchel bumping against hip.

"Soap bars in buckets and bread loaves on trays... melons piled in crates and wind chimes dangling from hooks...scarves knotted to pegs waft as flags in breezes...beckoning beckoning..." Rhynn chanted aloud over and over to an audience of no one but one horse, Pretzyl.

So it was in this state of mission that young Prince Rhynn now rode his agreeable stallion through quiet heather plain lured by the vision of the falls' tumbling water over high rocky precipice into the basin below. The sight of such powerful beauty humbled the prince to his bones as he sat in saddle watching water streaming into a basin that seemingly never ran over its rim but flowed onward in its journey down river winding through valley along mountain base stretching to a vanishing point but yet not ending. Ships always returned to the sea.

Pretzyl lurched sideways then reared shattering Rhynn's reverie.

"Easy, boy! Easy now." Rhynn whispered to his mount. In less than a heartbeat Pretzytl settled his hooves to the ground, muscles relaxing beneath cloth and saddle. "What is it, Pretzyl? What did you see that caused this startle in you?" A shadow happened on the pathway then as a lizard's tongue captured a meal of near-invisible insect and then all vanished from sight as reptile sought cover in a tuft of high grasses before emerging to comfort its belly on a smooth sun-heating rock.

"Calm now, Pretzyl. It was only a harmless hungry little reptile." Rhynn patted the stallion's warm neck. And the prince's gaze fell upstream to the lazy river glittering under high-noon sun away of the falls and drama of its fast-flowing-over turbulence happening in basin below. Dazzled by its shimmer and quite forgetting the gnaw taunting his belly the desire to eat berry tarts while cruising the merchant's shops evaporated in the moment as he thought of the satchel's tools and early morning's intent; that of finding his Mummy, Queen Latezia a present.

Ebo's words came to his remembrance as he guided Pretzyl off-trail through the soft heather toward the gentle bend in the river.

"One must learn to read the river, Jaguar! Just as the cat surveys the savannah your eye must scan the embankments and flow. Tiz important to see where the water slows in its journey for gold is heavy and will roll to rest under low pressure leaving light useless gravels to wash away downstream. Look for the highest watermark left by winter's runoff and driftwood left on high ground to dry in its waning wake. A bend in the river causes the flow to slow so look to these edges. Stop at large boulders for they trap gold nuggets in their break of the flow. Look for nuggets hiding in crevices crossing the flow for these cracks are riffles trapping gold. Pick at these places...use tweezers or tong to dislodge...then patiently, patiently above all gently swirl your pan free of muddy debris' bath." And little Rhynn rolled up his pants' legs and waded into the murk following Ebo's actions with his own pick and pan.

"Then I was seven and now I'm eleven." Rhynn spoke softly as he let the reins fall and released Pretzyl of satchel burden, crossbow and quiver. The stallion forgetting all else the way of this day, dropped his head rewarding a belly of the soft mossy grasses tickling soft nose. It took only a moment for the prince to load two scoops of riverbed muck into his pan. Feeling the soft mud at play between his toes Rhynn slowly swirled the pan of its water watching as large pebbles separated from the small as river's flow gently washed away dirt leaving anything golden to settle. Again and again Rhynn scooped mounds of mud from shallow pools and picked out rocks in cracks swirling these loads clean in his pan under slow-running water leaving only glittering flakes to glint in sunlight. His sieve sifted gravely sludge from rocks picked out from cracks until,

What's this thing gleaming I see through slimy mud coat?

Rhynn swirled the sieve in the shallowest of water rinsing the smooth rock rattling against rim.

Wow!

Rhynn's eyes beheld a nugget as large as his thumb radiantly glowing in golden glory resting on the cross-wire bottom of his sieve in his quivering hands. He is only three steps from the bank and when he'd climbed to dry ground from watery sludge it is to his knees he falls in a state of awe. Then raising his face toward lowering golden sun thanked the Holy Trinity for this rock-of-the-earth reaped from its rest in river's muddy crevice.

A great clanging and ringing of bells sounded throughout the valley carried on swift wind's airwaves through Belle Passe over falls and lagoon across heather plain. The sound came not mournfully low in tones but high-pitched to near-chiming...*ringing...ringing...ringing*

Pretzyl stopped his grazing to listen. The prince placed his find in the lidded tin cup and gathering up all tools in the satchel buckled it, crossbow and quiver to Pretzyl's back.

"Come, good Pretzyl, let's see to this happy racket happening in the village! A parade might be passing in the streets!" But when Rhynn happened upon the falls and Half Moon Lagoon it is the form of a familiar animal that captures his sight and halts his journey.

"Lightfoot?"

The king's horse turned its head at the sound of the boy's voice but its jaws kept to their task chewing young grass-blades rooted from a tuft. Lightfoot's soft brown marble-eyes lolled in their sockets then turned to gaze at the lagoon. Rhynn's eyes followed the gaze of the horse and he saw the naked body of his father gracefully gliding across its glassy surface.

Rhynn's legs dashed to lagoon's edge as his hands waved furiously clanging the gold nugget in tin cup...clattering...clanking...clinking...clanging

"Poppi! It's me, Poppi! Look what I found upriver just now!"

King Breretyn stopped his powerful strokes and bobbed where

he floated in Half Moon Lagoon's clear water and listened to the noise occurring on the shore. It is his son's voice that brings smile to his lips but his thoughts wonder at the cause of noise going on in tin cup and of the presence of Pretzyl burdened of satchel, quiver and crossbow.

The horse must have been lost in the trees when I passed by my child fishing

"Come see the nugget I found for Mummy's present, Poppi! It's magnificent, you'll see!"

Nugget? But what of your hook and the fish you waited patiently for?

"So, what's this in your vessel making all that noise?" Breretyn strode from the froth foaming at lagoon's edge to stand in sun's latent heat as thirsty breezes whisked droplets from his glistening skin. Rhynn handed the cup to his father and bade him unwind the lid. Taking a step backward in respect the boy studied the sum of the man's magnum parts and wondered what it is like to be king. The thud of the can's lid thumping on turf brought Rhynn's attention to focus and the boy studied his father's face for the reaction he wished might show there.

Breretyn's eyes did nearly pop their sockets and his mouth drew open but no sound escaped his lips. Rhynn waited a moment then prompted,

"It's big, isn't it Poppi?"

Breretyn blinked. He had not seen a nugget this size and glowing with such warmth since the one King Neptlyn found in a crevice upstream at river's bend and had made into one coin bearing the engraved image of the king's face fully looking on.Neptlyn had given the disc to him at his investiture and he'd kept it always in the folds of his shirt until the day a fair but injured maiden was pulled from peril away from the raised hooves of his terrified horse. It lay close to the breast of Parqai as reward for the artist's bravery that ultimately provided the king his exquisitely serene queen and the beautiful sweet mother of this child.

Breretyn dressed his dried body in fresh garments. The soiled linens of his earlier labor are quickly wadded in a ball and tossed to the bottom of his saddlebag.

"It's for Mummy's Christmas present! I was thinking of asking Sir Artist Parqai to carve a jaguar in the circular shape of a bangle to adorn her wrist. If I'm lucky raking the earth I'll find little green stones like the ones twinkling in your crown for the eyes! Then when I am not in her sights she shall look there and see her jaguar is still near her."

Breretyn being king after all, could easily reach into a velvet bag lying in the castle's vault and withdraw an emerald or two beholding dark wondrous gardens as eyes' pupils deep in their sparkling green depths. The gold nugget warmed in the king's palm and he marveled at the wealth of its entity not only in the weight it would add to his coffer but of the symbolic wealth-love-greatness swelling the heart of Latezia and Mummy. And being a father above all else he'd encourage his heir to rake and shovel his gardens' soil of the pebbles in gravel that lay there for great satisfaction is gained in one's soul set on a quest seeing through an end to his plan.

"You and I shall seek Parqai's expertise in the morrow, Rhynn! The idea you hold in your head will become real to your Mummy's wrist at Christmastime! It's a promise between us and our secret surprise as well."Breretyn and Rhynn turned to their steeds to mount before turning the way home.

It is then that the king noticed again the crossbow and quiver buckled to Pretzy's side and inquired of his heir as to the success of the archery practices in the shooting range and the number of bullseye points tallied thereupon target's red center.

"My points are dull, Poppi so my arrows don't stick but dangle a moment then fall to the ground. I stopped by the blacksmith shack right after breakfast early but Ebo was already gone from the place."

"Of course Ebo is gone from his work today for today is a day of great joy to our Ebo! The good blacksmith has given his fair daughter, Farayya's hand in marriage to deserving Emilio in the village's church this hour! Bells are chiming in celebration of it all."

The prince listened intently but the only sound Rhynn heard in his ears was the low growl in his belly for long had the breakfast of bacon passed from tongue down gullet to stomach through tunnels and beyond. The king heard rumblings going on in two bellies and wondered of his son fishing at river's edge downstream patiently waiting as his hand held twig, string and hook.

"It's too bad the fish weren't biting your bait today for I am quite in the mood for a hearty bite now!"

Fish? What fish? Was I to be fishing today? Rhynn turned in his saddle giving the king a penetrating puzzling look.

Breretyn startled to a slight chill at the deeply-perplexing but steady gaze of his son for he did not recognize this look in his heir's face at any other time gone before. But Rhynn turned away tending to his whinnying steed so the king turned his gaze back to that place by the embankment where earlier he'd happened across a boy standing in trees' shadows calling himself a raven.

In the onset of dusk the king saw only pale gray chimney smoke curling skyward given up of the brick fire-ovens in cottages' kitchens set off pathways winding the hill above the roadway across from river. Breretyn blinked at the dizziness threatening his posture.

Is it the sight of smoke puffing and scent of fish cooking on sweet Alder plank wafting on breezes tangling my reason?

A beacon high atop lamppost blinked intermittent green…white…green beckoning hungry husbands and children to table and plate...*green...white...green...white...beckoning*

"I can smell the smoke-room's work from here! Look there, Poppi!"

Breretyn sat upright now and focused his sight upon hearing the sound of Prince Rhynn's cheerful child-voice. His gaze followed the length of his son's outstretched arm to that point his fingers pointed.

"Smoke rises from castle's kitchen chimney! Cook Missus Tarryn says fish is to be on our plates at supper tonight, Poppi!I watched Husband Mister Tarryn fillet a fine fat one of its bones just as I downed the last of my milk before leaving the table to see Ebo, the blacksmith about sharpening my arrows' points."

Breretyn's ears heard not a tone of *this* heir's voice for the voice he hears in his head resonates the same tones as of *that* son speaking of *Ebo...patience...YourMajesty*

But the king kept his firstborn and heir riding-in-saddle-to-castle in his sight the whole rest of the journey as hunger gnawed at bone and muscle.

That's it then, this state of quandary I find myself in is caused by hours of labor and long cleansing swim with no nourishment between...hallucinations result behind the eyes of a man whose hunger overrides what his eyes see standing before...

CHAPTER 8

EVEN AT HER AGE NOW ON DAWNING MORNING OF MY SIXTEENTH birthday she looks like a maiden still and just as beautiful.

Prince Rhynn stands in ultimate silence at the doorway of his mother's parlor watching her elegant hand dip plume quill in indigo inkwell. Soft scratching echoes waft softly as nib spells out words on papyrus thick as felt and the color of vanilla cream.Her gentle silhouette sits before gilded desk. Sunlight beams over her being as a sheer golden veil given of Heaven itself highlighting the crown of her head as if a halo hovers there.

And the prince wonders at that long-ago morning and if it began exactly like this summer solstice day radiant in morning's soft early light and warming to rising sun's heat. His imagination's dream turned a page now to the chamber-of-heirs and the ancient mattress receiving his birth and first squall. A profound sense of worship came unto him at the thought of it all thankful in that moment for the unique gift of women and their right to bear babes can belong to no other.

Rhynn knows of palace birth-chamber's whereabouts but had not entered the room during his prowls up stairwells down hallways past suites' doorways through passageways and beyond.The space there seemed to swell beyond walls belonging only to queens laboring in their duty to gift king and kingdom of firstborn and heir. He wonders why he should be thinking so deeply of all this now and worries a trifle that his heart might run over itself at the thought of one beautiful Queen Latezia and Mummy bringing forth King Breretyn's son.

In that moment Queen Latezia sensed a presence on her parlor's threshold and glanced up suddenly as if hearing her name called in audible voice. She can't be certain if her ears heard the words or if some sweet dream is playing upon her imagination's stage. Her wide eyes stare at the silent figure standing stoic as a marble statue and just as white. Eyes of gemstone-green twinkle with life and a smile hints at his lips. Latezia's face softens in recognition at the sight of her child now grown to man in that flicker of time between blink and wink.

Since when did you grow so bold in stature and handsomely-fine in face, prowling Jaguar, my Rhynn, prince and heir…for it was only this day a summer's solstice away that I wakened from dreaming to behold infant-you in my arms.

"Did I startle you, Mother? You look as if a ghost is appearing before you here! It is only me, your dutiful son and king's lowly prince standing live in your parlor." Rhynn held forth his hand and Latezia rose from her chair floating forward to clasp her man-child against breast and heart.

"I did not hear you approach, stealthy Jaguar! You do look like a ghost dressed as you are in white fencing foil-jacket and pants like this! And your mesh mask would have hidden your visage from my eyes frightening me to near death had you not removed it from your head to hold it thus here. And your sabre…does it protect *you* or is it postured this way to protect *me*?" Latezia laughed lightly as she held Rhynn proudly at arms' length to give her eyes a grand look at this beautiful man. "I am pleased you stopped by my desk for I was hoping to catch you before you slipped off to your grandfather, the brick-maker's house. I have written my father a letter beseeching him to consider wintering here after summer this year for his age is increasing in numbers, and my mother's age too, of course grows in years unto frailty. They will protest, naturally, but with *you* offering my invitation with your own hand personally delivered…well… perhaps they will consider."

"Consider it done, Mother! I was just thinking a solitary ride about town in disguise just the thing before gathering my grandparents to my investiture this eventide and celebrations in the hours following."

"Disguise! What do you mean; disguise yourself… in what way…and from what? Predators…thieves…witches and ghouls? You are already *Jaguar*, Rhynn, so there is no need on your part to hide away from anything except… oh, I know! Twittering maidens blush and follow your footsteps whispering poems through pretty lips…"

"*Mother!* I am not afraid of girls! In fact, *I* seek *them*… they and the *ways* of them fascinate me beyond all reason of what is masculine-possible!"

Queen Latezia stared up at her son silenced at the forthrightness of thoughts his heart readily shared through his voice's unapologetic tone.

Rhynn laughed.

"Come now, Mother! Why this shocked look? I learned all this from watching how Poppi is with *you* is all, and how you fascinate him beyond words causing mush to soften his muscles and speech to flee his tongue when he is in audience of you. It's a phenomenon that happens like air which cannot been seen but is still real for it can be breathed in and felt swelling lungs as if standing as a solid as we stand on earth."

"Mushy muscles? Your father never once displayed any sign of a mushy muscle gripping his skeleton anywhere! In fact, his muscles are perfectly strong in all their work!"

Thankful that the conversation has taken a subtle turn Rhynn quicklyfollowed her line with one of his own.

"Father is a formidable fencing foe even in his years still! The king is agile and cunning then waits patiently plotting his next move. I learn much from my matches with him disguised as he thinks he is behind mask, jacket-vest and all. Which, I might add here is; if you happen to see a tall breathtakingly-handsome ghost lurking in your bedchamber, don't fear! It's only Poppi!" Rhynn's voice dropped to a whisper as his eyes beheld an entertaining range of emotions playing out in his mother's eyes and face. Taking her exquisite head in his hands, Rhynn feathered kiss on his mother's brow. Latezia allowed her face to linger in her son's gentle grasp feeling what another must eventually come to know.

And she remembered the day of Rhynn's birth and the words of her mother...*labor is only the first nudge along the way of a mother's letting-go...*

Latezia sighed.

Oh, Mamma...

Rhynn lifted her face meeting eyes' pale star-sapphire-blue gaze with his and was thrown by the melancholy he saw misting there.

"You are *first* in my heart always, Mummy, Queen and First Lady of my father, King Breretyn, and *His* Majesty'sonly love..." Rhynn's words trailed to whisper before uttering these words in his strong man-voice,

"If Grandpappy and Grandmummy are to be at my investiture on time I'd best escape this embrace and fetch them like a good son! Where is this missive you've drafted so I might persuade them unto your wish?"

Latezia turned away brushing aside a small tear falling as dew on high cheekbone with a swift motion of her hand. It took only a moment to roll up the scroll securing it with a black velvet cord. Its tassels tickled Rhynn's knuckles as he tucked her elegant entreaty beneath vest and jacket close to breastbone.

"Consider it done, Mummy! I'm riding through the streets like this; just like a knight in white armor atop a fleet horse whose name is Pretzyl!"

Latezia laughed softly but then silenced when suddenly all spirit vanished from the room. No sound of footsteps echo in the hallway. No door thudded closed in its jamb. The drapes did not billow in the wake of one leaving so quickly and the air remained stilled as if no one breathed here.

"Rhynn?"

How is it you flee so swiftly?

The queen dashed to the windows seeking answers in the courtyard below.

No clatter of hoofbeats sound upon driveway's cobblestones. Motionless sentries stand guard at high iron gates still closed. Royal greyhounds lazily rolled on the lawns in hedges' shadows as birds bathed in fountain's finer mists.

A mystery my jaguar is to me this day...I don't understand...my prince named Rhynn slinks away as a cat.

Latezia wrapped her fingers about the gold bangle gleaming up at her from its place on her wrist feeling warmth radiate to her palm.

"Oh, Rhynn."

"It is beautiful, isn't it, Latezia?"

Latezia's head jerked up at the quiet low voice sounding from doorway and saw there a tall figure standing still as a statue in dress white as marble gazing at her with eyes of jade-green softly glowing.

You're back! Where did you hide away just then?

And in a blink of her eyes she sees it is her king leaning against doorjamb, mesh helmet cradled in arm and sabre in hand posturing downward at rug.

My Breretyn and son...son and Breretyn...could be one and the same perfectly mirroring one and the other...father and son identical...Anabaa's long-ago words

"Beautiful?"

"The jaguar bangle Parqai made of the nugget Rhynn found that summer he turned eleven is lovely even this day as it sits resting on your wrist there as a real jaguar rests on a limb, is beautiful, my love, is all I am saying."

"Oh, yes...yes it is quite beautiful to wear and even more beautiful is way that it came into being and the cherished reason for it firstly."Latezia stroked at the jaguar's smooth head pausing to play at the points of its ears with her fingertips. "My favorite part of this project is our Rhynn's search for the cat's eyesplaying with little shovel and rake like that out in the gardens' gravels sifting through scoop after scoop then settling on these tiny quartz bits."Latezia turned the bangle on her wrist so the jaguar's eyes caught white light streaming through far window. "Charming how quartz shimmers in just the right ray."

Breretyn came to stand before his queen and lifting her head in his hands turned her face upward him. He looked into her eyes for a lingering moment holding her face this way as Rhynn had done only moments before... *placing a kiss*...Latezia closed her eyes in the memory knowing *this* kiss is Breretyn's kiss belonging to *her* only and understood by *no other*. Her fingers toy with shell buttons fastening foil and jacket and tugging gently at knots unraveled strings free. The queen's hands grazed bare shoulders then over scapulae down smooth spine skimming waist to fall unto rest crossed over Dimples of Venus as shirt fell away to the floor *not finding mush in any muscles anywhere there...* and in that moment cool air tickled at her own shoulders causing a shudder across clavicles falling between cleavage past sternum over belly and a quick gasp escaped her lips as taffeta dress rustles in its fall to the floor.

The king's eyes twinkled gemstone-green at this game each play as well as the other.

"Bathe with me, Queen, Latezia, most-lovely Love."

Pretzyl slowed his gallop to an easy-going lope in response to his master's command. The highway atop cliffs gifted rider and horse an indescribable view of King Breretyn's kingdom; high heather plain and far off Belle Passe, falls tumbling into silver-misting Half Moon Lagoon and the winding blue ribbon of river flowing past villages through valley along mountain base and beyond. Rhynn's eyes scanned wheat fields and corn rows to cattle grazing on hillsides and sheep bleating in meadow. Men gathering grapes to wood wagons move among vines, their bodies graceful as dancers bending low and then arms swaying away. Gardens flourish in yards behind cottages settling all lots. Flowering hedges and fruiting trees decorate street-sides. Bricks paving the walkways shine polished to a gleam by treads of many persons' footfall happening over time.

Dogs chase dogs up and down alleys. Cats dart up trees. Birds fly overhead all commerce exchanging and trading in merchants' shops oblivious to banter and barter happening in mercantile far below. Boys play ball games in weed-trampled lots. Maidens' feet hop-scotch dance on imaginary squares in the cobblestone street. Husbands gather in huddles beneath smoke rings as wives wrapped in patchwork aprons loaded baskets with pastry and supper.

Parqai sat at his easel hunched before canvas with palette in hand paused his brush-stroking hand in midair as he contemplated a scene.

"But the very best place is the cigar maker's shack for a sugarcane stalk can be had for a halfpence!" laughed Rhynn as he encouraged Pretzyl into a slow steady gait up the street. "I'll stop there first for the gifts I've planned for Poppi and Mummy, Grandpappy and

Grandmummy. I'll buy you an apple from the first fruit cart for you are a fine easygoing agreeable ride!"

Pretzyl whinnied in gratitude for his master's kind inclusion once his great square teeth finished grinding the orb's flesh to its core.

"Fancy a toke of my stogie, young man? It's my own secret recipe; tobacco grown in dark damp soil infused with blackberry and rum wrapped all about in sugar-soaked leaves when truly smoked leaves linger of sweet fruity earth on the tongue. Heaven-in-a-Bundle, I call it!"

Rhynn smiled at the cigar maker. The deep tan and crinkled leathery texture of his skin gave evidence of diligent toil under unforgiving sun's supreme energy and the fatigue of his facial muscles profoundly betrays their response to the gusto with which the man enjoys the fruit of his labor. Rhynn watched the man's onyx-brown eyes glint as glass-blower's marbles in sunlight.

"All your spicy sweet peppery mint nutmeg cedar cognac-dipped vanilla-infused stogies are Heavens-in-Blankets, good recipe-maker, sir," answered horseman on steed. Prince Rhynn waited a count of four before putting in his order for two ofthis day's secret blend. The tobacco man's eyes widened in surprise at the count of *two* today over the usual *one* so he quickly bound them together in strings before the young man realized he'd doubled up his desire.

"And I'll take two stalks of that sugarcane you hide in that sack laying in the shadow there, if you don't mind, good sir! It is my birthday today so I'm splurging, is all!"

"Well, well! A birthday! How many are you?" queried the merchant hustling two thick stalks onto thin papyrus then folding up all corners, tied them all about with cord.

"Sixteen."

"Ah, sixteen it is then, and may you see sixteen more!" chanted the crinkly-skinned man as smoldering cigar bobbed up and down between clenched teeth. Coins exchanged from royal fingers to gnarled-knuckled hand and that being that, concluded business.

Rhynn added the gifts of cigars and sugarcane to the scroll under his jacket patting the bundle of secrets hidden between cloth and warm skin.

Markets make their own music, pondered the prince as he listened to the cacophony of din and clatter playing an arrhythmic-tachycardia rhythm-beat.

It is a grand theme written on airwaves' imaginary staves that can be heard as verb and felt as noun.

Coins dropping in glass jars gentled clanking of coins dropping in tin cans. Mothers' treble clef voices calling children rang sweetly over husbands' bass rumblings arguing politics and weather. Boys' staccato shouts in street's ball-toss inspire girls' tenuto squealing in hide-and-seek games round about buckets sporting blooming flower-stems. Horses whinnied and dogs barked. Cats meowed from rafters and birds circling above chirped unwittingly overall.

Winds sweeping down mountainside across meadow through valley rose in crescendo up market's street whistling past tents, carts and shacks rustling leaves taunting branches' firm hold along the way of its selfish journey only to become a diminuendo memory in its fleeing up cliff along highway over palace turrets and beyond.

Silence

Dramatic how abrupt silence following a sudden gust can sound as thunderous

Rhynn patted the bundle growing warm beneath his jacket and nudging Pretzyl's belly turned into the street along the way to the brick-maker's house.

It was as if the little sirocco had not happened at all as all in the mercantile carried on as before. Tinkers and tailors, dressmakers, candlestick-makers and carpet-weavers' rugs, weavers' straw baskets in piles and needle-beaded hand-knotted colored glass strings hang from nails *glittering…shimmering…gleaming*

Not a thing changed in the wind at all except,

"Oh, now it's all smudged and wet paint is on me! Worse, I've lost my muse to a silly hide-and-seek game! Come back girl, where did you go? I can't get the eyes right if I don't see them again!" wailed diminutive artist Parqai as he grappled with canvas whilst balancing palette and brush. Rhynn halted Pretzyl's lazy lope to assess damages done to this man's work. It is true that the canvas brushed against the artist's shirt for alluring pigment shone there. But the smudge on the canvas appeared of no consequence to Rhynn's eye as he studied the subject blooming thereupon in colors so transparent as seemingly not to exist in paint at all. Rhynn blinked and stared harder.

This muse is a maiden dancing here…in the street there then away. Where are you, beautiful girl with eyes so arresting that Artist Parqai must capture you totally?

"Stop there, girl! Quit your twirling-about and look to me with those eyes so I might get the right pigments down before you turn away lost to your mother and mercantile clutter!" cried artist Parqai.

And a damsel did appear at the base of the artist's stool staring up at the brush in the man's hand swishing and dabbing then swirling and stroking. Rhynn stared at her face then back to the canvas where appeared the visage of *this* girl and a butterfly floating by her shoulder then stared back at the maiden staring up in wonderment, wide-eyed and mute at what she sees there. Rhynn turned his gaze back to the canvas and blinked, then stared again at what could not be happening here.

The butterfly's gossamer wings appear oscillating and the maiden's eyes glow hypnotizing the prince. Dismounting his steed Ryhnn took a step closer to the apparition then retreated two back.

How can this be? It's only pigment and oil swirled on bare canvas here. But that girl is real, really here! And Rynn looked again to the face of the muse standing silently by.

But not one girl stands here...there are two of them, exactly the same identical one to the other, the same! Look again! The eyes shine differently...one set glows softly as opals gleam...the other twinkles as pale star- sapphires shine.

"There are *two* damsels, Parqai; identical twins weaving about the flower vessels here yet you choose to paint only one."

"My canvas is small and I have only so much room. I must save space for the sky!"

"How did you pick one sister over the other? And what of the other left off the canvas is as much a part of the one chosen? Paint *both* faces on your canvas forgiving the sky for it is a given that sky encompasses all canvases' borders, all waters and the earth."

Parqai turned his face to the twins standing still, gentle hand catching bare white arm, graceful fingertips overlapping, for they stared up at the dashing young prince poised in his saddle with dazed wonderment. A dazzle of sunlight appeared in that instant as one halo encircling identical heads.

"What are your names, pretty damsels?" asked Prince Rhynn appearing to their eyes as a white knight mounted upon royal regal steed.

"I am Qeyyapi and my sister is Aotepi."

Moon and Star...Qeyyapi's eyes glow softly-brilliant as full moon's do and Aotepi's eyes twinkle as do all stars

In that moment a mother's chiming voice rang out calling her daughters come hither. Both damsels vanished from Rhynn's sight. When the prince turned back to the canvas resting on the easel he saw what he'd seen just a moment before; two exquisitely-painted identical faces but for one whose eyes glow as opals and in the other, star-sapphires. A rabble of delicate butterflies floats with diaphanous wings oscillating in sheer lavender-pink nimbus.

"This work pleases me greatly now, good Artist Parqai! Latch the canvas to my saddle here. Today is my birthday, after all, and I'm buying myself a present!" Rhynn pressed a heavy silver coin in the artist's warm palm.

Parqai gasped.

"That is but mere pittance as the genius showing in your work is beyond price."

Pretzyl sensed something magnificent had just happened in the way of Rhynn's growing up and it had nothing at all to do with the new strain of apple crossed 'tween *Delicious* and *Crisp*. His master's low voice softened into speech quite extraordinary leaving behind his boy-tongue of yesterday.

Magic happens in marketplaces; incense pleasing my nose, dogs flipping at my hooves, flies buzzing my ears too far from my tail. But today's magic is different and yet to be known.

Pretzyl dropped away from his horse-thinking deciding instead to just clip-clop along cobble roadway guided by princely hands holding reins dangling from bridle hitched to bit between teeth and lip.

The figures of a woman and two maidens walking along roadside carrying baskets between them roused Rhynn's attention as he turned the corner at Cluckers Corner. Sitting upright and focusing a keen eye on their backsides lest they evaporate from his view a second time Rhynn nudged Pretzyl to pick up the pace until shortly he pulled alongside this glorious trio.

Ah, they are who I dreamed they'd be! Happy birthday to me for it's a moon and star and radiant mother my eyes spy!

The three heard a horse approaching of course, and naturally turned their faces to glance up at the rider. Then all six eyes grew wide in astonishment at the sight of a royal riding their way.

"Put down the baskets quickly, girls, and curtsey for pity-sake! Tiz a *prince*, I think." Mother dropped down in an elegant deep bow the best she knew how in housedress and patchwork apron amid baskets and all. The girl-twins simply could not take their eyes off the prince as they did glowing like moons and twinkling as stars.

"Hello, Qeyyapi…Aotepi," winked the rider dressed dashingly in white fencing foil-jacket and gloves.

The mother near fainted away to the ground at such amazing luck finding herself with her daughters in private audience of one prime young prince. But reason quickly returned though outrunning her tongue.

How is it you know my girls' names?

"I am Prince Rhynn, son of King Breretyn and his queen, Latezia, my mother, as you righteously suspect. Live about here? I'm off fetching my grandparents, the brick-maker and his wife at their house on Rockledge Strip. It is my birthday today and my investiture happens at eventide. I'm inviting your family to come to my party…at my house, of course! Please say yes! I'll look for you from palace's plinth. I'll be the one in the little gold crown."

～◌

"You always could swim faster than me, Ravenz!" screamed Kyrro as he glided to the edge of Half Moon Lagoon, panting for air brushing water and slick curls from his eyes and face.

"That's because my arms are longer than yours!" hollered Ravenz. Then he softened his voice realizing Kyrro now sat on the grass beside him and that his own ears flooded their brims with water. "Sorry, I'm hearing the sound of falls in my ears right now."

"Lay back on the grass. They'll drain soon enough." Ravenz yawned as his eyes followed clouds floating east from west through sheer blue sky.

What is it like to be you, cloud? Where do you float away to and what do you see?

Fine moss tickled his shoulders and elbows and filled his downturned palms. Warm breeze swept droplets from his body growing warm. Sleep played at chasing wakefulness…tempting…hypnotizing

"I don't have time to lay back and loll! Father expects me within the hour! It's branding time and I'm to rope calves! Besides, there is an investiture happening at Kings Palace tonight! I'll see you there, good friend, at the party, of course!"

"We roped calves all morning, Kyrro!"

"That was just the south corral!"

Ravenz opened his eyes. *Kyrro?* He sat up and turned about searching for his friend whose voice still rang in his ears. But about him lay only a lariat-rope and vast heather plain. Grassy blades sweep gently against each other in breezes. A butterfly circled overhead seeking soft landing. Bees buzz about the business of gathering purple thistle's nectar for honeycomb later.

An eagle swooped low over Half Moon Lagoon then soared swiftly heavenwardbecoming a sleek dark silhouette in a veil of cirrus clouds before gliding into brilliant sunlight. Ravenz watched the magnificent bird halt its subtle wing-flapping to glide in wide easy arcs suspended by thin air's mighty loft.

What is it like being you, Eagle?

"Thief! Thief! Stop, rotten thief!"

Ravenz bolted upright from the tuft his head lay upon, torn from the sight of eagle's sky-poetry reverie to grasping lariat-rope laying snake-coiled at his side.

"Help! I've been robbed! Thief! Help!"

The sight of a man's shadowy figure racing up roadway chased by a faltering dwarfed man flailing a wide flat satchel in the air captures Ravenz' eye.

There is naught but armed guards, iron gates and dogs at the end of this line you've chosen, criminal. Thanks to Kyrro's rope and the skill I've learned by patient nature of him you will never have to explain your sorry situation to King Breretyn. But then again, you may prefer his audience over what I've planned for your soon-to-be-carcass!

In a flash happening faster than a lightning bolt strikes from cloud to earth the loop of Kyrro's lariat flew through the air lassoing the thief's knees instantly binding his legs together arresting all attempt of fleeing his victim. And in the way of roping calves that in the hours before high noon had seemed as sport Ravenz quickly encircled the ankles and wrists of this criminal now writhing on his belly biting dirt.

Artist Parqai approached the scene shuffling and huffing while gasping for air between wailings, "He robbed me! This wretched thief leapt at me from roadside's bush...back there...clubbing me fiercely on my nose and eyebrow here! He's making off with my coin!"

Ravenz waited till the man quieted his statement watching the bruise darken across the bridge of Parqai's nose as blood trickled from a gash over his brows over nasion along left ala-of-nares down nasolabial sulcus.

One look at the thief's tightly-balled fist hinted stolen property lay concealed in the hard pressed wrap of his fingers.

"What do you say, person? Do you have this man's property or not?"

The thief only lay on the ground in a state of mute shock. He was shocked firstly at how quickly his getaway came to a halt by way of this manner; the roped hog-tie state he finds his limbs in. The breath in his lungs expunged with force as body mass hit the turf. He inhaled soon enough but smelled dust and horse.

Tired of waiting for the criminal's reply Ravenz rolled the thief to sit up thus meeting the eyes of the artist, Parqai and his own. The man's mouth opened but no words came from his lips, too astonished were his eyes at the sight of one such Adonis standing in the middle of the road in plain sight of his audience totally oblivious of embarrassment by his state of complete nakedness without so much as a weapon more than this simple rope binding his limbs. The astonished thief blinked considering this condition; a single rope flying through pure air to bondage ankles, knees then crossing his chest securing arms and wrists together at his back.

Vocabulary followed.

"Wrong answer! Try again, fool." Ravenz spoke low and distinctly-clear. To add exclamation to his point he kicked the man's fist with such force the surprised fingers splayed apart. And in the yelp that followed a large gold disc fell to the ground.

"That's it! That's my coin! I told you he mugged me of my coin!"

Ravenz stared at the face engraved on the coin gleaming softly in the afternoon light. Even though dusty from rolling in the rut he saw the piece was indeed very valuable and a prize in its own right. The face engraved hereon *this* coin was of a full face looking on; eyes, nose, mouth and royal crown set on regal brow. All coins trading in the kingdom's commerce show profile engravings of kings' features. Ravenz suspected Parqai had hidden the coin close to his body and kept in a deep place not visible to any eye but his only.

"How is it you knew of this gentleman's coin, thief?" asked

Ravenz of the running-off man now arrested and sitting bound in the roadway. "Confession or not your words now weight the scales regarding the outcome of your day."

The robber inhaled.

"Long ago I came on a boat upriver to deliver goods to a merchant's shop when this man pulled a fallen maiden from beneath the raised hooves of a frightened work horse. The vagabond riding the horse jumped from his saddle to the cobblestones to kneel at the maid's side and that's when I saw him press *this* coin to this man's hand bidding him keep it with his person always. When I came back up the river today I saw this same artist-person sitting on his stool and remembered that old day gone by and the gold piece."

"Is this the way of it, Parqai, sir?"

"The story is exactly as the thief says. The damsel I pulled away from under the vagabond's horse that day is King Breretyn's queen, Her Majesty, Latezia."

Parqai reached down and picked up the coin from the place it fell to in the dirt road and rubbed the face of it tenderly against the clean side of his paint-smudged cleft-in-twain shirt.

"Look at me, thief! My name is Ravenz. I could peck out your eyeballs one by one swallowing the orbs whole as each one would comfort my belly for a long, long time. But I have decided you must keep both your eyes for you will need them to see me. I will haunt you from all skies above your head to all manner of terrain you crawl on. My eyes watch from the shadows of an overhangs' eave and branches of all trees. It will be me in the roadway and pathway and all passageways seeing everything.

"I will not free you from bondage for that is your work. Use your teeth to gnaw through that rope and by day's end you will come to the way of your fate. You will remember my name all the hours of your remaining days."

Ravenz turned away from scene in the road and did not look back.

Serenely indifferent to his naked state Ravenz strode to Half Moon Lagoon considering a dip in water welcome medicine in light of sun's blazing afternoon heat. Breeze seemed to have forsaken the day and his brow itched as did his tongue parch. He was just stepping into the water when he heard a frail voice calling,

"Raven bird, young man, sir! Stop!" Ravenz turned around and saw diminutive Parqai waving his hands in the air. So he waited patiently where he stood, feet cooling in shallows lapping at his toes until the man stood quite close. And then he saw Parqai's open palm and the royal coin resting there.

"You must take this coin from my hand! You *must* take it, please! It was given to me for an unselfish act such as yours today. It is true the vagabond gave me this coin as it had been given to him for just such a deed. He told me to keep it to my breast always till such a time I might pass it on to someone deserving. Take it. It is...*karma!*"

The little man turned away clutching his satchel when Ravenz had a thought.

"Wait! Do you normally walk this way, Artist Parqai?"

"Not at all. I generally avoid this road taking the high way to the palace instead. I am late to the investiture this eve so I took a shortcut. I am late setting up my canvas and brushes there!" Ravenz looked down at the bloodied face of the artist and with his hands scooped water from the lagoon to cleanse and sooth the wounds he sees there.

"Take my shirt, sir. It is fairly clean still and on your body will become a painter's smock to reasonably present yourself at the castle tonight."

In the next instant the transformation was accomplished and Parqai sped away on his journey up roadway through King Breretyn's iron gates thinking the whole time he smells faintly bovine.

Then artist saw a vision unfold in his mind of a project to come;

that being a portrait painted of

a youth-bull holding a calf close at his breast, lasso rope dangling

remembering one named Ravenz.

         ~❍

"Ah! Ah, ah! OoohAahhh! Ohhh…ooooahhhhh!."

Ravenz halted his foot-run mid-flight up Falls House's back steps hearing feminine wails filtering through his bedchamber's cracked-open window.

Intruders!

A chill crept down Ravenz' back even in high afternoon's heat. Goosebumps rose on his arms as knuckles showed white beneath finger's taught grip on the hand railing.

Ravenz did not breathe.

Anabaa is in the marketplace…Constance and Qiaona are attending the queen in the castle…

The balled-up tattered artist's shirt sailed over the side of the railing without so much as a whisper landing on a weed tuft below.

"It's coming again! How can it…ah…come so soon after the last…oh! Oh! Ahhhh!"

"The pains are quite frequent. It won't be long now." The comforting voice seemed nearly inaudible but familiar in tone and cadence.

Anabaa?

Ravenz' ears strained for more conversation.

"Bako!"

Bako?

"Where did my Bako run off too? *I want Bako!*"

Lizbett! Lizbett is in my bed...her bed...why is she in my bed...her bed...how...what the....?

Ravenz leapt the last three steps in one single bound rushing through doorway over threshold past kitchen to bedchamber archway feeling fortunate having slipped on his pants last minute before leaving Half Moon Lagoon. The curtains hung drawn across the window though opened.No air whispers through. A woman lay on his mattress; arms outstretched, hands gripping headboard's two high posts with hands clenched, head thrown back on his old flat pillow, legs flying up in the air or slapping the sheet bent at the knees. Her bare bulging belly glistened sliver with fine misty sweat. Soothing Anabaa sat at Lizbett's side on the old carved chair that had been in this room since long before Ravenz. Anabaa did not look up to his dim shadow falling across rug and plank floor nor did Lizbett turn her gaze from ceiling to him.

Tiz only the great wondrous miracle of birth happening here to my Angel Lizbett; a common enough pain causing cries as music accompanying nature's sweetest work

In the space between heartbeats Ravenz knelt on the rug at the head of his...Lizbett's old bed and taking her arm by the elbow gently unraveled her fingers from about the post.

"Hold fast to my hand, Lizbett! Keep your eyes fixed on my face always looking in my eyes." Lizbett turned her face to stare in confusion at Ravenz, at this man tenderly stroking her arm while clasping her hand.

Who are you, gentle green-eyed stranger-man comforting me? You are not Bako! Where is Bako? I've seen you somewhere in my days gone by.

Anabaa spoke next. Rising from the chair she flew to the foot of the bed where a chest sat with lid closed. In a swift lift of the lid a mound of towels lay heaped by the bed. Steaming water in a basin appeared set on bureau fogging mirror and wall.

"Bako is off fetching Ebo, his father and mother, Fairie, Ebo's wife! He'll return quickly enough as their house is not so far away."

"Since when did Bako sail home from the high seas?"

Ravenz queried softly of Anabaa so as not to raise anxiety in Lizbett.

"They arrived on dry land just two days ago to prepare for the birth of this child in the house of Ebo and Fairie when her waters broke today in the mercantile street and…well, since Falls House isclose by and I'm here… all this is happening! The child comes early. Its delivery should be weeks off yet! Thank Heaven for you here, Ravenz! I am alone as Qiaona is tending Queen Latezia and Constance tendsthe queen'smother this hour. Prince Rhynn's grandparents are marching to the plinth at the left hand of him at eventide."

The muscles across Lizbett's softly-glowing full-moon belly contracted in waves causing her head to jerk up from the pillow and her back to arch. Fingers like steel talons grip Ravenz' hand mashing all bones as cartilage into a mass of muscle, tendon and skin.

Ravenz whispered,

"It is me, *Ravenz,* Lizbett!"

"What? A raven! What bird? Why am I hearing talk of birds?!" hissed Lizbett through clenched teeth.

"Turn your face and look into my eyes!" Ravenz nudged at

Lizbett's arm as he held her hand at his face. She could feel the soft muscles of his lips feathering the top of her hand and his breath waft onto her skin in quick puffs of air. He watches the contraction's deep seizure ebbing as her breathing slowly returned to natural easy respiration.

"I can't believe my eyes seeing you here in our room like this, Lizbett! You are so beautiful still…just as I remember you in your white lacy dress that sundown at the church before Bako took you away. I have slept in this room every night since remembering you above all my day's memories."

"Ravenz! Oh, it is *you*, little Ravenz! I see now, my eyes focus better between the pains. How beautifully you have grown in manliness, Ravenz! And your green, *green* eyes! They twinkle as two emeralds yet, even brighter at this hour in summer solstice high light! *Wait!* It is *your* birthday today, Ravenz!" Lizbett's head nestled into the pillow as she pressed his hand against her lips. Her eyes softened to mist as she stared at his face. From the corner of his eye Ravenz watched a new contraction advance mercilessly through to its entirety then receding away to a dim memory, if only to return in intensity a moment later immediately reminding…

"I am sixteen today, Lizbett!"

"Ah, sixteen…I remember the day you were born, Ravenz! Why, only yesterday I picked you up from the mattress of petals your sweet baby body lay on in that dark basket. Your eyes shone green as gemstones then as you looked to the sky and the world around. Where is your shirt, Ravenz? You sit at my bedside half naked." Her belly's muscles tightened in one great long spasm causing an interruption in her query. But Lizbett kept her eyes fixed on Ravenz' face as she impatiently waited the ordeal through to its end. "Has the washing day passed one day too long?"

Ravenz laughed softly leaning closer to the pillow. Lizbett's tawny curls tickled his face now as it did one summer day in the lagoon years before when she'd swept him from shoreline into her arms' embrace swaying him back and forth, back and forth as watery ripples teased at his heels and little pant-legs.

"I went swimming in the lagoon, today! It was so hot at high noon...and my shirt..."

"It is time, Lizbett!" Anabaa spoke directly but in low calm tones.

"So it is Half Moon Lagoon's sweet fresh scent on you! There is no finer fragrance ..."

"*Lizbett!*" yelped Anabaa in controlled stern tone. *"Push!"*

"Why-ever for should I push? Push *what*, Anabaa? Can't you see I am in conversation with our Ravenz here?"

"Well, pardon my rudeness for interrupting your reminiscences but if you are to see the face of the child you've only prayed for all these long years then you had best hush your speech and *push now!PUSH!"*

Sweet weak bleats rose into a full-blown squall as new tiny lungs filled with oxygen inhaled; a simple and profound response to birth's great work. Anabaa held an infant in the air watching its arms flail tiny balled fists and little legs kick up heels.

"Cut your daughter's cord, Bako...that's it...right there!"

Bako! Daughter? It's all over...so soon? I am a mother of an infant girl!

Lizbett blinked clearing the haze from her eyes. Then her ears heard Anabaa's familiar lyrical voice,

"You may bathe your granddaughter, Ebo and Fairie! Those towels on the bureau should suffice."

Lizbett turned her gaze to the face of the man, Bako whom she loved beyond heart's reason and pressing his fingers to her lips whispered, "It's all right, isn't it Bako, you were here for the birth of our girl-child seeing she is beautiful and truly well?"

Ravenz vanished as ghost from the business happening in the room what with bath and lather gently splashing, tender words softly spoken as serene mist and Anabaa gathering baskets and linens going about the work of midwife and all...

He did not look back.

The pyramid grew by one spit-ball-of-moist-twine more.

Vocabulary followed.

My teeth ach to the tips of their sockets and my jaws cramp...my tongue is raw and my throat is parched. 'Gnaw your way through your bondage,' the birdman says! Easy for himto say!

Horses' hooves plodding upon dry dirt road play bass to the high squeals of a wagon's turning wheels bouncing in out deep ruts made during a long-ago surprise rainstorm. The robber quit his lament looking up at the sight of a dust plume rising as a handsomely-matched team of five magnificent horses, one royally-differingPretzyl, hauling a gleaming black carriage rolled to a halt only feet of his hapless body sitting bound in the roadway.

Thank you for stopping

Then he blinked his eyes three times focusing hard on the face of the driver holding reins over these steeds.

"You!"

"Excuse me? Have our eyes met on some other way? Forgive me if I don't readily recognize your face." Rhynn sat in the seat of his grandfather's great carriage wondering more of the cause of this man's predicament than at the fact that somehow they had crossed paths in another time.

"Ha! Totally funny, raven-man! You stood over me only two hours ago…naked and unabashed…threatening to pluck out my eyes!"

"Really"

"You called yourself a raven…" The robber stopped his explanation upon seeing the perplexed look cross the driver's face as puzzlement deepened the jade-green of his eyes.

"So what happened here to make you think it is I who bound you up in a cowboy's lariat and leave you in the roadway thus to chew your way to freedom?"

"A dwarf man…clubbing…bloody eyebrow…a coin…thieved…" stammered the robber not wanting to divulge the whole secret lest some pity might gift his way.

"A *dwarf* did this to you? You say *he* bound you like this and robbed you of *your* coin?"

There is only one dwarf in my father's entire kingdom and he is diminutive Artist Parqai. He sits upon a work stool in the marketplace tall as any giant among all peers in this realm.

Rhynn stared a long silent moment at the face looking up at his own.

"I discern no injuries to your face for no blood flows from any tear in either eyebrow's skin. Your nose appears quite free of swelling or purple bruise."

Sensing his hope of early release fleeting the robber sighed reconsidering the raven-man's dark promise.

"Now, how does the tale of this woe go? Begin again, sir." Rhynn spoke directly, distinctly low, eyes unblinking, waiting patiently where he sat in driver's seat.

There is no other way for me now but to tell it rightly for he is in the roadway and passageway, coming at me from shadows and branches and sky overall will this man, Ravenz haunts me

After twitching in itches caused by the rope's scratchy twine the thief sighed and began his story again.

"I ambushed a dwarf-man as he walked this way clubbing his brow with a branch then seized his shirt...tearing it. A coin rolled onto the ground freed of torn cloth. I fled up the roadway with it in my fist until your rope flew from the air encircling my knees causing my fall to the dirt, is all." And the robber looked down at his knees and saw that he was quite close to breaking through to his freedom. *Only three or four more bites...* So the thief bent his face unto its task baring his front teeth to commence gnawing on twine.

"I agree with the naked raven-man that you sit in fair sentence for the act you committed. Your incisors are wide and their edges appear sharp. Carry on with the gnawing, unless, of course, you would prefer that I cut you loose and haul you to the castle's court to appear before my father, His Majesty where you may plead the harshness of your punishment beforehim."

The thief's eyes rolled back in his head as his body swayed side-to-side upon hearing this news.

"Look me in the eye, thief! And know this; I am Prince Rhynn, son of King Breretyn and his queen, Latezia but to you always will I be Jaguar. My haunches tighten watching your footfall whatever path you tread in nighttime's blackest hours and on all days' sun-illuminated roadways will I stalk you from all shadows and branches, cliffs andevery valley."

The thief dropped his gaze to the ground at the jaguar-man's covenant-oath spewing out a spit-ball of twine adding more soggy lint to the pile pyramiding at his side. *Only a few more bites...just another bite more...one more bite...one more*

When he dared raise his face to the eyes of the prince the thief saw naught but long empty rutsstretching to a vanishing point both coming and going.

~⌇

Prince Rhynn rose from his knees to the choir's mighty crescendo. The crown on his head felt heavier than he could have imagined in all his boy-dreams fantasizing the day when such crown would adorn his brow as does the magnificent sovereign crown gracing his father's head. Even now with his muscles grown strong and powerful in confidence due to disciplines of fencing and archery, hunting and swimming the prince held his head stiffly upright hardly breathing for fear a sneeze or twitch might cause the object to slip off his head falling into an embarrassing clatter across the plinth. He took advantage of the entire last stanza to accustom himself to the little crown's weight, itself symbolic of his station's responsibilities because of his birth to these two people; King Breretyn and his queen, Latezia. A shudder dared cross his shoulders but then suddenly warmed away beneath ermine and sable.

I will meet each challenge head-on without flinch and with much thoughtfulness, without temper and with fair disposition will I tend the throne of the kingdom upon my father, King Breretyn's...

"Long live the king! Long live the king!" chanted the choir. Drums beat. Horns blew. Fireworks' explosions lit up the night sky with a trillion blazing stars.

Kyrro stared.

Ravenz is...Rhynn? This whole time?

Crowds cheered.

Rhynn stared at the engravings deeply cut into the square flat surface of his signet ring and saw a sheaf with four heads bound two times with rope around the middle, tassel dangling. Each head depicts a different symbol.

Grape cluster: *earth's bounty*. Fish: *water's bounty*. Bird: *air's bounty*

And a Jaguar…tiny emerald eyes glint from its perfectly carved muscular face.

Ravenz lay succumbing to drowsiness in the swaying hammock hanging between porch posts in candles' soft glow through his bedchamber's window. The curtains hang swished aside and the panes flung open inviting sweet summer night air into the room. Voices within purred like cats dreaming as dark silhouettes passed by bedposts to headboard's pillows and back again arms tenderly exchanging to one another a bundled girl-infant cooing.

And in Ravenz' palm warmed one large golden coin with engraved royal face gleaming in full moon's white glow, the eyes luminescing as two stars softly shine.

Looking to the night sky beyond dark rocky ledge to a tree's subtle-swaying branch Ravenz sees two white eyes blazing in the face of an eagle perched regally there.

You are Ravenz-prince-bird-royal of the valley kingdom as your brother-twin is royal Prince Rhynn-Jaguar-cat of high castle's kingdom as I am royal-supreme in my kingdom sky.

Chapter 9

NOCTURNE

Ah, there you stand enchanting queen…when you left me just now I knew it immediately as if each extremity had been jerked from its socket leaving my entrails to empty and my heart to wither for want.

"Which one of them will become the wife of our son?"

Latezia startled a little at King Breretyn's voice, even low and soft as it floated to her ears at this midnight hour in the parlor she'd slipped into since turning away from fireworks' sparklers, musicians playing endless dance songs and uprising voices offering phrases in high celebration and enthusiastic cheer. Her heart melted at the mere little thought that the king had noticed a brick-maker's daughter's absence from such a spectacular gala swirling on the lawns about fountain through hedge mazes and out over cobbled courtyard.

Were you watching me at play with our guests, husband, Your Majesty? Or did you startle when remembering me suddenly aside your duties and come looking for me in a crazy panic? Every time I sought your eye your face was bent to hear words spoken through your loyal subjects' lips.

Latezia feels his warmth suddenly comfort away such thought breaking darkening spell as his arms wrapped about her pulling her against him. The slight weight of his chin grazing the crown of her head stilled all ponder as her eyes focused instead on Parqai's ethereal portrait of two damsels' identical dreamy visages standing amid a whir of butterflies' wings.

"*One* of them? They appear both as the *same* girl!"

"Look again, Love, look at the eyes, most especially."

Latezia closed her own eyes instead as her head rested in the hollow of His Majesty's throat between clavicles' notches-to-sternum. It is the place where once at a damsel's age she had felt such simple comfort from an accident's pain in a gentle working-man's arms, the place where she closed her eyes to the sun and thoughts of soap and jade-green eyes kept time with an old workhorse's bumpy gait, and slipping into dozing had simply entrusted her battered being to a stranger's kindness...*somehow knowing...knowing something more was yet to come.*

"I know the one she will be even now, from this canvas I can tell you Rhynn's choice exactly, Latezia."

"How so...so perfectly do they reflect each other in color and curl of tendril, curve of lip and gentle chin and soft slope of shoulder...but then you are king above all, of course, and see things beyond simple subjects' gaze."

"My heir will choose the one with a star in each eye...white stars gleam in blue irises as does a star gleam in blue-sapphire cabochon.She is the one having eyes as his mother's eyes. When he sees her he sees you, Latezia."

"Oh! In here! They are in here!" Rhynn's voice rang through his parents' meditative contemplation as did the sound of dance slipper-clad feet swish upon marble tile turn their heads to the archway. A trio of beauty in their son's company widened their eyes as recognition set in.

"Father! Mummy! I've met the most gracious lady-persons! Let me present Missus Tsagalakis and her twin daughters, Qeyyapi, and Aotepi."

It did not escape King Breretyn's keen gaze that Rhynn presented

Qeyyapi with his hand gently resting to the small of the maiden's back and that his heir presented Aotepi by her hand clasped in his and lifted slightly unto his awed parents' faces.

Three females dropped to the floor, taffeta and silk billowing as clouds about their bowed beings, arms swaying as swans' wings and faces turned to the royals' hems.

"Your Majesties, King Brertyn…Queen Latezia," chanted lyrical bird-like voices. And then they each rose quite dramatically as practiced for an hour's time before mirror and mother since an errand's return from market was interrupted halfway by a prince-royal riding horseback.

Moon…Star

"Your timing is impeccable for we were just admiring Artist Parqai's grand portrait of your exquisite daughters just now, Madame! Step up between us here and see for yourself his work's beauty." Breretyn extended his hand to the maidens' mother and as Latezia and the king swept aside, ushered Madame Tsagalakais before the canvas smelling faintly of fresh oil-paint.

Daphne Tsagalakis, being humble beyond most simple-humble and greatly awed beyond supreme reason at experiencing the day's events beginning with the interruption of her foot-walk home by a cantering horse's hooves upon gravely cobbled roadway and the sight of what appeared to her eyes in that moment; a courteous rider seeming as a prince-royal riding in saddle and the kind invitation he extended herself and two daughters for a little house party given in honor of his sixteenth birthday-investiture to finding herself swept up in a stunning gala happening at glorious Kings Castle's vast courtyard and lawns and now being ushered by a royal hand into a private audience in the palace Parlor-of-Portraiture with Their Supreme Highnesses, King Breretyn and Queen Latezia, most superb parents of newly-minted Crown Prince Rhynn, to standing here now, knees weakening before this before-unknown-to-herself portrait of... *her own twin daughters!* The astonishing surprise of the entire day of it all overwhelmed her mind causing Daphne to succumb to a dizzying vapor fogging her senses.

Quaking knees buckled beneath Madame Tsagalakis' weight causing her body to slump against the king. Arms possessing muscles of steel gripped about her ribs causing faint air to escape her lungs. She felt her person swayed away in a singular motion before being set upon a chaise bolstering fat pillows. Candles' flickers dance brilliant aureole above her head and her ears heard voices swirling as autumn dry leaves rustling in winds' sweep up canyon and down corridor.

Mother! What happened? Are you sick, Madame? Fetch Bazil for ice! Oh, Mother, what happened just then?

Daphne lifted a trembling finger pointed to the portrait.

"How did it come to be here, in this place?"

"An artist in the mercantile sat as his easel painting when the wind gusted fiercely and dust got in your eyes," chorused her twin damsels.

Latezia, having sensed Daphne's oncoming faint at the sight of seeing her daughter's faces painted so divinely on canvas by Parqai's sensitive brushstrokes, grasped at the woman's wrist noticing her fingers relaxing their fast hold to a little glass jar bearing odd green spheres resembling eyeballs but with bright red pupils at their core.

Latezia held the jar to the light of a near candle's dazzling flame.

"Breretyn...what are these?"

These

Daphne lurched up coming out of her daze under the shock of Bazil's tender ice poultice rendering shivers across her cheekbones.

Oh, no! That's my pitifully-humiliatingly-bitty hostess gift for the queen...of all women! She scrutinizes it now before blinding illumination!

"Well, well, they look to be some type of..."

Daphne interrupted the king. "Olives, Your Majesty. They are simply green olives, is all. The red you see there is only pimento pepper stuffed in pits' place. The whole of them bathe in brine." She sighed, looking down at her empty palms. "It is to be a gift to the lady-of-the-house, you know...for inviting me and my daughters...here...tonight..." Her voice trailed to a bleat almost as a child's embarrassed whine.

"*Olives!* How sublime! Pickled stuffed olives such of a color and size as I've not seen in *any* time! This is an exquisite gift, Madame, and rare...a remarkable gift most unselfishly given to our little household. Come! Let's all to the kitchen and we'll give them a try!"

～

The far-off strains of dance music played on night's airwaves cause a stir in Ravenz quite unlike any feeling experienced any other night before.

I was born this day sixteen years past. Was it upon nighttime's full moon that my face saw first light...and did music play then as it does now...so enchanting...bewitching...alluring me?

Twosmall stars luminescing more brilliantly and closer to Ravenz than all others appear perfectly round *as eyes.*

I soared

"Fly above me, Eagle!" Ravenz whispered his command to the solitary dark form majestically perched on high rocky ledge.

The hammock tilted under Ravenz' weight as he slipped over its side silently-effortless as a bird rises wings into flight. His buckskin suede jacket hanging on wooden peg under the eave offered acceptable dress to his shirtless bare skin. Leather sandals hastened his foot-tread down steps under lamp's light through gateway onto gravely roadway winding along river past Half Moon Lagoon mirroring moon's silvery high shine. Mist billows diaphanous cloud upon cloud as hushed encore-veil to the roar of the river's tumbling falls. Beyond heather plain radiance shone in an arc above the castle casting a near-daylight glow over the king's lawns, hedge mazes and foaming fountain as constellations clustering in black sky's hemispheres twinkle overall.

Mute sentries standing guard before flung-wide-opened high gates stare away at the goings-on happening in courtyard and on lawns. Running his fingers through sun-dried disarray-curls Ravenz strode forward under cover of kind darkness toward His Majesty's castle.

Sparkling fireworks lit up the night sky illuminating the castle's turrets before falling to earth as a trillion miniature shooting stars arc and descend. Musicians strumming harps' strings, buglers bugling, trumpet players tooting and drummers drumming…dancers in silk and satin twirl, arms gather and sway, graceful heads bent bashfully aside…eyes too nervous to look-lock…too curious not to…

Laughter rang through great Champagne Hall's high open windows. Goblets clink against each other boosting voices' goodwill chimes. Tables groan under silver domed platters and waitpersons in waistcoats carrying gilded trays glide in circles beneath crystal chandeliers.

Rhynn reached for a scone but the tray bumped aside as Kyrro's face suddenly rose before his.

"You've changed your shirt, Rhynn! Now you look just like Ravenz again!"

"I am Ravenz. I gave my shirt to Parqai at the lagoon

earlier…after a little mishap. And then Lizbett delivered herself of Bako's infant daughter in my bed at eventide. I just got here, Kyrro. Did I miss much?"

Kyrro eyed Ravenz with a look such as Ravenz had never witnessed in any gaze extended of his friend's eyes at any time in all his years' days past. A slight shiver ran down his spine in spite of the jacket covering his otherwise naked back.

Kyrro laughed. Heartily

"The way I see it the only thing you are missing is a grand goblet of the king's new royal purple champagne effervescing its bubbles misting all faces tickling eyeballs!" Kyrro raised a massive clear vessel to his lips draining it dry in one supreme gulp of an elixir of such exquisite color and clarity as Ravenz had never beheld in any brew.

"*Purple* champagne?"

"Ah, indeed it *is* purple, Ravenz, as the royal brew is infused with macerated blackberries' nectar!"

Kyrro burped.

And in the fume-fog that followed, Kyrro vanished from view just as a tray of roast quail-on-toast passed before Ravenz eyes.

Ravenz gripped the waitperson's gloved wrist before it too, vanished as mysteriously as seems to be the way of the night's happenings.

"I fancy a bite, kind server. Wait, please, till I make my choice." The waiter looked up into Ravenz' eyes and did not flinch under Ravenz' long deep gaze and longer hand-grasp. Ravenz released his steely grip then to pick out a thick crisp toast loaded with syrup-glazed deeply-caramelized bird.

The server waited for Ravenz to take his first bite then twitched his nose.

I may smell of Half Moon Lagoon's fresh watery bath, of windblown hair and sun-bronzed skin and of spending an hour in birth-chamber holding a woman's hand in her greatest work delivering a child.

"Thank you, kind server-sir, for waiting on me so unselfishly here."

Strength gradually returned to muscles aching for nourishment for long had the day passed since morning's hard hours roping claves then bathing in lagoon's rehabilitating water. The work of settling a robber to justice and comforting a victim unto reasonable solace to the sweet surprise-joy finding Lizbett in deep labor's throes upon his...*her*...bed...and hearing an infant's first wail depletes a man.

The last crumb did not escape to the floor.

～～つ

Low light glowed through the crack between door and stone floor. Grandpappy and Grandmummy jerked their heads up at the sound of the door suddenly opening and startled as comics at being caught red-handed devouring biscuits and slurping warm milk.

"Now just you stay set there, Mamma. Don't go getting up on our account. Breretyn and I are just nibbly, is all and we have in our presence one Madame Daphne and her two lovely daughters having come here for Rhynn's party," babbled Latezia as she fastened an apron about elegant silk and tulle glittering ballgown.

"Shuffle on down the bench there, good father-in-law! Make room for your grandson and his lady-guests here!" A quick hustle of bustles slid along ancient royally bum-polished benches as biscuits were passed and glasses with milk splash.

Daphne Tsagalakis could not help herself staring at their Royal Highnesses, King Breretyn and Queen Latezia, both aproned; she lifting tureens' lids and he with his sleeves pushed up pulling bowls from cabinets and ladles from drawers dishing braises from kettles still warm from the ovens' smoldering coals the whole of the time oblivious of tiara and crown appearing together in castle's kitchen as choreographed dancers gracefully reaching and arcing, serving and passing over and about one another as any plain-townsfolk husband and wife in any house's humble kitchen in the world anywhere.

The king sliced cheeses. The queen stacked flat crackers. A jar popped its lid. Green pimento-stuffed olives rolled onto rimmed platter.

Except one

The king raised his hand, fingertips holding the green orb and with red pimento-pupil showing forth to his guests, popped the orb into his mouth closing both his eyes.

Daphne held her breath.

Only when positively certain the king had chewed through and swallowed the entire orb and his eyes opened and refocused themselves did she dare ask a simple question.

"Does…the recipe…please His Majesty's…palate?"

"Bravo! These are a true delicacy such I must have in my kingdom in all future time! How is it you came by this one jar and, if I dare dream, might there just be…*many* jars more?"

Everyone at the table grabbed at the olives and cheeses and crackers creating such a flurry of motion Daphne had to glance away…if for only a moment while she righted her vision and composed her thoughts.

"My husband tends the olive trees in our motherland. He set us to sail here in hope of finding a far-reaching market for his harvest's bounty. My girls and I stepped foot on dry land only yesterday and today we ventured into market in quest of learning if such a kiosk might be welcome in the street to display his jars when a great wind blew up nearly sweeping away my basket of bread loaves and supper and then a rider on horseback stepped alongside us on roadway and well, he, I mean, Prince Rhynn, your well-mannered crowned son here, invited us to his house tonight for a little party in his honor. The olive jar is the only gift I have in the house, what this event being short notice and all." Daphne quit her speech because she is out of words and out of air.

In the course of the conversation that followed plans were in put in place for a kiosk to be erected on the morrow for an afternoon's display of a cartload of jars bearing splendid green spheres resembling eyeballs with red pupils showing…bathing in brine…*supremely sublime.*

"I will write to Mister Tsagalakis, your good husband in my own hand explaining my desire and implore him to send more jars over the sea so all in my kingdom shall partake of such excellent delicacy."

Daphne near wilted to a faint on the spot where she sat at the luck of this day, what being discovered along roadside by a prince-royal.

And just having to have not one but two daughters surely close to his age adds joy to my luck for a simple invitation to a little party ensued…and now…all this!

"I'm off show these lovely damsels about the house, Mummy! Thank you, Poppi for the nourishment served here…and for your olive gift, Missus Tsagalakis!" Rhynn slid from the bench pulling Aotepi along by her hand. "Good night, Grandpappy, Grand-mummy! Kiss! Kiss! Sweet dreams!" And as the way of things seemingly happening in King Breretyn's kingdom the kids disap-peared from the room as vapor vanishes in air.

Grandpappy cackled first.

"That boy is going to marry that star-eyed maiden!"

Grandmummy seconded his phrase.

Breretyn added punch to his father-in-law's line.

"He just hasn't told us yet!"

Daphne's head hit the tabletop.

Breretyn leaned over the table in a valiant effort to raise the woman's face from the ancient elbow-and-dish-burnished oak tabletop. No bruise showed on her porcelain skin and no fluid ran from her nose. Her eyes appear as those of one daydreaming so tranquil seem their focus.

"Daphne will be fine, Breretyn, gentle husband. Fainting is a uniquely feminine phenomenon. As soon as she revives I'll show her to Southwing's Camellia suites."

~⁓

"I am going back to join the party in the courtyard, if you don't mind, Prince Rhynn. My feet feel like dancing and my head is full of wakefulness yet. Shall I see you again before we take leave?" Qeyyapi dropped into an elegant curtsy keeping eyes coyly downcast for the count of one-and-two-and-three-and-four before rising to hold Rhynn's eyes in her soft steadfast gaze.

"I'll be seeing you at the breakfast table, of course! Your mother, yourself and Aotepi are guests of King Breretyn's Camellia suites, along Southwing's corridor." Rhynn's voice trailed to whispers as Qeyyapi's feet sped along stone hallway up stairwell down mirrored hallway across glassy marble foyer through wide open high French doors under portico down circular stone steps across pebble courtyard drawn by the sound of the great fountain's bubbling and misty-fog-rising enchanting her ears and hypnotizing her eyes far beyond any true meaning of *spell*.

Ravenz sees the damsel's eyes before he saw her being. Two eyes glowing as full moons beam out to him across fountain's shallow rippling basin-lake. Mist rsies as a translucent veil shrouding her form to darkness but seemingly enhancing her eyes' magnet pull.

Stay there, beautiful eyes for I will swim across this tiny ocean to better understand your gaze!

Qeyyapi stares

You! How is it you arrived here before me when it is my sister's hand you clasp so tightly in yours, fingers entwined as you dash her away down passageway through castle's secret getaways? How is it you look at me with desire burning in your eyes when it was Aotepi you persuaded the artist to paint on the portrait next to the head of which one of us even he knew not?It was her face you looked upon when you extended your party invitation to my mother and into her eyes you gazed when we rose from our bow. You have already forsaken your crown and cloak for a suede jacket! Why this valley-boy disguise? What is the meaning of this game you play in darkness with me...as Aotepi dreams?

"I am Ravenz."

Qeyyapi blinked.

"Excuse me, but I thought you said your name is…"

"Ravenz. Why have I have not seen you before in the king's court or anywhere in His Majesty's realm?"

But surely you saw me for we share a whole day linking one crazy moment to another ending in this place but yet you say this thing.

"Your eyes look like two moons beaming through the fountain's mist but now that I'm close they appear as opal cabochons shimmering." Ravenz stood so closely to Qeyyapi his ears hear her heart beating. "They mesmerize me. What is your name?"

You smell different...like clear water, sun and breeze...not of precious bergamot and rare myrrh like before and your skin is bare beneath that thin suede jacket looking as if left to hang outside weathering elements. Is this a disguise or a trick of light happening in fireworks' glitter and full moon's gleam?

"You enchant me. Are you a statue as these marble ancestor-kings standing here are statues? Is that why no sound passes between your lips? Why is it I hear you breathing but hear not words?"

"I am Qeyyapi."

"Ah, the maiden does speak! Qeyyapi…Qeyyapi…what does it mean…Qeyyapi…wait! I know now…it means moon, of course! Incredible! So incredibly beautifully do your eyes shine as the full moon beams!"

Trumpets' blasts and drums' reverberating startled the crowd from its dancing to gasp,

"What's happening? Why this interruption? Look! Look up…at the balcony there! See, the butlers are at the doors…opening…swinging them wide!" Warm dancing bodies dressed in silk, satin and taffeta brushed against Ravenz crowding his view as they squeezed ever tighter in their forward movement in hope of securing a better look.

Ravenz retreated.

The girl named Qeyyapi ceased to exist in the sea of heads swirling before Ravenz' eyes. Curls, ringlets and waves bound in ribbons and pearl strands, tendrils tied up in flower-bands, nosegays tickling his nose to the point of sneezing caused Ravenz to turn back about the fountain, crossing cobblestone courtyard over deep dew-damp lawn through high iron gates onto roadway where night's natural symphony serenades his ear; crickets in far-off thickets chirp, frogs down at the riverbanks croak backup-chorus and a nightingale carries lead vocal throughout all. Overhead an eagle circles in wide arcs, magnificent wings spread seemingly beyond their tips, white eyes luminescing as two stars keenly watch the valley-prince glide silently along dry road, dust pluming in his wake.

The eagle swooped to the earth in such a grand dive Ravenz halted his footfall, holding his breath.

What is it, Eagle? What do you see in the roadway?

The bird settled itself in the ruts, pecked at something limp as if a snake then let it fall away from its beak. Ravenz dashed forward in curiosity. The eagle rose slowly flapping its mighty wings in no apparent urgency as it weaved its great self about in the air diving and swooping here and there seeking a rodent or hare.

"It's only a cowboy's lariat rope...wait, there's two! Oh, I remember now, the robber must have chewed himself free. But what freedom can possibly come of being watched by a raven every hour?"

Wrapping the ropes into a loop over his arm Ravenz turned onto the path at the lamppost below the beacon softly blinking *green...white...green...white...gently beckoning*

"Oh, look up! Look there! Tiz King Breretyn and Queen Latezia escorting Crown Prince Rhynnand a *maiden* to the railing up yonder!"

Aotepi's eyes searched the crowd until they caught sight of Qeyyapi standing in the fringe of fountain's finest mist.

"Qeyyapi! Come up! Come up here and stand with us, good sister! Stand with Mother!"

Qeyyapi stared, blinked, and then glanced over the crowd searching all faces for *that* one named Ravenz who just a moment ago looked identical to *this* Rhynn.

So confusing is this night! One-him-crowned-royal dressed now in ermine and sable where a moment ago he-valley-boy wore naught but a thin buckskin suede jacket...how can this midnight transfer occur so magically-quick...happening in a breath and heartbeat...is truly happening...or is it not?

A candle burning low cast dim light through the window above the hammock swaying between porch posts. Ravenz laid his head upon his body-warmed jacket now folded in quarters. Parts of its corners tickled his shoulders. Occasionally a dark silhouette passed by the window holding a bundle to shoulder then fading from view as quickly as shadows vanish. Now and again soft voices exchange low-spoken words soothing a newborn's cry.

The coin in Ravenz' hand drew warm in the folds of his fingers so he opened his palm in the moonlight to behold Artist Parqai's golden medallion laying there.

The girl with moonbeam eyes I saw through fountain's misty haze is real…isn't she? She really happened before me in one short night hour before she vanished…as a full moon evaporates in day.

King Neptlyn's engraved golden face gleams in the warmth of Ravenz' palm and his eyes glow.

Ravenz dreams.

CHAPTER 10

LATEZIA'S FOOTFALL BRUSHED THE LENGTH OF MOUNTAINWING'S western corridor passing closed doors to suites and chambers long vacated of widows, orphans and wardens, the infirm and their nursemaids. The air hangs close even in early July afternoon's ultimate heat. No scent of winter lingers anywhere; no sweet spruce needle or pinecone lay forgotten in any corner. No peppermint oil wafts on any airwave. Even biscuit crumbs left behind had undoubtedly been digested within minutes of the New Year's infant hour.

Thirteen empty rooms...perfectly beautiful silent chambers...lilac scents air and lavender scents linens encasing pillows and sheets inviting dreamers...dreaming

Latezia turned a knob.

The door swung wide away from her hand as suddenly as if a gale catches a windowpane unto shutter-slam and clattering. Icy air breezed across her face though no drapery billows in its wake. Snowflakes kiss at the glass even as brilliant summer sunshine floods the room through tightly shut windows. Flutes toot and little bells jingle, batons tap on drums and mandolins' strings hum.

Mummy! Look here...over here, Mummy! Jagger is playing with the elves in here! See how we run in this round-about-way! Look there, Mummy, the stockings are stuffed over their tops ...all the toes drag to the hearth! Biscuits and tarts...clove-apple juice ...pears floating...silver cups brimming...painted horses gallop on wooden hooves...trains going in circles...glassy-eyed dolls in satin dresses smiling...some cooing...some wetting...blue teddy bears and pink stuffed lambs! Mummy, is Christmas night coming a day early? Say,

'Yes' Mummy cuz Jagger can't wait!

Chuckles and giggles and soft nursemaids' voices chime.

Chase me! No, meee! Come find Jagger, Mummy! Over here...no, here! Look under here...way back here! Ravenz flies up here...catch Jagger's tail...Ravenz flies...flapping wings...Jaguar slinks...come catch Jagger...come back, little flyaway bird, Ravenz!

"Mother!"

"Ah, Ravenz."

"It's me, Jaguar!"

"Oh. *Jaguar!*"

"And Rhynn! You look ill, Mother! Are you sick? Your face is so flushed in this hot empty vacuum! Why are you standing *here*...in *this* room? I've been looking all over the palace for you! Come out of this place to summer's fresh air. See the doorway yonder? Tiz left open...the afternoon breeze wafts through corridor now."

Latezia fainted.

"Qiaona! Mother's fainted! Fetch Bazil...and ice!"

Latezia moaned. And shuddered

Ice! Sweet winter's ice...cold...hard...wet ice...solace...winter solstice...snowflake...muskrat...

"Green-eyed scamp...are you trying to freeze me when I wish only to melt?"

"You are hallucinating, Mother! I am Prince Rhynn, your jaguar son. Focus your gaze on my face!"

Latezia stared up at the eyes peering at her face and sees green.

Oh, myBreretyn's wondrous jade-green eyes comfort me as a traveling gypsy man's eyes once peered into mine...long ago...a hurt and dazed damsel.

Latezia bolted upright.

"Stop stroking me with the ice bag! It's so freezing cold! I'm shivering, for pity-sake!"

"Mother?"

Latezia looked into Rhynn's eyes a long moment then slumped against her first handmaiden, Qiaona smelling faintly of Her Majesty's precious rare oils.

You've been dipping crystal stoppers into my perfume vessels again.

"Oh, *Rhynn!* It's *you!* Beautiful Rhynn! My baby! So beautiful is my little Jaguar." Latezia reached forth her hand and brushed an errant curl from her son's brow. "I was just dreaming a small Christmastime wish, is all…missing the giggles and cheer wintering children bring here. It's so quiet and still now and all doors are closed…so tightly. I just wanted to hear little voices and watch them play again, is all, Rhynn."

"You are lonely, Mother. The house is too big with its one-hundred chambers. In all my dream-prayers I call for Aotepi to come back, God speed. I will fill every chamber with infants…so many for you to chase down hallways, through corridors to catch and snatch up in your arms, I promise! But the month is summertime which passes soon enough and those in the village planning on wintering here will be back in these rooms before first snowfall. Poppi promises!"

The queen laughed.

"Why am I sitting on this silly stone floor? Come! Let's be off to the kitchen for lemon water and ice! Now, what were you saying about 'looking for me'? Why were you calling for me, Rhynn?

"I just wanted to let you know I'll be at the university tonight!" Rhynn, his queen-mother, Qiaona and Bazil close behind just-in-case sped down stairwell across landing into mirrored marble hallway through side corridor slipping into kitchen sliding along ancient bum-polished benches. "I will be in Kings Observatory mapping Southern hemisphere's Sagittarius for Naval Academy's celestial navigation lectures, is why I was calling for you."

~⊃

"The lamb rack is roasted through, Ravenz, and sits on the sideboard should your appetite step up the plate. You haven't eaten at all since the eggs Constance fixed earlier breaking your fast."

"You have either read my mind or else heard my stomach's demand because I am on my way to your table this minute!" Ravenz slapped shut the physics journal tossing it aside the abacus then gathered three kohl pencils dropping them into a tin can, points up.

The dam-lock-channel-conceptual blueprints please him hugely so he'd slid the grid papers between two heavy sheets of papyrus.The quest for this magnificent seaway stemmed from a singular idea nurtured in his developing curious brain since his fifteenth summer when he'd rowed with Admiral Bako and serene Lizbett in his little wood boat gliding in river's unceasing flow past villages here and there until his eyes beheld ships docked at the quay and many more anchored offshore wasting weeks' days waiting to unload.So many tiny boats jammed the river in efforts to gain cargo's best produce…jockeying…jostling…tangling all oars the whole of the way forth and back.

Ravenz does not want anything smudging the drafts.

But it is the written proposal that has his mind stymied as he sat the last hour thinking through many compound-complex sentences running long in strings linking important composite vocabulary tempered by the addition of impressive Greek-symbol formulae qualifying mathematical-equation-calculations supporting his argument. When all sentences chased around each other in circles, tails catching up to the heads, is when Anabaa poked in at the doorway mentioning nourishment.

When did you grow into this man, little bird-baby Ravenz? Your shoulders...so broad and your limbs are long... Ravenz glanced up. *Your facial bones are angular now and your chin is square. A slight cleft shows there and shadows tease in the hollows of your cheeks...such incredible green eyes I have not seen in any man since King Breretyn's face... and his firstborn heir.* And she shudders then, eyes closed, body pressed against doorjamb, hands grasping at the wall.

"What is it, Anabaa? Are you ill? The air is still warm from sun's high heat and yet you shiver."

Ravenz' hand grazed Anabaa's face as his arm clasped about her shoulders. "Sit with me while I have my supper. You have been cooking all day in summertime's high heat. Come, let's to tall goblets of lemon water and ice." Fingertips pressing gently beneath her chin, Ravenz tilted Anabaa's face to meet his gaze. "I bought a sugarcane stalk at the market today!"

~⌒~

"Qeyyapi? Are you awake?" whispered Aotepi from her narrow thin mattress beneath her sister's sagging upper berth.

Stop listing, ship! You have long ceased your cradle motions and now dare toss me onto hard plank floor. Stop heaving, sea! Settle yourself into gentleness. My hands grow tired hanging on like this.

Aotepi wondered how it is that Qeyyapi could possibly slumber on upper mattress seemingly oblivious to the squall's quest churning current crosswise current... and *dream*! Even her father's deep even snore amazed her as did her mother's soft even breathing seem as a comforting lullaby in an earlier childhood time when she'd wakened from startling dream to seek solace in her parents' bed.

But I am not a child and my parents sleep on the other side of this simple wooden wall.

The ship heaved. A trunk slid across the floor slamming against cabin door. Qeyyapi lurched up.

"Aotepi! Are you awake? What was *that*?"

"It's our trunk tossed into the door because this storm refuses to give up, is all. The waves have been angry for hours, since dinnertime. I'm weary of its ceaseless temper!"

Qeyyapi yawned and shifted her weight causing the slats to squeal as they strained in their brackets. Bits of mattress puff out as fat sausages in the cracks. A blanket hangs at an angle over the upper edge appearing as an obtuse curtain to Aotepi's berth.

"Do you think he'll still remember me, Qeyyapi?" Aotepi fingered the deep purple-blue sapphire on her finger feeling the stone's hard flat surface and beveled edges caught in thick gold clasps at its corners. The band circling her finger is wide and elegantly engraved in patterns the prince called filigree. "It's been twelve months since he saw me on the road that day and those two summer weeks went by too crazily-fast! What if he doesn't even recognize me, Qeyyapi? Worse yet, what if he didn't wait for me and took another? It is entirely possible, you know."

"Hush, Aotepi! Of course he will remember you! Prince Rhynn never let go of your hand the whole two weeks we spent in the mercantile kiosk and we almost missed our ship home because of his clasp!" Qeyyapi drew silent a moment plumping the pillow and turning it to the cool side. "Besides, he put that ring on *your* finger, didn't he? Why would he do such a thing if he never wanted to see it again? It is most valuable by all accounts... from his story anyway...it being his Queen Grandmother Myrinna's jewels, wife of King Neptlyn, mother-royal of King Breretyn!"

"Prince Rhynn was just newly sixteen, Qeyyapi. Boys that age don't know what they are doing."

"Like us being sixteen-and-three-quarters-now know what *we* are doing, of course!"

"Don't jest! I would be sad if when he sees my face disgusting expressions flood his muscles and he turns his eyes away. What if his dream-visions of me exceed my true real beauty and I am but just another maid in the street?"

"You are *not* just another pretty face in his kingdom's street! You are *unique*, Aotepi! *Nobody* in the whole world looks *anywhere* nearly as exquisite as *you!*"

"You do."

Aotepi pressed the ancient sapphire to her lips feeling subtle warmth radiate there as if just plucked from the earth and polished to brilliance only moments ago.

Qeyyapi lay silent a long while allowing her body to sway to the waves' rise, crest and fall as a baby lays helpless in a cradle rocking at others' will.

"Aotepi? Is it possible that we being identical twins one of us can see another whom is identical to someone one of us loves and that *her* heart also lurched that night becoming infatuated beyond relief under fireworks' mystery thus yearning every living hour to see his face once more?"

"Qeyyapi? What on earth are you babbling about?"

"That night, at the castle party I saw another who appeared to my eyes a man identical in visage and stature...*exactly* mirroring Prince Rhynn! So stunned was I at his gaze on me I near froze even in midsummer night's heat. I knew you swooned in the presence of the prince and I stood confounded at the sight of *this* person I thought to be *him* and was about to inquire of the nature of this cruel prank he could play on one of us against the other until he drew close to me at the fountain and spoke his name."

"Which is?" Aotepi's voice came curt and flat.

"Ravenz."

"Ravenz! Like raven, *the bird?*"

"It was when he stood before me that he smelled different, like river water, sun and air…no rare oil wafted from his person at all as Rhynn smelled so heavenly of musky myrrh that night. And he wore sandals and was naked beneath his thin buckskin jacket. But I swear on my life, Aotepi, he was *positively identical* to the crown-royal Prince Rhynn!

"At that moment commotion happened with trumpets blaring and drums beating, then *you* appeared on the balcony with the king and queen, Rhynn in his capes and new crown, and Mother stood up there looking down at me, too! I was dumbfounded stupid at the sight up there at the railing but when I turned back to look at the man, Ravenz was lost in the crowd. I saw him no more."

"We worked in the kiosk two weeks selling Father's jars and you never saw him once then?"

"I glanced up and down the street every day and my heart lurched at the sight of the one I thought might be him coming but when he approached closer his eyes were only on you, Aotepi. He was always Prince Rhynn! He looked at me too, of course, but as oppositely as if I am winter and you are summer. I knew he was never *him*."

The trunk shuddered back across the cabin coming to rest jammed between bed and wall.

When the ship up-righted itself bobbing a moment between swells, Qeyyapi softly queried,

"Is it possible twin babies conceived in one single egg, even though cleave into two complete singularbeings, can see the other's desire as her own? Is such transferred interpretation possible? Are we two joined…*as one* to the ultimate depth of our souls, Aotepi? Is that why I saw Rhynn's face in another so...*hopefully?*"

"But you said you heard his name spoken through his own mouth as Ravenz and all else about him appeared different."

"Sush, Aotepi! Listen!"

"I hear nothing. What am I listening for?"

"That's just it, Atoepi! The tempest has quieted! The ship lists no more! The ocean feels as a mother's arms gently rocking."

Aotepi heard a new sound floating in the darkness above her head; that being soft even deep breathing of a sister in slumber.

You and I are joined at our heart, Qeyyapi. You are systole and I, diastole.

⁓

Lightfoot ambled through the deserted mercantile bobbing his head to the rhythm of four new steel horseshoes echoing on cobblestone pavement. Tarps covered open-air kiosks and latched shutters covered shack's shelves. Long had conversations ceased for hunger and fatigue drove men home to table and ingredients gathered here by their wives in afternoon's light. But the smells of days' business remained as ghosts lingering in shacks' wood, in carts' bins, on kiosks' shelves, in rusty flower pails and wicker breadbaskets harboring a scattering of crumbs left to fortunate birds. King Breretyn smiled a great smile. Then he opened his mouth wide and whooped a great whoop as a schoolboy hollers upon scoring a goal.

"Yes, Lightfoot! Soon this ancient street and all these bumpy stones shall be smoothly paved flat with fine tarred gravel and grand stores shall line the avenue! Tall buildings skimming the sky shall be built strong of brick and mortar, glass and steel replacing all this shabby clutter of rough wood and tattered tarp! My hydro engineers have designed magnetic-steel-blade-turbines to whir in fury under dam's powerful water-force causing a magnificent surge of sparks unto illuminating our streetlamps and drive our industry's machines!

"This vacant trampled-weed lot will become a spectacular stadium where all persons can gather and play! It will be done, Lightfoot! I have approved the diagrams and signed every blueprint! Indigo villages in my realm will become great shining white cities from mountain through valley unto plain along winding riverbank to ocean's coast! You'll see, Lightfoot!" Breretyn rubbed the horse's neck then playfully scratched his mount's ears.

Lightfoot whinnied.

Moonlight shimmers as silvery ribbons upon the river's lazy-flowing surface. An owl hoots a call from its high perch in an outcropping of trees upstream fore Dog-Leg bend. Somewhere above the king's head, on a rocky ledge or in deep eave its owl-mate echoes in return.

A beacon high atop lamppost at pathway's end and gateway's entrance blinks

Green…white…green…white…gently beckoning

"We are almost home, good and faithful stallion! And I am nearing you, most beloved Latezia."

～

Ravenz dropped sinker, hook and line into the deep black slow-flowing current then sat upon the damp mossy earth against tree trunk's foot. Birds had long quieted their young with bellies filled of insects and worms. Only an occasional hoot of an owl or two wailed across river to echo off rocky ledge. Ravenz closed his eyes allowing all senses to focus on the smooth twig gripped in his palms. Bottom-dwelling fishes teased at nibbling the old baited hook causing a shimmy in the line and a tug on the twig.

Ravenz opened an eye.

Silver-winged insects oscillate in congress above a thatch of water-grass, blade-tips seeking light above water's glassy surface. Moonlight beams upon the surface as silver ribbons streaming along.

In one month I shall present my ideas to Kings University round table of engineers. The Minister of Trade and Dean of Admiralty, Head of Kings Naval Academy will attend, too.It can be done! My great seaway canal will be done! Ocean-going vessels will sail long up the river's great channel-lock-system delivering goods and supplies faster and closer to all cities.

A whinny and scuffle of hooves upon dirt road followed a long agonizing man-groan as a body thudded heavily upon the ground. Ravenz lurched up grasping twig, straining his ears to hear more. Only gasping and hoarse throaty sounds escaping lungs and larynx floated up in the night.Then silence.

Ravenz seized the twig flinging the line from black water's depths to land spiraled over granite rocks then bounded up bank's side to the roadside. The sight of a rider-less horse in the road rearing on its hinds and then kicking its fore hooves startled Ravenz to gasp. Reins flew free of guiding hands like long streamers flailing in air. The empty saddle gleamed in the moonlight.

Where has your rider gone? Why do you kick hysterically like this? Are you abandoned here, horse?

Ravenz rushed forward to the horse but ground to a halt, fear clutching his chest, breath stuck as a rock in his throat.

A crumpled man lies in the ruts in this darkness!

Ravenz turned the body face up to the moon's glow, stared, then grasped at the royal shoulders lying as mortis in dust.

"Your Majesty!" shrieked Ravenz violently shaking the king's shoulders and banging his fists against royal arms and chest. "Your Majesty! Wake up!" The king's face appeared tranquil as one does in deep sleep. Ravenz reared back and tilted his face to the Heavens calling upon all stars clustering together in constellations to part their way clear so his plea could be heard in Great Maker's sanctuary.

But no words escaped Ravenz' mouth. Only calmness and clarity settled over his being as words from a page written long ago streamed as sentences before his eyes. *Anabaa! Tiz your words I see and am coming to know in this moment...*

Ravenz tore at Breretyn's jacket ripping free of its buttons then with sure firm fingers pressed into king's carotid artery and counted.

One-and-two-and-three-and-four-and five

Nothing

In a flash faster than lightning bolts to the earth Ravenz thrust his fists deeply into the king's chest causing ribs to squall in their cage but yet he did not stop his earnest thrusts.

"Three-and-four-and-five-and..."

A gulp of air and a lip-lock later Ravenz forced air from his lungs into those of the king.

Rise...fall... Once more, breathe!

Ravenz exhaled deeply into the king's still motionless mouth feeling the man's lip muscles lax and soft beneath his.

Again and again Ravenz thrust down on King Breretyn's chest counting aloud as a young schoolchild...*more pushes... more breaths*...over and over only breaking away to check for life's pulse in the king's neck many times between.

Ah, Latezia, white bride of my dream...you hover over me, my beautiful one. But why are you hurting me so with such anger in your arms as to punish my heart causing ribs' fracture? What kiss is this with such fierce air expelling from your hard lips bruising mine? Your iron finger jabs at my neck…here on hard mean mattress smelling of dirt and dust billowing!

"Are you trying to kill me, woman? Quit this horror!" Strong arms shoved at Ravenz throwing him backward onto his elbows.

Ravenz stared. Relief surged through his being as great joy rushed forth his lips.

"Your Majesty! You awaken! Angels, flee to Heaven's gate and deliver my thankful message!"

The king stared into the eyes of one he must know but not his Latezia's enchanting gaze he desires so greatly.

"You are not my gentle wife! Who are you…I know your face… Oh, *Rhynn!*"

"I am Ravenz."

"What happened to me? Why am I sleeping in dirt on the roadway here? Why were you pummeling my chest so desperately and forcing air into my lungs like that? Your poke on my neck is causing a dam in my artery!"

"I was night-fishing at the riverbank here when I heard you drop dead of a quit heart onto the roadway where you ride Lightfoot, Your Majesty, is why you lay here in the dust. I could not find your heart's pulse throbbing in your neck so forced its blood through your being with my fists as I breathed my lung's air into your empty lungs over and over just as Anabaa has written in *The Book of Knowledge and Practice*…as told in the beginning!"

"Who? I *died?!* I lay here…*dead?*"

Onrushing thundering hooves happened on the road as a horseman approached upon galloping steed.

Ravenz froze with massive dread at the thought of one mistaking a mischievous crime committed on King Breretyn's person. In an eye's blink Ravenz vanished over the side of the road sliding down bank silently slipping beneath river's black surface to glide downstream until that place where the flow slows over shallow sediment bar...to the climb river's bank crossing roadway up pathway to lamppost's beacon urgently blinking.

Green-white-green-white-green...

The king peered into eyes he thinks of as ...a raven's? But they appear now as an eagle's white incandescing orbs drawing away just as two others come into focus just inches from his own.

"Ravenz." Breretyn raised his hand to the image. "You appeared soaring up as an eagle just then."

"I'm Rhynn, Poppi! Your *jaguar*! Look at my finger and see the signet ring you placed there!" Rhynn held his hand before Breretyn's searching gaze. "What's happened here? Why are you laying like this on the gravel, sleeping *here*?"

"*Rhynn*? You said you were Ravenz just now! And now a jaguar comes! Am I truly dead as your raven says I *was* and do I live *now* as this jaguar thinks?"

"You are *alive,* Father, living and breathing and seeing *me,* Rhynn! Look here, Poppi. Lightfoot sniffs at your ear! And Pretzyl stands here, too. I was riding home from the observatory mapping Sagittarius and I found Lightfoot whinnying and fractious in the road!"

Breretyn lifted a hand to stroke the horse's soft brow. Running his palm down Lightfoot's strong nose then holding the steed's warm face close to his own the king smelled munched weeds on its breath. But he kept his eyes open in a steadfast gaze on Rhynn.

I am Your Majesty to the bird but Poppi to the jaguar.

"Find this man, Raven in *you*, Rhynn! Find your *other* being for *he* is the second part of you who knows of a way back from death as is written in *The Book of Knowledge and Practice*. Promise me!"

"*What?*"

Lightfoot nuzzled the king's ear then gifted His Majesty's royal face a lick of his generous tongue.

Thank you, faithful horse for that shot of confidence!

"Help your father up, Prince Rhynn! I have a bride I must get home to! And don't forget your fish, there!"

"*Fish!* What fish? I have been peering at stars through glass lens all night plotting the fourth quadrant of Southern hemisphere at latitudes between plus fifty-five and minus ninety degrees!"

"It's been a *very* long journey, good Rhynn, Honorable Heir, but the hour is late and I am starving."

Lightfoot held high his magnificent head as King Breretyn's royal head lay alongside his thick neck. The king's slumping body warmed his mount's mighty back.

I saw two spheres floating in the sky above me…one bright as the sun…the other softly gleaming as a full moon…in afternoon's high light…at Half Moon Lagoon

～✲

Ravenz shuddered.

In the blackness of this nearly moonless night he stripped his body naked of river-soaked shirt and pants kicking off sloppy mud-caked plimsolls forsaking the heap aside Falls House old wooden steps. In one giant lunge Ravenz' long legs leapt the entire flight landing upon threshold then into darkened kitchen down shadowy hallway. Only dimming candlelight glowed under bedchambers' shut doors belonging to Constance, Qiaona and Anabaa. Faint deep breathing of ladies in slumber drifted on night's airwaves; sweet fumes given up in dreaming upon pillows.

Ravenz slid his hand between pillow and mattress feeling for an artist's gold medallion resting on cool sheet.

Ah, coin! You turn molten in my palm! It is true what you told me when you pressed this disc into my palm that day, Artist Parqai, that the coin bearing King Neptlyn's visage holds karma unmatched in any other!

Ravenz slept.

~~⌒~~

"Guards! Fetch Nicoli! Quickly! My father, His Majesty is ill!"

"Why is your voice so commanding in midsummer night's balm? Your tone disturbs me and vexes my peace. Why has Lightfoot quit his gentle gait rocking me as one in a cradle sways? Take me to my bride, noble steed! She waits at the fountain there…fair young shimmering Latezia waits in fountain's mist! Latezia! Latezia!"

The clatter of advancing hooves echoing through the courtyard and the sight of the palace guards dashing up the great stone steps under portico into foyer caused a chill in Latezia as this is not the custom for sentries to enter the palace in such urgency at this hour.

Unless…

"Nicoli! We have come for Nicoli! He must come with us at once! Prince Rhynn's orders, Queen Latezia!"

"He is in his bedchamber across foyer down yonder hallway…" Crisp staccato footsteps retreating as batons rapping snare drums fade down marble tiled way.

What has happened? What of Rhynn ordering Nicoli up…the man is Breretyn's…butler. Oh, no! Something has happened to my Breretyn! Where is my king?

Latezia dashed to the great oak doorway searching the courtyard from atop the stone steps.

Darkness Starlight Ghostly mist rises from fountain's never-ending cascades. Crescent moon hangs by a magical cloud-thread in deep nocturnal vault.

But the gates are swung widely open and guards are rushing the hallway loudly calling! Latezia beheld the shadows of two royal horses and riders...one riding tall and one slumped over.

"Mother!"

"Rhynn!"

Latezia sped down the great stone steps and as an angel in swift descent she floats around fountain across courtyard to halt before royal horse she recognizes as easily as one knows a child.

"Breretyn!"

The king's head lifted a trifle from where it lay as a rock against Lightfoot's thick neck and his dry eyes fixed their gaze on her face.

Ah, Latezia! It is you I see playing in fountain's bubbling mist...splashing as a mermaid...my little silver fish swims under spouts' streams...I adore how the mist crowns your pretty queenie head in this moonlight and how you glide to your king.

"My Latezia..."

Latezia gasped, clutching her heart.

"Breretyn! Sit up! Come to my arms, king-husband."

"Father is ill, Mother! I found him sleeping in the roadway just past the trampled weed lot where children play...before mercantile street's entrance...on the back road winding past Half Moon Lagoon!"

"Sleeping? What do you mean? He was lying on the dirt gravel,

191

sleeping? Where was Lightfoot?" Latezia grasped at her husband seeking his hands from under his belly, but they gripped saddle's horn too tightly. In that moment a flat board clattered to the cobblestones and Nicoli's calm deep voice rang out,

"Your ride is here, Your Majesty! The rest of the way home is but a short trip across courtyard and up step's incline, is all."

"Ah, faithful Nicoli! You've come to meet your king at trail's end."

Eight quick hands grasped the king's body as eight strong arms lifted his being from Lightfoot's warm back to hard cold tabletop-board.

"What manner of mattress is this, Nicoli?! You dare jest with your king here! My journey was long. I am starving for the fish my raven has stuffed in his pocket there!"

"I am Rhynn."

What fish? Twice now my father speaks of a fish and a raven. He hallucinates in fatigue and from famished belly.

Breretyn's arms fling free of his chest to flop over the sides of the plank carrying his fevered soul beneath high lampposts illuminating courtyard and steps.

"Stop running! Set the king down!" shrieked Latezia. "Oh, Great God in Heaven, what happened here? What manner of creature tortured your ribs causing this heinous bruise to flow as a lake beneath skin? Your shirt's buttons are severed free of their clasps…some have fled their threads! Breretyn, what happened? Oh, my love! Why are your lips swollen like plums ripening to deep purple-blue? Pray, Your Majesty, tell me, Latezia, simple brick-maker's daughter!"

Breretyn gazed long into the eyes of the one true beauty ever to enrapture a man's captured heart and prayed immense thankfulness to the Angel Hosts congressing above his head for his great fortune in Parqai's rescuing a damsel beneath Ploughorse's highflying hooves.

"Clasp my hand, Latezia! Oh, I see now, you hold it already clasped to your pale warm cheek. The fairytale goes, according to our Ravenz that I dropped dead of a stilled heart too tired to keep beating the whole way of the trip home. I landed with a loud thud onto the roadway slipping from Lightfoot's back causing a fear in my steed. Our son sat night-fishing at river's bank and hearing calamity happening came rushing to the place I lay sleeping in grave blackness and thrashed upon my heart through cartilage and ribcage to rise it from slumber. I wakened to the fiercest kiss anyone can possibly succumb…and feeling my lungs expand to near-bursting with an air such as I did not draw in. And the raven receded from my eyes when Rhynn appeared at my side to help me mount my worried Lightfoot. See the bundle in his pocket there? It is a fish he caught with his little string and old hook to smoke on Alder plank."

"Is this *true,* Rhynn? King Breretyn lay…in the roadway… *dead?"*

"The part of the story I know to be truth is Father lay *living* where I found him lying, Mother! I know nothing of the first part for I was charting a constellation at Kings Observatory this night! See, the bundle Poppi speaks of is only my grid sheet scrolled up and bound in cords."

"Carry my husband into the *Parlor of Portraits,* sentries! Nicoli, bring the king a stein of strong broth from stovetop's middle steaming cauldron! And bring a spoon!"

"Comfort the king onto the chaise, diligent guards! He is familiar with this room and the plump pillows will ease his distress!" whispered Prince Rhynn in newfound tones of authority.

The guards bowed low their heads at this command immediately lifting His Majesty onto cushions and pillows waiting patiently there. When Latezia turned back to offer her thanks she saw naught of sentries and hard board but only Rhynn clasping King Breretyn's hand.

How is this happening? Is any of this real? This evaporating away and suddenness of things changing is far too surreal this night!

"Come Latezia, and clasp my free hand. Your palm is so warm and strength lies in your fingers encircling mine. Oh, I see my hand now, tiz already resting against your soft flush cheek!" Breretyn turned his face to Artist Parqai's magnificent portrait of *Queen Mother and Infant, Firstborn and Heir* and heaved a long sigh.

"Through an astounding knowledge I have been granted the supreme gift of a second chance at this life to relay one singular message to you, good wife, queen and mother-royal of my firstborn and heir." Breretyn stopped in his speech to gather in air.

Latezia gripped the king's hand fearing to breathe, listening to his words softly spoken,

"It is true, my beauty, just as Artist Parqai has painted this drama of you and our prince resting on chaise as it sits here that he did see two cherubs hover above you *exactly identical* as a mirror reflects its image back to exact *first* image.

"One cherub is a raven and the other oscillating there; Jaguar. *Two* men live in our Rhynn. The breath of our Ravenz gave me life again and the strength of our Jaguar saw me home to you. Such metaphysical phenomenon requires quantum faith to comprehend, my love. I have never told you this but I wakened on the heather plain in the hour of our infant's birth to see two spheres hovering over me in summer solstice sky; one appeared as the sun, the other, a moon; Ravenz and Rhynn."

"I too, beloved husband, did dream of cherubs fluttering above me; one coming closer, the other lifting away. When I wakened

194

from the birth it was two heads I saw lying with me on the pillows. One head is my infant child and the other belongs to my king. But now I know the meaning of my dream's riddle; Ravenz and Rhynn. And we love them both the same."

"One and the same...both together in one, so *well loved.*" Breretyn turned his eyes to gaze through the window seeing brilliant stars twinkling in constellations according to coordinates blueprinted in The Almighty's own hand and marvels at divine genius arranging such exquisite light in patterns appearing as lace.

Latezia lay her head near her king's shoulder closing her eyes as in dream's prayer.

Prince Rynn held steady his father's hand warming his own and felt the king's thumb press hard upon the flat surface of his golden engraved signet ring.

"You are my parent and sovereign predecessor and I your firstborn son and heir, Rhynn and Jaguar. It is my sovereign promise to find this man, Ravenz who gave one ultimate moment of life to your heart for our mother, Father, Poppi, King Breretyn..."

Rhynn's voice hushed at the sight of his father's face turning incandescently radiant so white did his skin glow that the prince drew back and stared with eyes fixed only on Breretyn's staring eyes.

"Father...what do you see?"

"I see my father, Neptlyn, His Royal Graciousness standing atop yonder blazing stairway beckoning...*me!*"

Ah, my good and dutiful son, Breretyn, tiz time to take your seat at the Table of Kings for you have served well our kingdom's loyal subjects! Come! It is but only the first few faltering steps... then the rest all simply...fly away...

"Poppi?" Rhynn felt the fingers clasping his hand relax their grip then slip away as the king's hand fell as a feather to the chaise.

"Father!"

Latezia lurched up as one rudely startled out of deep sleep.

"What is it, Rhynn? Why do you scream so violently when your father is resting?'

And then in a flash she found the answer in her Prince Rhynn's eyes and a great sobescaped from her heart past her lips to echo off all walls, foyer and hallways beyond, cries so mournful and inconsolably- long…lasting far into a forever midsummer night.

A spoon clattered and skidded to a halt upon glassy marble floor. Broth splashed over stein's rim wetting the knuckles of one trembling hand.

"I am too late! I have not ministered unto my king in his great hour of need…too late!"

"You are just in time, honorable butler, Nicoli, sir for your greatest service is required in His Majesty's deepest hour of need.

Nicoli rested the stein aside a vase of wildflowers still scenting the parlor reminiscent of sweet afternoon's bright summer hours earlier picked by way of the queen's own hand.

Nicoli bowed deeply, then said humbly,

"It is my honor to dutifully tend to your father, Your Majesty, King Rhynn!"

CHAPTER 11

*Q*UEST

A coin spins swiftly at first as if dangled by a tightly-wound invisible string held by invisible fingers high in stratosphere's dazzling incandescence.

As the coin's crazy silent twirling slows to a hypnotizing sway an engraved visage appears on the face of what surely must be gold but gleams brilliantly now, luminous as platinum. Thoughtfulness emanates from the being's forehead beneath sovereign crown set upon royal brow. The face engraved thereon houses wise eyes and a kind mouth. The lips form words as a voice tries to speak but no sound comes forth as now the vision of a second face emerges, though diaphanous aside the first; eyes of jade-green glow in the face of one King Breretyn.

Lips part Words escape platinum-gold element's cold engraved mouth to waft as warm vapor to Ravenz' mesmerized eyes.

Two of you live as one. Or one of you living as two

Tiz a riddle…a riddle…riddle

Ravenz and Jaguar King.

The coin spins in a dizzying fury then evaporates into blackness as a yoyo is snatched up in a palm's tight grasp.

Ravenz lurched up from this nightmare off pillow and mattress staring into a darkened room still echoing words breezed as a summer squall through walls' cracks and down chimney.

What is it, Your Majesty? Why did I just see your face on Parqai's gold coin just now? What is the meaning of this insane dream?

Even in summer night's warm air a chill quite as ice settles on Ravenz skin causing a shiver.

The coin! Is it gone from me?

Ravenz' hand thrust beneath pillow madly searching the sheet. Inexplicable relief flooded his being as fingers enclose Artist Parqai's golden medallion. Holding the coin to his heart Ravenz backed away from the bed to stand on the rug before unadorned window seeking illumination by way of slim moon's dim gleam.

This is the same coin the artist pressed to my palm that day, but now only King Neptlyn's face is engraved hereon just as before. What meaning lies at the heart of this dream that I saw King Breretyn's transparent visage hovering here?

⁓

"Oh! Look, Qeyyapi! Isn't it beautiful? Just look at all that divine land!" Aotapi sat in morning's brilliance before the porthole. Her hands gripped the round framework as her breath fogged the glass. "So much exquisite dry land, beautiful quiet still ground waiting so patiently for our footfall!"

"Aotepi? You have been holding that pose since I bid you sweet dreams only eight hours ago! Now that we are anchored, if what you say is actually true and you aren't just sleeping in some half-wake wishing-dream then you haven't slept a wink yet and you'll fall slumbering onto your little cot when it's time to disembark!"

Qeyyapi turned away from the wall and kicked off the blanket watching it fall to the cold plank floor becoming in that moment a warm rug. She yawned as her arms stretched to the ceiling, palms grazing white-washed thin smooth boards before swinging her legs over bunk's side. It was then that her eyes see what Aotepi saw; a long sweep of cream sand banking curving seaboard foaming white at its fringe and beyond lay green trees rising upon a thousand green hills rising unto purple mountain's myriad peaks piercing white puffball clouds blanketed overall by morning's lavender sky.

The sister knelt with Aotepi before the porthole gathering in the warmth radiating from one another as is the way of such closeness. She brushed her own hand above Aotepi's fingers feeling a magnum royal sapphire ring press into her palm.

Aotepi's *Prince Rhynn*

Qeyyapi closed her eyes and inhaled new air; sweet heather wafting from gentle plain and riverbanks' trees exuding musky resin, Half Moon Lagoon's fresh-tumbling water heating under a rising dry sun…illuminating the face of a man called *Ravenz*.

So this is the meaning of wakefulness…true awakening experienced now so ultimately…sublimely rising

"Ravenz," whispered Qeyyapi so softly only warm breath wisped a tendril resting on Aotepi's temple.

Are you real as Aotepi's Rhynn is real as is evidenced by this ancient stone we gaze upon every hour remembering two men exactly identical as the one we know is certainly real? Is Rhynn just Ravenz? Or are they to be Ravenz and Rhynn? Can I possibly hope for a simple slice of luck coming my way that there might just be two of them as Aotpi and I are two?

"I do believe the storm has hastened our journey's days over these open bumpy waters and we are only hours from stepping into our beautiful dreams, sister Aotepi."

⁓

Rhynn stood in the doorway of his mother's bedchamber watching gentle drama unfold in slow motion before his eyes. The only constant in the room is the furnishings sitting in service this morning the same way as it had sat in place since the day he'd toddled in as a small child testing his limbs. The four-poster-canopy bed's linens remained as they had lain yesterday over mattress and pillows in wait for King Breretyn's return and still smelling faintly of freesia. But no bodies had dreamed away any night hour tween silk sheets and satin duvet. No cherished secrets evaporated in love's fume between two heads lying close on plump pillows.

Decanters filled with petals' attar remain trapped beneath jewel-knobbed dipping sticks reaching into vessels' depths. Rising sunlight streaming through high windows capture precious emollients' amber hue casting soft shading over vanity's tabletop.Rainbows on walls are rays fracturing through diamond-cut crystal's beveled edges.

Armoires' gilded doors stay latched together by polished brass clasps and tapestries hang pulled asidewindows as if still yesterday, forgetting the night had happened at all.

Hazy forms of three heads moved about one motionless being sitting in a silvery fog on the chaise before yonder window facing courtyard and cascading fountain, vast lawns and blooming hedge mazes over high iron gates guarded by sentries standing-at-arms, staring...*out*...*in*...staring at nothing at all. No dog chased a rabbit. No cat exercised a mouse. Butterflies sat stilled of jittery flights resting wings folded instead. Dragonflies took the day off. Only songbirds in high treetops offered sweet invocation unto morning...*mourning*...mournfully chirping sweet notes meant to hearten.

"Oh, Rhynn, Your Majesty! We did not hear you enter!" whispered Constance as she dropped into deep bow sweeping the floor with her hand. Rhynn quickly bent forward kneeling instead to grasp Constance's hand mid-sweep even before she raised an eye to meet his gaze.

Constance gasped glancing up into King Rhynn's face.

"Come, Lady Constance. Let me help you up. There is no need for bowing before me like this. I am still Rhynn, after all. Tell me, how is Mother?"

"Lady Qiaona has been with her since before the daybreak and she has not moved from the chaise since you set her upon it last night. Zayyana has been with her in all time through nocturne's long hours and not once did she close an eye unto any slumber. The queen sits devastated, Your Majesty. Her heart will be gladdened when her eyes see you." Constance swept aside of the king and waved her hand in a feathery gesture toward the chaise.

Rhynn rounded the edge of the chaise coming to kneel at his mother's knee.

Latezia had not changed from her dress of yesterday and her shoes remained tied to her feet with satin bows just now showing fatigue in their loops. Only her long golden ringlets fall to rest upon her shoulders for the pins holding them up had been gently removed allowing this freedom. Ribbons remained woven in locks as before rendering unto Latezia the look of a damsel skipping down mercantile street. Her gaze seemed fixed on the fountain and did not flinch when Rhynn's shadow formed at her feet.

"Mother? Mummy, it is Rhynn, your little jaguar!" Rhynn placed his hand over the bangle encircling his mother's thin white wrist. Cupping her chin in his free hand Rhynn turned her face toward his and called her name again.

"Queen Mother Latezia, it is your son and King Breretyn's heir, Rhynn sitting here, Mummy! Look at me, please, for I have something to say."

Latezia's face did not move but her eyes' gaze settled on Rhynn and a glimmer formed there if only for a moment.

Ah, those green eyes in that noble face live before me bringing light to my bleak hour. You live in our son, my Breretyn, as surely as if you are sitting before me yourself! You planned this all along, didn't you, my king, so my heart would be eased at the sight of your memory living forth in our Rhynn.

Latezia reached out her hand and brushed an errant curl from her man-child's brow.

What a beautiful man you've grown into, my little jaguar! The bones in your face are angular now and your chin is square. A little cleft forms there and shadowing plays in the hollows of your cheeks.

"What is it, Rhynn? I see thoughts forming behind those eyes but yet I hear no words introducing them. Is there something you wish your mother to know, Your Majesty?"

Rhynn startled at hearing his mother's voice referencing him now in sovereign terms and he felt novice in this station. Every hour since his birth he'd sensed an importance in the weight of his title, *prince*, but now he feels quite at odds with the arrogant *sound* associated with the office of royalty and of *kingship* generally.

Did my father in all his sovereign years feel as I do now wishing to disguise myself as a simple subject working as any laborer alongside men working honestly and humbly as he did?

"Father's monument is to be raised at the reflection pooltoday, Mother. His statue will stand in the line of his ancestors aside his father, King Neptlyn. It has already been carved according to his exact wishes blueprinted in ink penned by way of Poppi's own hand. Look for King Breretyn's marble effigy to be standing there in pool's sweet aqua-mirror come eventide as is his promise to you, Queen Mother."

Rhynn pressed Latezia's hand to his lips thinking of her not as the wife of a former king but forever as his adored Mummy.

"I must take leave, Mother, and see to an end a promise I made to Father just before he drew his last breath. It is a challenge I immediately embrace but which may take me a lifetime to come to the heart of it."

Latezia did not comprehend her son's words for they seem as an enigma to her.

Perhaps it is the way of kings to be in a state of conundrum once the office is settled onto their souls.

"Go, King Rhynn, and sort through the way of his wish for this is the meaning of governing one's kingdom."

King Rhynn lifted Latezia's hand feeling the fine bones of her fingers lying limp in his palm. He noticed the bangle had turned on wrist's axis and that the jaguar's head dandled face down. In the space between his heart's beats the cat's face upturned to the light catching morning's beam in its tiny quartz eyes.

"I shall return to your table at suppertime!" Rhynn playfully kissed about the jaguar's golden ears. "I love you, Mummy!"

—

"Easy with that crate there, young buck! That one is the king's personal cargo; goods commissioned by King Breretyn, himself so the story goes! Just set it down real easy-like and none of us will lose our heads!"

Ravenz likes longshoreman Robyn even if the man is toothless except for one large front incisor hanging down over four smaller anterior teeth standing up and two opposing molars showing in left quadrant when he laughs. He wondered at the cause of Robyn's lack of dentition and if the condition is a design flaw showing up in child development after his birth or if his lack had simply been caused by an architectural-planning omission at the time of conception. Whatever the cause of it Robyn never commented but only carried on in jovial attitude grateful for new days dawning and grateful still for cold malt at days' end.

"I can read, Robyn. I see the king's name branded on wood in block letters right there!" Ravenz brushed his fingers through his hair feeling ocean's salty breeze cooling his scalp. Sun's temperature threatened to rise to new heights though the morning hour is still young. "Don't worry, I'll be careful. If I have to I'll row this crate up river to the palace myself! I know the way." Hearing no retort Ravenz glanced around for Robyn. The only sight catching his eye is the longshoreman's backside disappearing into the shadowy hold. "You can't unload all that yourself, big guy!" Ravenz bounded up the ramp only to grind to a halt at the top of it.

He stands motionless as granite staring long into the ship's hold seeing a thousand identical crates with the name, BRERETYN branded in black ink on the sides waiting to be unloaded. Only a half dozen smaller crates stood off to the side bundled together by way of a rope's crisscross binding. The name, Tsagalakis, sprawled out in black paint appears on all small crates on all sides.

"So, those belong to the only passengers on board? I don't see any other passenger cargo among all these crates here."

"That would be all there is, buck! This ship's been hired out entirely by the king himself just for his own specially commissioned cargo! These people just happen to be the only passengers invited along for the ride, is all! King probably commissioned them folk, too! Their name is beyond my tongue to say so go ahead, you say it, schoolboy!"

"I am Ravenz."

Ravenz cooled in the shade of hull studying the name but did not recognized it from any conversations or acquaintance happening in the mercantile in any of King Breretyn's villages either up or down the river or along mountain's foot or across valley or plain.

"Well, well! If it isn't who I think it is! I would recognize that stance anywhere! Ravenz, turn around this minute and give Lizbett a great big hug!"

Ravenz didn't get a chance to turn about for feminine arms

reached about his waist drawing his body against the woman who'd played with him since his birth.

You still smell the same, Lizbett. Your fragrance has never changed even as you have just endured weeks in a ship's airtight cabin or paced the deck in salty air. And your voice! It charms still ringing young as a maiden's; soft as little bells chime.

"What a gift it is seeing you down here at the docks unloading us, Ravenz! I didn't know! But then Qiaona and Constance always said you flit about here and there all through the kingdom rolling up your shirtsleeves pitching in helping out and all!"

A small child's holler echoes through the hold as the word, "*Mamma!*" came blasting over the airwaves. Bako appeared before Ravenz holding the tiny golden blue-eyed suspect high in his big admiral's arms, his strong hands still burning from minding the master helm in lofty wheelhouse.

"What a greeting this is seeing you here, Ravenz, especially after that treacherous storm we endured! Thankfully we rode the turbulence out in the hurricane's eye.By the grace of Almighty's hand gentling the waters my good ship made it here early, it seems! And, oh, this is our princess, Aurelia! You remember…I think you were there at her birth last summer at solstice eventide… in Falls House?"

The robust child in Bako's arms studied Ravenz' face with an honest sober childlike gaze until Ravenz winked. Aurelia giggled, eyes twinkling.

I see Lizbett in you, pretty baby…and how she must have looked in one's arms

"I will remember her always, Bako.Aurelia and I share the same birthday." Ravenz reached for the tyke's hand and felt little soft fingers wrap about his thumb. "Hey, what's in all these boxes His Majesty commissioned? Seems like a lot of the same thing far as I can tell."

"Olives!"

"Olives?"

"Jars and jars of olives! And bottles and bottles of olive oil, too! Seems the king got introduced to the things sometime last summer and ordered an amount sufficient for every village in the entire kingdom! As I was here with Lizbett preparing to deliver our child he sent my ship back loaded with bales of hay just to pack all these jars in so none would break and no oil would be spilled! It will take some days to deliver it all. We'll deliver a crate to a village as it is unloaded so the rest can stay put in the hold waiting turn. It is safer this way and less stressful in the whole unloading process as fatigue causes accidents and irreplaceable damages."

"So, who are these Tsagalakis people? Any relation to this olive business happening here?"

"Ah, you are funny, Ravenz! Of course Tsagalakis is responsible for all this! Mister Tsagalakis came along to oversee the distribution, of course!"

"Will you stop by Falls House? Qiaona, Constance and Anabaa want a visit!"

"It will be after we drop off all these crates along the way here. King Breretyn's stash sits at the deepest end of cargo's hold, far up there, so his will be lastly delivered."

Aurelia reached out her chubby arm to grasp Ravenz' other hand tugging hard on two of his fingers.

"It seems our princess is smitten with a certain longshoreman named Ravenz!"

"Ah, Admiral, I bet she finds a lover in every port!"

And she'll leave each one as he stands on plank boardwalk gazing

⁓

"Now don't you just be a pretty one, sailor man!" A wispy young girl of indiscernible age swiveled seductively about Rhynn as he stood in a swab's costume Nicoli managed to rummage together off a closet's shelf pressed among masquerade masks and harlequin jackets, glittery fairy wings and furry-trimmed tulle gowns. Rhynn stared at the girl

Sailor…so the disguise works

"But you don't smell of salty air or boiler room sweat." The girl's nose brushed across Rhynn's back and her breath tickled his ear. He shuddered.His scalp sweated icy chills beneath tattered gingham kerchief tied in knots at his temples. "Maybe you swab topside the king's pretty yacht, is why you smell so…different."

How can you tell what I smell like, girl, for this hovel smells of soapy ammonia and stale potpourri in a poor attempt at disguising the base scent of grime and man!

Cigarette smoke wafts in the air creating ghostly apparitions in candles' dim glow. Voices spoken softly and low as muffled grumbles rise and fall from long chaises scattered about the room's partitions. Laughter evaporates as cheap champagnes' bubbles in thick air as response to a comment just as quickly forgotten. Maroon damask tapestries shut out day's light keeping the mood of nighttime in and absorbing all secrets to woven silence.

Time is money to you, after all. But my time is wasting!

Rhynn grasped the girl's fluttering wrist as her hand rose to tease at the kerchief's knot. The thinness of her bones shocked him and her skin looks sheer as vellum and feels fragile as rice paper. He fears her brittle fingers might shatter in his grasp as balsawood sticks splinter.

The girl gasped feebly and stiffened.

"Stop dancing!"

Rhynn gentled his command to a whispering plea, "Take me to a room."

"Ah, sailor-man gets right to the point, I see." Rhynn did not let go the girl's wrist for he intended to examine the dermis binding muscle and tendon or if any tissue at all should lie along such a porous shaft. But he needs light.

Daylight

It took some moments for Rhynn's eyes to adjust to the darkness as he followed the cat-eyed girl haltingly at first letting his free hand sweep the wall as their feet swept carpeted hallway past doors shut tight against sport misconstrued as romance-in-dance.

The door closed. And latched shut with a snick as bolt fell into bracket. Rhynn blinked, searching the darkness for furnishings, candlelight, or window where curtains might hang waiting to be swished aside letting sun in exposing all.

"It's dark in here!" hissed Rhynn. Then remembering the root of his task spoke more gently to working-girl. "Take me to the window, Miss...what is your name pray tell, so I may treat you properly as a well-named beauty should be treated just as beautifully?" Rhynn's lips brushed her temple feeling a fine pin-feathery tendril tickle his nose.

Ah, sailor-man speaks flattery but his hand hurts my bone...why is he clasping as one hungry?

"Tell you mine if you tell me yours!" teased wispy breath against stubbly cheek.

"Jaguar"

"I am Lilli."

In that moment shady forms of a shabby iron-frame bed feebly supporting sagging springs standing next a small vanity came into dim view. A simple childlike drawing depicting sheep grazing in pasture hangs by a wide ribbon from a hook in the wall. No chairs occupy either side of the bed but a little tufted stool sits apologetically before a mirror seeping its silver. Rhynn counted to five the number of vessels containing turpentine-based chemicals camouflaged as *Cologne Splash* lined up in gauche glass bottles topped with pewter screw-off caps.

Pathetic…so not Mother's gem-encrusted-sphere-topped-bevel-chiseled crystal decanters holding Stephan's oils so purely ethereal

Rhynn smells musty cloth.

In one swift step he pushed Lilli against the windowsill holding her there with his thigh firmly pressing into her back so as to ensure no escape. Lilli's eyes grew startled and searched Rhynn's face for a leading expression as to where this encounter might go…and end.

Rhynn reached for the swag and in one swift grip of his hand yanked at the fabric dangling from tin rod resting in tin brackets ripping the entire ensemble from the wall. Bits of plaster and dust flew to the floor following the clatter and clang of cheap hollow hardware bouncing upon old burnished plank.

Lilli gasped.

Rhynn stares.

The room remained in darkness for a sheet of black tar paper nailed to the wall shuttered out sun's brilliance trapping darkness inside.

"Do you know what day looks like, Lilli?"

"I don't know what time it is…what means…how you say…*day*?"

"Look closely because you are about to find out!" Faster than light travels Rhynn freed the pane of its tar paper captor exposing a blast of dazzling sunlight, sheer high-noon-blue skies, wispy angel-hair clouds and green trees hosting songbirds trilling unabashed and free on branches.

Lilli blinked. Then she gazed out at a whole new world with eyes wide in utter wonderment.

Rhynn studied Lilli.

You are young, girl, and your skin is transparent, nearly clear showing veins barely trickling heme-leached plasma seeking oxygen in pure-air-starved lungs. Your eyes show as boiledyolks floating in pale albumin. Your bones are fragile as thin glass for no sunlight is allowed on your skin. I will rescue you from deathly deficiencies but I need something from you in trade.

Rhynn looked out the window and saw far off to yard's distant side three fat women in brown aprons with their heads bound in scarves fastening laundered sheets on lines with stout wooden pegs. Nothing but sheets hung from wire lines facing sun's warmth. Lines yanked along squealing pulleys roll out bleached sheets hanging to flap in day's floating breezes.

And hundreds of sundried sheets washed-clean of secrets exhaled in passions' selfish feast stuff rattan baskets hauled inside to unload… and load

"Lilli? I need something."

The girl stilled her breath as if standing on the brink of a spell about to be broken.

"Would you happen to know of a man named Ravenz?"

"What?" Lilli's face registered disbelief and surprise at Rhynn's obtuse question. "What should this *Ravenz* man look like, if perhaps he wasn't as generous as you in telling me his name?"

"He would look exactly as me, if one of us were to look in the mirror seeing his duplicate reflection looking back."

Lilli simply looked at Rhynn's face with a passive expression of her own not giving away any hint at all of having engaged any such person.

The girl is good, mused Rhynn, *and she plays her role well keeping the characters as just mannequins bouncing through their pitifully-sad dramas upon her narrow stinking stage keeping time to the squeals of tired springs' protests...unceasing...*

"Jaguar?"

Rhynn bent his head closer to her face in a pretend-effort meant to encourage forthcoming admission.

Who are you, Jaguar man, with your sailor eyes of such hue as I have never seen in any face in all my living hours? It will be this memory of your face looking at me as I behold it now that I will transpose over all others coming after.

Lilli laughed. Out loud, loudly laughing as a baby giggles just discovering its toes. As clear as glass bells tinkling does honest pure laughter ring in the room rounding all walls filling ceiling's every crack.

Rhynn did not blink waiting where he stands before window holding his pose pinning Lilli where she laughs.

Sobriety follows hilarity eventually.

"No, Jaguar, sir, I have not seen this man, Ravenz whom you seek. A man reflecting identicalbeauty as you display in your singular self has no need hiring my services for he is far blessed in the way of getting all this for free."

Of course, she must be right in this thinking. If Ravenz is in me as my father believes then why in Heavens' name would I seek answers in a place such as this...unless...there are two of us...but then, as she rightfully states, "Why?

"Time has come, Lilli." Rhynn softened his grip on the girl's wrist but not his capturing stance. Instead, he tenderly massaged the red marks his fingers imprinted on her frail wrist and thin palm holding her hand in his as if precious rare bisque rests there.

Lilli's eyelids softened their wide-open tight muscular hold to that of dreamily-gazing one might interpret in any other as longing.

A silver coin glinted before Lilli's eyes briefly shattering the edges of a dream forming.

"What's that?"

"It is fair payment for truth, is all."

Lilli reached for the coin proffered by Rhynn's hand. Her eyes studied each side front and back and all around the engraved circular edge as if never seeing such an object ever before.

"This is my first time seeing this thing you name payment-coin." Her entranced voice trailed away to a feathery whisper barely audible.

"How so, Lilli? You work here, right?"

"Clients always pay the man sitting in the closet at the entranceway, from sidewalk steps coming up from outside."

Rhynn pressed the coin into Lilli's palm enclosing her bony fingers about it one by one. Clasping this balled-up sickly fist in his, Rhynn steered the meek girl free of his capturing pose to cross filthy bedchamber floor through doorway down hallway past others locked, through front doorway into brilliant sunlight so blinding to Lilli's weak eyes that her body slumps the length of his sliding straight to stone portico threatening a tumbling and clattering of all her bones to heap at steps' end.

Rhynn swept down catching Lilli up in his arms. Her head dangled backward and bobs lifeless showing knotty bones in her white skinny neck. Slender pale arms hang like chicken bones at her sides. Nubby knobbed knees point skyward. Her feet turn in no particular direction at all but flop to the rhythm of Rhynn's steps as leaves flutter down a street in afternoon breeze.

Dubai sits waiting patiently in Kings Carriage strumming an old mandolin he spotted hanging on a merchant's wall. It had taken some doing to finely tune its tatty strings but soon enough the instrument's voice rang clear and true. The king's driver is lost to a state of poetic music-making when a door burst open and calamity happening on the stoop splinters his trance.

"Good gracious, Rhynn! What is the meaning of this? You insisted I bring you to this place in disguise and now you run out the front door with...with..."

"Lilli just fainted in the sunlight, is all. Her eyes are weak from lack of seeing it! Make way for her in my father's coach, good driver! Don't argue!"

Dubai raced to the king's side even before the pretend-swab's sandals reached the bottom step. Quickly gathering the girl's arms to cross her chest he reached to steady her bobbing head in his hands.

Dubai's heart lurched at the sight of Lilli's wan face.

"What goes on here, Rhynn, I mean..."

"All the wrong things go on here that will come to a halt by hour's end! It is the meaning of my first order of business in the office I've inherited as is my intent of carrying forth Father's... King Breretyn's great reconstruction plans. Now, open the carriage door and listen carefully to my words! Follow my instructions exactly as I give them! Understand me so far, Dubai?"

"Of course! I hear well! Now tell me, what am I to do with...with this girl?"

"Take Lilli to Mountainwing's west side and carry her from carriage to the chamber of Lady Constance. Lady Constance is to draw Lilli a bath foaming with oils poured from vials only she knows where to find. Then seek Lady Penelope, a seamstress needling in tailors' north quarter as she has dresses hanging-in-wait.Request two or three! With lace! Stop by the kitchen on your way back fetching broth from middle steaming cauldron. And take a spoon!" With a final fling of the old gingham kerchief onto the carriage floor Rhynn ran his fingers over his scalp tousling scrunched wavy curls to life.

"Now, go!"

"But what about you, Rhynn, Your Maj…"

"I've got something to find yet for it wasn't in this place. But Lillie's life could end here if you don't hasten!" Rhynn slapped at the team's hinds causing a whinnying response in horses' turn-away to the highway leading to ultimate fairytale castle on magnificent green hilltop.

Lilli slowly came unto wakefulness in cooling shade of the carriage's canopy feeling the gentle jostling of wheels turning on gravely roadway wondering at the meaning of this dream she floats in.

What of this scent…these smells…something like flowers in air so light and void of cigarettes' stale smoke and candlewax melting? And what is that sound like music's notes but not quite? It's like a song warbled but not by one's voice…I must see the cause of such sweet noise.

Lilli opened her eyes to see birds in joyful flight high above a stranger's head; driver Dubai sitting tall in the driver's seat holding reins so elegantly guiding horses.

Guiding horses!

"Who are you and why am I here…lying in this thing? Where are you taking me and what happened to the sailor man, Jaguar I was with just then?" Lilli felt muscles' cramp paining her balled-up fingers so released their hold to reveal Rhynn's gleaming silver coin.

"I would be one going by the name of Dubai, Miss! I have been instructed to take you to Mountainwing's west suites where Lady Constance will tend to your immediate needs. You will be bathed and clothed in a new dress with lace, and nourished with a nice rich broth extracted from kitchen's steaming middle cauldron. Tiz duck today, I believe, Miss. Lilli. Quite satisfying!" Dubai turned about on his seat to look back at the girl.

Dubai stares.

The girl on the seat is a waif to be sure, starved to extreme thinness and milky beyond all shades of white at the lack of direct sunlight allowed most other damsels' peachy-pink cheeks. Yet her face shows true beauty hiding beneath skin so finely-smooth as does any maiden's fair beauty show in the gentle-way of growing up freely.

But her eyes! What amazing eyes I have not seen in the face of any maiden...golden, they are...and shimmering just as the element, gold gleams!

"What is this mountain place and who is Madam Constance?" demanded Lilli, sitting more forward on the royal carriage's deeply tufted velvet seat.

"Why, it to His Majesty's castle I am taking you, Miss Lilli! And it is one *Lady* Constance who will minister unto you according to King Rhynn's command."

Lilli's yellow eyes rolled away in their whites and her head slumped to the side as her hands went nearly limp except for the sake of the coin did she keep fingers' grip.

"I have been teased by a...*king?* In a brothel a sailor-man...now you say, 'king'... visited me...but *not quite* visiting me...asking me things...and then...*this!* How am I to get home? I don't know where any of this is!"

"Oh, you are definitely heading home, if King Rhynn has his

way! And he does, I might add, come from a long line of strong kings used to getting their way! The place you have been freed from will cease to exist after today. You are now in the king's care and it is to be in Mountainwing's suite your head shall dream tonight."

Lilli gazed up into the kindest face ever to hover so closely to hers, except the sailor-man's, of course, and she feared to blink for fear Dubai might evaporate away as all others gone before.

"Well, are you coming into my arms, or not? The king has ordered me to carry your loveliness from coach to suite by way of my arms as not one of your feet, or toe for that matter, must touch the ground till you have been bathed in royal fragranced oil and gowned in a dress of pure fine lace.

We've stopped?

Lilli peeked out from beneath the canopy shelter and beheld Kings Castle in magnificent splendor. Grand turrets pierce the sky. Twittering birds flock in flight from branches above fruiting trees to alight in limbs bearing blossoms so huge as to be one giant bouquet.

"Such grandeur I did not know exists, nor air so sweet or time this pretty.All I learned of was the way of ugly black night. Tell me, kind sir, does day end in the house of kings?"

Dubai flew up stone steps under porch awning over threshold down granite hallway up stairwell across landing through sunlight beaming as Heaven's ribbons streaming through high arch window falling softly on white glassy marble echoing his swift footfall, gracefully stepping as a dancer's soft-soled shoes glide the whole while of the way calling,

"Lady Constance! Lady Constance! Miss Lilli needs urgent care, Lady Constance, My Lilli needs tender...my Lilli needs...my Lilli" in rhythmic cadence quite as a lullaby's words falling like feathers in Lilli's ears.

A candle...a bottle...oleoresin spilling...a flame igniting...torching tapestry and sheet, mattress and rug

Rhynn emerged onto the road looking up the deserted gravel way seeing nothing but earth meeting sky at horizon's enigmatic horizontal line. He shuddered. But his being shuddered not from breezes sweeping down corridor up canyon but from his eye's horror witnessing abuse suffered in one disgusting pox-of-a-hovel blighting his realm. But the king stands in absolute solace knowing stained shabby rugs set on decaying plank floors and filthy mattresses in black rooms robbed of proper time by dust-laden tapestries hiding tar paper forbidding great sun's warmth and all days' promise billow skyward rendered there by way of greedy cinders as famished blaze reduces nightmares' whole to nothing but a heap of ashes.

Husbands scrambling for pants would come to correction at the ankles of wives. Others jump in the river seeking refuge. More than a few suffer singed heels. And Lilli might live.

Rhynn did not look back.

Last night...did last night really happen? Why do I feel this odd dreamlike attitude settling over me as I kneel on gravel back road?

"Why do I kneel like this on the roadway, Poppi? What happened here? Mummy just sits by the window looking out...just looking. This is only but *one* road in *one* village, Poppi! How am I to rule over one thousand others in one hundred villages? How did you rule all this alone, and King Neptlyn before you rule? I am here...sitting under kingdom's heavy crown...alone."

No you're not!

Rhynn startled, eyes opening wide and ears listening.

Two live! Find this man, Ravenz in you, Rhynn for he is the one harboring astounding knowledge in the way of restoring life after death, if even for a brief moment's time so a misconception in one's first life may be understood in the second…a treasure lost might become found.

"Restoring life…what is the meaning of your riddle, Poppi? I don't understand…*restore life?* You were living when I found you lying in road's dust. Here! You lay, *here,* Father, is where I found you and brought you home on Lightfoot's back to Mother!"

Rhynn glanced about the ruts he kneeled in searching the dust and gravel for a clue.

"Who is Ravenz, Poppi? What happened here to make you believe me to be a raven when I am Jaguar to you in all our play?"

Look harder!

Rhynn saw things cast aside in ruts what appear to his sight several small flat discs seeming as buttons torn from their threads through fabric's holes. The bold letter, *B* sits engraved on each button's face.

Father's jacket buttons sewn by tailors in Northwing's quarter! Someone was here! I did not do this astounding thing… I know in my honest true nature I live only as one man my father named Rhynn.

Rhynn looked to the sky and seeing one pure cloud hover above his head, yelled,

"Forgive me, Father, my selfish wallowing in child-tears' puddle. But I saved a woman's life, today, Poppi! You'll see!"

An eagle, wings full-spread glides gloriously about the cloud in loops as hypnotizing as rings circle Saturn. Round and round floated the bird until in an eye's blink it swooped from the firmament to skim over river before lofting Heavenward over high tumbling falls and beyond.

Ah, spectacular! Where did you come from just now, giant sky-king? Does a fish's coppery scales glint in your eye as you swoop along river like that?

Rynn's gaze fell to the river where sun's brilliant beams sparkle as a million diamonds strewn along endless watery ribbon.

Fish…in Ravenz' pocket!

"Fish? What fish, Father? That's three times now in these past hours' time I hear about fish! It wasn't a fish in my pocket last night but a constellation's coordinate-map."

Rhynn rose from the place where he'd gathered the buttons still clinging to remnants of thread and fabric cleft of Breretyn's garment and strode to road's edge looking down over grassy thatches and moss to riverbank to hazy shimmers of frolicking insects carrying on in hot summer air above watery flow.

There appears a thick rotting string strewn over the rocks as a sleeping snake warming its lengthened-out belly in sun's high heat. But at the end of it is not a snake's head and fang but an old rusty hook showing its glinting recently-sharpened point. The remains of bait lay sagging, withered and leathery at tip's piercing.

So there was someone fishing here at this bank in the night who heard tragedy happening upon roadway here…someone harboring astounding knowledge…but whom?

"I stand here in a swab's disguise searching for a man named Ravenz whom you believe in your eyes' memory-blink is *me*, Rhynn! I made you a promise I intend to keep until I come to the end of this mystery." Rhynn pulled up rotting string, tiny cannon-ball sinker and carcass-baited hook balling the whole of the rig up in his fist, stuffed the mess of it all in his pocket crowding dusty buttons to the corners. "The person I seek is close by, Father! I know this seeing his string, ball sinker and hook so old as to have been used before at this place many times many days for too many years. *I am Jaguar!* With cat-stealth will I stalk Ravenz to his nest in tonight's black hours and see with my own eyes the face of the one mirroring mine."

Rhynn's belly hurt. His head throbbed. Eyelids too tired to stay open and too weak to close clung above eyeballs too dry to roll in sockets too tired to tear. But his feet dutifully carried on with their singular task hauling all royal else above ankle and knee, femur and spine to any place at all that matters circuiting skull's command.

"Is this the meaning of kingship, Poppi? Tell me, please, so I'll know what is real and what really should be…"

"Hey, look! It's Ravenz! What luck! We can finally win a game now! Ravenz is here!" Shouts rose from trampled weed lot as hazy figures clustered before Rhynn's eyes. One player held a harpastum ball under his arm while another playfully tried wrestling it free.

"You…are who?" Rhynn forced a blink. "Oh, I know you now, Cairo! Forgive me, I've been in a daze resting on moss in trees' shade down at riverbank there and completely forgot about this game we planned here. I think I'm taking ill as I don't seem to remember the way to my house.My stomach is queasy and fire burns in my head. My eyes feel like hot coals and my throat steams. My ears are near deaf for fluid floods over the lobes. My limbs are weak and I can barely stand let alone tread one more step. Help me to my house, good friend! Save my life, Cairo!"

"I am Kyrro!"

Rhynn slumped to the ground, feigning delirium.

"Is he dead?"

Someone plucked at Rhynn's upper lip with a twig.

"He sort o' smells dead."

"He isn't dead! See there, his chest rises and falls with breath."

"Take the ball, Rokkyt! Start a new game without me. I'll carry him to his house. I'm the biggest. Tiz not far. Go! I'll return quickly enough."

Iron arms hoisted Rhynn from the gravel and in a weird sense he feels his body tossed as a hog belly-down over a shoulder as broad and strong as an ox's. He opened his eyes to see Kyrro's heels and feels his legs crossed over chest and bound at the knees by hands' clasp. As if carried through clouds by seraphim Rhynn's body flew in this state down roadway to pathway under lamppost's high beacon dimly blinking in afternoon's high light...*silver*...*silver*...*silver*...quietly beckoning...through gateway up stepping-stone walkway to stoop before thick oak door.

"You're here, buddy." Kyrro spoke gently and without any hint of exhaustion set Rhynn down on a straw mat.

Rhynn peeked up at the place Kyrro brought him to as...*Ravenz'* home.

A carved wooden plaque above the door read, *Falls House*

Tiz the place near the fishing spot, Poppi, not far up from river at all! So close...close to all this...all this time!

"I'll be fine here, kind friend. Let me gather myself in doorway's shade. I feel better for the lift and somewhat recovered. I just need food, is all, and some water. I lost track of time pursuing errands and, well, got disoriented by hunger. Go back and finish the game. See you tomorrow?"

❧

"How's Mother?" whispered Rhynn as Qiaona lifted her gaze from where she stands braiding ribbons through Latezia's golden ringlets. Qiaona's eyes grew wide at the sight of the young king regally standing on the chamber's threshold. Not since King Breretyn lived had she seen a man as beautiful. Her breath caught in her throat. But it caught not because *this* man is King Breretyn's firstborn heir and now His Majesty, King Rhynn but because of another, also beloved; one equally-identically-beautiful *Ravenz.*

Great God in Heaven! The kingdom is blessed twice at once with nobleness and grace and as such does each reign; one in castle on hilltop and one in valley house.

"Lady Qiaona? It's me, Rhynn! Do I startle you holding a supper tray like this instead of Nicoli as I am dressed in these black pants and shirt? This isn't my usually normal attire, I know.If I'm not suitable to sit with Mummy like this for supper then I shall go eat at kitchen's long table.

Qiaona smiled setting aside hair brush and hairpins leaving ribbons to rest where they'd been woven through braid and tendril falling among ringlets to graze shoulder and satin.

"Come in, Your Majesty," bowed Qiaona waving her hand to the chaise. "Set the tray here on this sideboard. Oh! I see two plates domed and goblets, also two."

"I promised Mummy I would be at her table for supper, Lady Qiaona, is all. So, I think this means as long as I'm here now and the tray is set with nourishment, it is suppertime. I will sit with her, if it's all right with you, of course, Qiaona?" Rhynn looked at Qiaona as a child seeking approval.

You are still Little Jaguar to me and I will never get used to saying these words; KingRhynn

"I will visit Lady Constance in Mountainwing's suites. I heard of a girl-visitor arriving this morning by way of Zayyana's concern and if you don't mind my leaving your Queen Mother Latezia now, I shall see if her needs have been met, Your Majesty." Qiaona bowed.

"I just popped my head in on Lady Constance and Nurse Zayyana just now. My driver, Dubai sits with Lilli plucking comforting sonatas on his mandolin. Lilli looks pretty and well-dressed in Penelope's lacey dress!All are feasting on their suppers from picnic trays such as Mummy and I will now! Go and be with them."

Qiaona turned taking three steps toward the doorway.

"Oh, wait! Do you want to know what I did, Lady Qiaona? I saved Lilli's life today!"

Rhynn held the spoon to Latezia's lips letting the steam rise under her nostrils. Broth's fragrance wafted teasingly there taunting her mouth to open unto her belly's apatite. But his mother's eyes remained fixed on the window as her jaws stayed shut behind stoic cheeks.

"What does your heart wish to see there, Mother and what do you really see through windowpane and beyond? Look at *me*, I am your Rhynn and Jaguar, Mummy! I promised you I would be here and…"

Oh, I know! Father's statue should be standing at the Reflection Pool of Ancestors! Rhynn dropped the spoon in a tinkling clatter upon silver tray and strode to the window looking down.

King Breretyn's marble statue stands in line next his father, King Neptlyn and all ancestors gone before. And it is carved exactly as Breretyn had commanded the sculptor use his chisels. The king standing in reflection at poolsidestands not in grandiose swaying robes of marble fur-and-velvet and heavy crown weighting his brow but as a peoples' servant dressed in a blacksmith's shirt rolled to his elbows, hair caught up in shabby cap pulled low on his brow. Borrowed boots shod his feet and worn leather gloves lay clutched in one hand. A bridle dangles from the other. The eyes appear twinkling iridescent-jade-green though one seems to wink at the sight of one son standing at windowsill looking down.

Bring Latezia to the window, Rhynn, so I may behold my beautiful damsel-bride!

"Come, Mummy, and look down at the pool rimmed with royal king statues! Come up from the chaise, tiz a surprise! You'll see!"

Latezia spoke the first words in many hours' time as she extended her hand to her king-son, firstborn and Breretyn's heir.

"I hear my name being called as in a serenade from yonder courtyard through cascades' bubbling ripples lapping against sandstone edges. Help Mummy up, Jaguar! His Majesty is calling my name!"

Latezia rose to stand transfixed at the window, palms pressed against pane, lips feathering glass, breath steaming over all.

"Ah, tiz Breretyn! I knew it! I just *knew* it! My love plays for me above cobblestone courtyard disguised as a gypsy man dressed in Ebo's blacksmith attire! But now you gleam clean of borrowed clothes' smelly scent, your people's hard-working king...*my* Breretyn! How you tease a brick-maker's daughter, enchanting me so!"

Rhynn slipped away from the room as a jungle cat slinks away from its lair with paws silently gliding into hallway across foyer down stairwell through passageway around fruiting trees past arena and stables through gate in the fence onto back road heading to Belle Passe and Half Moon Lagoon.

The roar of the falls camouflage the crunch of his footsteps upon pathway's fine gravel as storm clouds darken the moon's glow through shrubbery. Jaguar adjusted the holes in the matte black face mask to fit his eyes and quickened his pace toward the eerie green snake-eye beacon blinking in Ravenz' gateway lamppost. The signet ring encircling his finger dug into the bone's thin flesh, so tight is the leather glove enveloping his sovereign hand.

Stop here, Jaguar, and breathe...breathe...breathe.

Rhynn pressed the naked fingers of his right hand against the jugular vein pulsing below his mandible...steady, slow, rhythmic...

In the chest of any other man beats the heart of a practiced assassin, but in me beats a promise my heart made. You are the man I want, Ravenz! But I, above anyone must be absolutely certain of your innocence. It is your face I must see with my eyes!

Falls House

No light shines through any window and no moonlight illuminates yard, walkway or stoop. Only dark forms of shrubs and two small trees occupy the lawn add natural ambience to the little brick house. Rhynn felt his way along the wall to its corner until a window's glass pane reflecting few stars and a cloud-filtered moonbeam showed his hand about to rest on a backstairs hand railing.

I'm an idiot! If Ravenz who is identical to Rhynn lives here then why am I, Jaguar, slinking about this house wearing a criminal's coward-mask?

The black mask flew through the night's black air to land between stoop and bush atop a mat of discarded rags left to sleeping dogs as comfort against damp earth's night chill. But Rhynn's eyes detected pigments glinting in dried paint stains on torn fabric and wondered if Ravenz is somehow an artist.

But I've seen these colors smeared just this way once in the mercantile…like Parqai's paint…the afternoon wind blew his canvas against his shirt. And now these exact hues shine through in the faces of Aotepi and Qeyyapi. Odd that I see Parqai's torn shirt crumpled here…stained. But what of the other garments laying damp and smelling of river water, mud caking pants' hems and the shirt hints of decayed bait…burlap shoes molding?

Rhynn leapt the steps in a single bound at the sight of a cowboy's lariat-rope hanging looped over a hook next the door.

Not one whole rope hangs here but two pieces of one rope!

Rhynn held the remains of the rope in two hands examining shredded ends. Each piece bore the ragged appearance as if a rat had gnawed through its twine seeking fibers for a nest.

The bound thief's confusion at the sight of me driving horses in the roadway is unraveling unto sense.

Rhynn turned the knob. The door opened unto darkness. But a silver candlestick gleamed from its perch on the tabletop and with a strike of a match Rhynn had stuffed in his pocket the kitchen came alive in candle's glow. Hallway's wooden floor shone softly-burnished with footfall's wear and doors to bedchambers stood slightly ajar in their jambs. Rhynn passed them all until one caught his eye; a masculine room...and man's clothing hanging...a desk littered with papers and books...an abacus and protractor, compass and ruler...

Ravenz' room

And in a single step Rhynn came to stand in little Falls House library before a feminine gently-designed cherry-wood desk polished to deep hues over years' time and a petite chair patiently awaiting a lady-person's rest upon fine needlepoint cushion.

Rhynn moved closer peering at a closed tome resting atop the desk. Gilded engraved lettering shone up from leather binding in the flame's glow and in that instant Rhynn's hands shook as he'd never before felt any such shaking in any of his life's days gone before.

The Book of Knowledge and Practice

⁓

Clouds blanket the moon. Only the bravest stars huddling in constellations' outreaching corners hold gaseous torches feebly twinkling dimlyilluminating river's obsidian surface. No owl hoots for a tardy mate. Loons opt for slumber in marsh nests. Insects vanished to places only insects know where and Ravenz sitting in little wood boat rowed silently past villages' deserted streets and halcyon houses. Barely a candle's flame flickers in any window. Even lampposts dotting river bends fatigue in their ceaseless blinking.

One…more…green…white…green…white…one…more…boring …blink…blink…

"I'd blink tiredly too, if I were a beacon trapped on a lamppost standing in place blinking on and on evermore." Ravenz spoke softly into nocturne stillness until he looked up catching sight of two small blazing-white orbs swooping closer to his boat than any two stout stars shimmering in night's black vault. On rushed the orbs increasing in speed as wind blows over one's head and do majestic wings swish over Ravenz' head catching up his hair in airstream's wake.

"Ah, Eagle! You dive and soar at me as if teasing me to play!" Ravenz stopped his rowing resting the paddles across his knees and settling the rowboat to bobbing in the slow flowing current.

But my arms are tired of paddling and tired from unloading crates and more crates. Let my eyes follow your magnificence in flight as you entrance me so with your swirls and swoops.

The eagle circled above Ravenz' head then scooped low over the water as if suddenly sighting a top-feeding fish unlucky in this late hour. But no fish caught up in Eagle's steely talons for both remain tightly-gnarled balls uninterested in hunting supper. Up to the heavens swooshed the bird flapping its giant wings in urgency such as one fleeing a predator's terror. Around and around, back and forth up and down the river soared the eagle over Ravenz' head is if relaying a warning unto an outcome yet to be known.

"What is it, Eagle that has you so agitated? Is it me, mighty sky-king, who bothers you so? Am I late for some promised event I've forgotten in a few days' absence?"

But in that moment the eagle vanished into sky's darkness soaring off to seek perch on a rocky ledge looking down through one lowly-lit window at one young king-twin bent low over a page in a book.

Calligraphy and sketches quilled in indigo ink meet Rhynn's gaze as his hand lifted aside the tome's soft leather cover. The candlestick clattered against the desktop releasing faint tapping tones till it settled itself on four wide round feet. Flame's nervous flicker softened into a serene glow calming Rhynn's attitude and quieting his hands.

The Birthing of Babies and the Midwife's Duty

Drawings of a woman progressing through stages of birthing-labor sit among columns of script describing great muscular seizures with regard to time measured in segments. A paragraph wrote of amniotic fluid draining through birth canal thus increasing pain's frequency and intensity of deep muscles contracting. A womb's dilation measured in centimeters meaning imminent birth showing as a series of gradient circles beginning small as a pea to large as a saucer. Finely-painted baby hairs lay in tiny swirls across what must be its scalp. The word, *Crowning* appears written below.

Descriptions of preparations in regard to steaming water, clean linens and towels litter the pages as does an interesting caption below a picture of an alchemist's bottle seemingly filled with a clear liquid.

Chloroform Alchemy Regarding Pain Control in the Birthing of an Infant

The passage described the effects of an alchemist's near-magical anesthesia-like potion when soaked into a cloth and held over the nose then inhaled by the mother inducing a deep sleep in her brain so profound as to obliterate all sense of pain and knowledge of a procedure about to occur.

Rhynn studied the sketch of a nursemaid sitting aside the headboard of a woman whose head rests on pillows, their hands clutched together as second midwife holds a cloth over laboringpatient's nose. The next picture depicts arms and hands falling limp and eyes closed unto slumber; tranquil as shows on a face of one dead.

An infant expelling into the hands of the midwife is drawn next to a sketch of the same infant held up in the air, mouth open in an *O* squalling and chubby legs kicking up tiny heels. A column describes a bathing basin warming with hot water taken of scalding cauldron and the procedure for properly cleansing a just-birthed child. The baby, wrapped in clean linen and placed at the breast of the mother is gently encouraged to suckle.

Rhynn turned the page.

Multiple Birth and Dismay

What? Dismay at witnessing more than one child being born of a single womb is a surprise? In what way...

The script tells of the midwife's post-natal-patient in-wait for the afterbirth sack to dispel from the its body in a normal way but the midwife instead observes a foot emerge...*purple, it is, nearly black even...*and then two feet extrude pulling an infant's body and head into the hand of the dismayed midwife. The infant is perceived stillborn and in haste the midwife rushes the tragedy from the birthing chamber so mother awakens from her induced deep sleep to see one perfect robust newborn babe cradled in arm suckling at breast.

A sketch depicts the weak body of an infant paint-brushed in a watery black solute as to appear unto the shade of purple. The paper beneath the picture waves slightly as is the way water air-dries on pulp. The caption beneath reads,

Smothered-Cord Oxygen-Depraved Fetus

But to Rhynn's reading eyes there appears a change in the tone from one of clinical direction to that of storytelling. Long sentences containing anxious sounding words run together as panic grips the attending midwife. The author writes of footsteps hastening through secret passageway down stairwell through long dark hallway searching for a place, but where?

There are no such houses in any of the kingdom's villages large enough and in need of secret passageways and long hallways except in the castle's great labyrinth of corridors, wings, suites and stairwells.

The whole way of trip the distraught midwife calls upon the Creator for mercy and direction, pleading over and over as the blue infant is clutched in her hands against her breast. Then in a miraculous event candlelight suddenly illuminates a doorway leading to a dank mop room where water dripping in a sink's drain resonates hollow in long deep pipe.

Mop room? Why flee into a mop room seeking divine interventionin such a place?

Pictures showing a room's tile floor and mops lining walls standing before discarded heaps of mildewing rags and overturned draining buckets support the author's text. A drawing of a skull-capped woman clutching a bundled apron to her bosom kneels on the tiles.

Rhynn turned the page.

Across the top of this page in elegant black lettering is scripted these words,

Breathe the Air in Your Lungs into Suffering Infant's Nose

The drawing of an apron lay cast aside in a crumpled heap on the stone tiles as an infant's face is held to the mouth of the kneeling midwife. Her lips encircle the nose and mouth of the wee babe and her cheeks are drawn puffed-out with air intent on inflating empty infant lungs. Hands grip at the child with fingertips sketched as those of a masseuse's hands massaging a body's vertebrae and sternum. The second picture showed the infant's lungs ballooning with air.

The script ran on describing the process of breathing air of one's lungs into the lungs of another unconscious unto near death, pausing to massage the heart into pumping in natural rhythm returning lung's oxygen through arteries to organs vital to living…until the victim shows life by way of kicks and chirps…and a pink hue returns to the skin of the infant chasing all trace of blue-black away.

Kicking commences…and chirps sound…? Blue-black… Ravenz! The midwife writes of the black infant as little bird, a…raven!

"That's it! Here lies the astounding knowledge Father spoke of as he awakened from a black sleep he remembers not. And the ferocious kiss of air forced into his lungs as a hurricane suddenly blows in…over and over did the air of one's lungs force through lips' bruising seal about Father's mouth as hard fists pummel sternum's cartilage annoying ribs…is all written here as Ravenz knows and just as a midwife wrote of in the beginning! Only one man lives in me, Father. Only one man lives beside me identical to me as I am one living identical to him just as he is also one.

"The first of us to see birth's light is me, *Rhynn!* The smothered black-bird twin is named *Ravenz* growing strong in childhood and manliness mirroring me causing this conundrum in you and all others. The chloroformed mother is Mummy birthing in the ancient chamber-of-heirs! In her anesthesia state she would have no remembrance of the birthing experience at all, only waking to see one perfect babe cradled on her arm. But who is this midwife who learned of this extraordinary thing restoring life into one dead in such a manner as this and writes of such knowledge so another may practice?"

Rhynn's voice wafts throughout Falls House as midsummer night's gentle wind softly flows through cracks down hallways into chambers whispering low as to ghosts.

A truth flashes in Rhynn that the tome resting on the desk before his curious eyes causing his mind to ponder speaks more honestly of an act of circumstance falling into a midwife's hands causing torment to war consciousness' reasoning because a dark secret hides in her heart.

"What my eyes behold is a confession penned in disguise."

The wooden rowboat slowed to a stop over the place in the river where water flows slower over shallow sediment bar. Moon's gentle glow overcame storm's threat banishing black clouds into hiding until a later night's fury. Silvery moonbeams lay strewn upon river's glassy surface rendering them the appearance of endless mirrors reflecting and beckoning in quiet dark beauty known only in night hours.

"I am home, Eagle! My bed awaits my tired body's burning muscles and numb bones." Ravenz looked to the ledge where the dark silhouette of the great bird sat perched, wings tucked down and royal bald head bent low so two scintillating white eyes could look into his. "You have calmed yourself, I see, and sit still in rest. 'Till morning then, Sky-king!"

Ravenz saluted the bird and turned the knob.

The eagle did not blink.

CHAPTER 12

*T*RUTH

Latezia shifted the black lacey veil shrouding her face to a space of tulle sheerness where her eyes could focus between two appliqued roses better surveying the bits of intricately-cut stained glass arranged in high holy-picture panels above the chapel's altar. Even in this dark hour without benefit of sun's enhancing rays through the panes all colors still shine luminous in their soldered brass confines seamlessly as if a continuous painting brushed there by a master artist's hand. Candle flames burning in wall sconces cast their own glow outward in reverse of a day's sun shining in still highlighting panes' hues of purple and red, green and orange and yet the effect on one's soul in the deepening vesper hour is just as serene.

The window's colors lift my mind like an anesthesia's vapor but my feet feel as heavy granite, like magnets even, nave's elements pulling them hard to the aisle. My head and arms feel light as a marionette's body suspended in air by imaginary strings. My eyes float up but all my lead toes weigh down my two soles.

Latezia stared at the altar.

I see a million flickers casting a million shadows dancing to madrigals' low chant and a harpist tenderly plucking…yet why is the altar so far away as to appear a vanishingpointgoing into blackness in sanctuary's candlelight? How can I say my prayer if the altar isn't there?

Latezia reached forth her hands as one grasps at precipice's brink.

Look up, Latezia!

Latezia lurched at the sound as if Breretyn's live voice had uttered the command.

"What?"

See balcony beckoning above yonder steps leading up stairwell there? Leave the nave and come to me by way of the steps up stairwell. Sit with me in the loft, my love. Tiz nearer to Heaven up here than lying face down on cold stone upon colder earth before an ancient tree's carved-trunk altar!

In the mystical way a puppeteer plays strings dangling from his fingers did Latezia glide up the stairwell unto balcony not stopping in her ascent till she floated down as an achene into a seat offering a view of the chancel. Her hands clutch the railing.

"Brereytn? You called my name but yet I don't see…"

Let go the railing and give me your hand, Latezia for I sit beside you on velvet cushions

"Velvet…cushion?" Latezia lifted the hem of the veil filtering her eyes' gaze to clearly see a mound of plush velvet cushions at her side.

"Oh! How lovely are the colors, so fatly stuffed and covered in thick velvet soft to my palm's touch!"

Latezia's hand warms as if enclosed by the hands of another who has loved her. Her eyes close as unto a dream commencing and her ears hear a heart's low rhythmic beating reverberating in the loft as an orchestra's prelude to a drama about to erupt across a stage except the curtains remain closed…or yet…not closed at all as Latezia sees King Brereytn's face so close to hers and feels his breath on her cheek as cool as night's air but still warm as day's wispy breeze.

I am not gone away from you at all, my queen, most beautiful Latezia, but wait at path's end wherever your feet tread…will you see me waiting. You only have to listen just as you have opened your ears unto me here and you'll know…you'll see.

Latezia prayed just as she intended when slipping away from the palace in the moonless hour awaiting Chapel's high steeple bell tolling a telling-tone over somber valley, gentle flowing river and solemn mountain top. But she prayed not face down, forehead upon cold rock but face up and warm, nose breathing faint-scented myrrh.

"Ah, my Breretyn, tiz not a mystery I'm dreaming...at all!"

Latezia's lips part in a smile and sapphire-blue eyes now shine in the vault as twin Polaris stars beam.

"Forgive me, Holy Father of my fleeing Chapel's nave forsaking hallowed chancel and humble altar for a little space in balcony's vault close to Heaven's door where my Breretyn comforts me."

～つ

Falls House. And rest.

Ravenz closed the oak door against the moon and stars and all else belonging to night and listened to the sound of silence in the absence of Anabaa's quill scratching script across papyrus, Qiaona rattling kettles upon stovetop and Constance humming enchantingly overall.

Even darkness has its own sound if properly listened to in tranquil time as this. But I am tired and seek my bed.

Only quiet white moonlight sifted into the parlor and hallway through curtains diaphanous as mist illuminating walls' linear planes and floors' burnished planks.

My body seeks slumber in sweet night.

No dim candlelight glowed beneath any bedchamber door.

Except one

Ravenz froze.

The door swung aside as if by a ghost's hand. Ravenz stared into his bedchamber seeing all furnishings sitting before him exactly as any day and night gone before but for the kitchen's candlestick bearing flickering taper resting on his desk.Not a thing appears disturbed of its place; no book lay overturned on its spine nor any clutter happened on desktop. The mirror reflects no one's person but the being of himself looking back unto him.

I don't see anyone but yet I hear…someone has been just here or…is here still…in my place. Whose' hand opened this door ushering me enter my own chamber?

Then Ravenz' gaze fell to the pillow to see an old fishing line entangled in a loosely-knit ball about lead sinker and rusty hook still clinging to withering bait.

Who has brought in Ebo's old rig from my yesternight-river-play suddenly interrupted, that I cast aside on rocks for an event forgotten?

An icy chill swept over Ravenz' scalp causing a clatter of molars in sockets and great rattling of vertebrae along shuddering spine to femurs, patellae to spindly fibulas and tibias.

My coin! Someone has stolen the artist's coin!

Ravenz' hands claw up the pillow from blanket and sheet to see naught but tufted mattress in faded gray-blue ticking void of Parqai's golden medallion.

"Looking for this?"

Ravenz lurched up turning at the sound of a voice coming from the mirror but…

The mirror? No one is in a mirror except me and I stand here at bed's side holding a pillow mid-air! So why am I there holding Parqai's coin in my hand like that when I see it's gone from its secret place here?

Ravenz tossed aside the pillow but the image of himself did not reflect the motion at all but remained standing where it stood holding forth a coin in its hand.

Ravenz blinked.

"Come! Take the coin from my hand as it belongs to you, good brother."

"I am Ravenz."

"I am Rhynn."

Ravenz stepped to the side and back then took a step forward waving his arms but yet the image did not respond. But the hand still holds forth the gold coin glinting in candle's glow.

"Ah...*Rhynn*! His Majesty calls me Rhynn and so too, the queen, Latezia does say to me when calling me Rhynn and me answering, 'I am Ravenz.' 'Oh! You are a bird now and not a jaguar!' And all others, too as does Ebo say, calling me cloud-hopper and terra-crawler in all my child-play. Is this a mirror's reflecting-trick game playing with my eyes? What means this duplicity...and...*brother?*"

"Move to my side and face the same direction with me and you will see."

Ravenz stepped forward and to the side of the one standing identical to him, gazes locked onto each other, eyes moving in synchronization as magnets pull lead balls until Ravenz turned his face away and stared in the same direction as Rhynn.

Ravenz looked to the mirror seeing two identical faces staring back. One face speaks words through its lips though his do not.

"The mirror hangs *there* and its face does not lie. What we see reflecting to us is what all others see when they look upon us; one is the same as the other appearing to all eyes as one and the same, identical are we to each other.

"It is I, *Rhynn* who holds King Neptlyn's coin in my hand but it was given to *you* by the hands of another. I believe a thief lies at the

237

heart of your story. Take it back, Ravenz. It's...*karma.*"

Ravenz' lips move in response to a question forming long in his mind, since the idea of an identical-other coming to stand here happened upon reading Anabaa's confessional prose as a young child just having mastered the magic of reading words.

"How is it you just learned of this truth, Rhynn, that we are identical twin brothers as you righteously say?"

"I learned the truth of this enigma in my hour's reading *The Book of Knowledge and Practice* in library-parlor. Our story is camouflaged as clinical theory written by the midwife's own hand. Our mother, Her Majesty, Queen Latezia is to be delivered of King Breretyn's twin heirs but on the day of our birth, me firstly, a nightmare occurred in the womb suddenly thereafter severing you and I from each other in all our days' light. Until now.

"You are the second twin to be born of our mother but along the way of your birth life smothered from you and all oxygen snuffed away from your lungs. You were born dead of her body. The midwife's hands clutched a purple-black bird-like lifeless infant to her bosom. But by way of incredible knowledge she restored breath in your lungs and pulsing beats in your heart's chambers. In her arms you came alive. She named you Ravenz."

"But what of the fishing line, sinker and hook? How do you come by this knowledge that these things are mine and how did you come to this place to find me and thus...*us?*"

"Our father died last night, Ravenz."

"King Breretyn dropped dead of a quit heart falling from Lightfoot's saddle onto the road as I sat night-fishing at river's bank but I restored breath to his lungs and his heart to beating just as Anabaa has written in the book's beginning! The king shoved me aside calling me Rhynn. 'I'm Ravenz,' I said just as a horseman on galloping steed approached the place where His Majesty lay and

238

taking the king up in his arms and setting him upon Lightfoot's back, King Breretyn lived then is all I know."

"You speak the truth. I know it is you. Look into my other hand."

Ravenz stared from coin-in-fingers to buttons-in-palm.

BAnd torn threads.

"After leaving Kings Observatory I happened upon nervous Lightfoot in the roadway and our father lying in gravel. He called me a raven and wanted to eat the fish he thought to be stuffed in my pocket. I feared he suffered confusion in an injured brain and prayed for enough wellbeing to last the way home so Mother could see. It was in the *Parlor-of-Portraiture* he wished to rest before Parqai's masterpiece painting of *Queen Mother and Prince*. Our father made one last request of me and that I am to find this man, Ravenz who is identical to me, even if he lived as an imaginary-other inside me or lived as another beside me for he is the one having knowledge of restoring life. In the soul's secret place Father knew he had died on the roadway. This was King Breretyn's last command to me.

"I discovered Falls House by way of Kyrro's unselfish concern and manly strength. Kyrro carried me here from the playing field as one carries another suffering delirium believing in his eyes I to be you. And I discovered the truth of us in the midwife's confession. And I've come to the end of this riddle unraveling all persons' confusion regarding our mirror-identities perplexing their eyes and tangling their thoughts."

"I am Ravenz and have never been any one by any other name. I have never suffered riddle's tease as you have being called a raven, a jaguar and Rhynn."

"I am Rhynn, Jaguar and King. You are my identical twin, Ravenz and as my brother, equally royal. Kings Castle is yours."

239

"Royalty is a state of mind, Your Majesty. Since first memory have I romped the palace's hallways and stairwells, passageways and corridors. I have dreamed in Mountainwing's suites and in royal chambers. I have listened to the queen's music boxes tinkle and strummed the king's lute. I have chased puppies through hedge mazes and lifted kittens from limbs. I have been nourished at royal kitchen's table. I have been tutored by way of King Breretyn's saddle in the arts of riding and hunting and learned to draw letters and words by way of Queen Latezia's hand as I sat in her lap. I live as a prince in this valley house and in hilltop mansion. I know the realm as Peoples' Castle and this valley, mountain and plain as Peoples' Kingdom."

Ravenz bowed his head slightly only to catch sight of Rhynn's own head dropping in bow.

"Come with me to the chapel, Ravenz. Time is now the bell-ringer must put the bell to tolling for our father, His Majesty, King Breretyn in his mourning hours.

A jaguar king and raven prince…or…a raven prince and jaguar king, identical one to the other in the way a mirror reflects identical images the same…*but one royal head turns back, eyes searching rocky ledge locking gaze with two small white stars closer to Earth than all others*…stride side by side over Falls House threshold under portico down stepping-stone pathway beneath lamppost and beacon-blinking through gateway onto roadway along riverbank past playing field through deserted mercantile street under moon's serene glow to Chapel's vestibule up stairway through stairwell to bell-ringer's chamber.

Listen, Latezia! Tiz the bell's toll! But never mind the melancholy tone, Love, tiz only a necessary short prelude to Evening News so seemingly important to mortals. Shush now, my beauty! Our jaguar, King Rhynn is here…in the belfry with Ravenz!

The eagle waits.

Anabaa knelt under sanctuary's noble archway pressing her palms to her heart. In whispers uttered Heavenward silently as feathers lift in breeze she prays the same prayer seeking blessing for all women with child and all mothers delivered, for unborn babes and babes newly born.

Anabaa paused in her words and crossed her heart, then clutched her hands together entwining her fingers into knots. Falling forward over her knees Anabaa's forehead grazed the nave's tiles.

"Forgive me. Forgive me. Sanity hangs in my conscience's warring crosshairs." The midwife's body rocked back and forth then swayed side to side as a little ship lists on high sea in hurricane's wind. Suddenly as if caught by a rogue gust Anabaa's body reared up, face to the ceiling, eyes wide open beseeching and pleading as her knees inched forward up nave's long cold granite trail only to fall prostrate across all steps, arms outstretched and hands clawing at the ancient tree-trunk altar. "Forgive me...I meant no palace malice..."

Gong...gong...gong...gong...

"What means this dismal ringing? What message does bell's clapper tell?"

Gong...gong...gong...gong...

"Wait! Is a funeral tone interrupting my prayer...is the noise my ears hear?"

"Anabaa! Anabaa! We've been looking all over for you only to find you here, lying distraught at altar's feet!" Qiaona and Constance grasped Anabaa's shoulders lifting her face to the light.

"I always pray here in the vesper hour, Constance. I'll be home soon enough."

"The queen has gone missing! Latezia has fled the castle...slipped away in the dark!"

"So?" Then seeing inexplicable angst in the eyes of Constance and Qiaona, Anabaa gasped and dropped her head to the tile. "It is Death's tolling tone chiming in steeple's tower. Tell me, who is it the bell tolls for?"

"King Breretyn is...*dead*, Anabaa. He sleeps of a heart gone...tired and quit. And Latezia is vanished of her chambers!"

Latezia...the queen...Latezia...

"I hear my name called but yet I don't see! Why is my name echoing here, in *this* place?"

Look to the nave, chancel and altar, my love! You'll see!

Hazy orbs drift in candlelight's golden fog settling over nave, altar and chancel occupying all hallowed space above granite tile and marble walls, stained glass windows and arced ceiling.

Latezia gripped the balcony's hand-railing, staring through black gauze veil searching the scene unfolding in the sanctuary below. Three bodies huddle on chancel's platform. Two others stride the nave's long way to the altar.

Toss aside your mourning veil and look down, Latezia!

The black lacy veil floated away from Latezia's brow wafting downward in holy air's gentlest current. As a dry leaf falls from a branch to the ground did the veil come to rest on nave's path at the feet of Ravenz and Rhynn.

In that moment two identical faces turned upward to gaze at the face in the balcony looking down.

I see two identical cherub-faces on granite pathway there. One is my Rhynn standing there the same as the other...but which one...and who is the other?

Latezia cried out,

"Jaguar!"

"Mummy!" Rhynn stared up.

"Your Majesty." Ravenz bowed.

Anabaa, Constance and Qiaona clutched one another paralyzed in trance.

Latezia leaned against the balcony's railing hands clinging to smooth old wood, face looking down and eyes staring into identical faces of two sons.

"How can this be, Breretyn? I behold two faces exactly the same! One is the same as the other is the same as a mirror reflects an image over and over!"

You were right in your birthing dream, Latezia. Two cherubs did hover above you. The one that drew closer to you is Rhynn, your firstborn and my heir, sleeping in your arm. The cherub lifting up and floating away is the twin, Ravenz who faded to darkness in your womb.

But the midwife, Anabaa restored life to your raven-babe causing his heart to beat and lungs to inhale. She has the knowledge to do this thing and through her writing the whole story of it down did our Ravenz read of her deed and comprehend thus restoring life to me in the roadway for just a little more time, enough for me to understand our dreams' mystery.

Anabaa brought Ravenz back to us, Latezia! He has been here since the beginning, since the day Parqai painted two cherubs in the portrait! You've chased him in circles around chamber down hallway up stairwell and corridor and about fountain and shrubs and hedge mazes as he called, 'Ravenz flies here, no up here, now perches here, no, under here the same as you chased little Jaguar in the very same way as he called, 'Come catch Jagger's tail, Mummy! Up here, now, here, no, under there!' the whole while of the way chanting nursery rhyme lines.

I have been with one or the other every day I lived as one went with me to pick grapes in the wine-maker's vineyard and the other helped me sheer sheep in a shepherd's fold or attend mares foaling in stable. One or the other, Rhynn or Ravenz has been with me in all villages and mercantile, factory or stall and field learning the ways of his king's people. One called me, 'Poppi.' One called me, 'Your Majesty.'

"By what way did you come to this answer, Breretyn? I am a simple girl, a brick-maker's daughter and yet I knew it even then. I just *knew* it! A mother always knows of the tiny souls growing in her belly."

Heaven is Trinity's library, Latezia! All answers rest here simply awaiting saints' queries.

Latezia looked on the faces of Qiaona, and Constance as they cradled the midwife, Anabaa in their arms huddled at altar's foot. And she saw devotion shine in their eyes and love halo their heads.

Come down from that dark place to chancel's light, Latezia! Comfort our sons at the altar...where I wait...

"Wait for Mummy there, Jaguar and Ravenz! I'm coming...running down stairwell...up nave...to gather 'bout you all!"

⁓

"Take one last look about the cabin, Qeyyapi! Father is back from the livery and waits for your trunk! Where has Aotepi gone now?" Daphne swirled about the cabin as a frustrated hen cooped in a day too long, skirts catching about her ankles tangling in overlaps between her shoes.

"We've taken one last look about the cabin seven times already and Aotepi waits in the doorway, right behind you! I would think she'd be the first of us down the gangplank what with that giant sapphire rock burning a tattoo on her finger! She can't wait to plunge her hand in matrimony water!"

"That's enough, Qeyyapi! Your sister has held herself together patiently-well through all these long months with nothing but a few weeks-worth of delicious memories to hang on to, and the prince's ancient sapphire ring helps keep those alive!" Daphne sighed at the memory of past summer's short weeks almost as if the royal encounter in the castle had simply been a dream after all. With her skirts calmed and draping over calves as deep lace ruffles graze the toes of her new shoes, Daphne exhaled.

"Tiz all right to stare at the gem, Aotepi. The prince placed it there as a reminder that what happened last year was not a silly wish made in your girlish heart but as a real promise you can feel with your finger and see with your eyes. Qeyyapi wishes she could be just as lucky as you, is all. Tiz only natural your sister's heart burns with desire the same as what smolders on your finger." The cabin door shut with snap of the latch. "Come along, girls! The temperature is rising! The sky is summertime-blue! It is high time we leave squawking seagulls nose-diving in our wake!

Daphne Tsagalakis sprinted ahead of her daughters, eyes only upon her husband's face holding his gaze in her vision as her feet sped toward a wondrous future.

"Do you think Prince Rhynn will remember my face, Qeyyapi? Really, in your *heart of hearts*, do you think he'll recognize my face among all others...and not be disappointed?"

"Aotepi! It is me you are talking to! What is this insecurity in you? We are the *Tsagalakis* sisters, identical *twins* even! That little detail in itself automatically doubles our confidence and strengthens all bonds. Listen to me! The prince's heart will set ablaze the moment he sees the stars burning in your eyes! No maiden in any kingdom in any other realm has your exquisiteness, Aotepi!"

You do, Qeyyapi. Your eyes glow as two moons in a face as lovely.

"It is this truth Prince Rhynn holds fast in his heart's memory. You'll see, Aotepi!"

And my eyes will search every face in the kingdom for two eyes I saw once through a fountain's mist under a rain of silvery fireworks on a castle's lawn in moonlight, like Aotepi saw in a prince's face.

Qeyyapi raised her face to the sky and closed her eyes shutting out all blue's mysterious depths and every hint of cloud, mountaintop's ridge and trees' canopy allowing her body to feel each cobblestone the cart's four wheels roll upon in its journey past kiosk, shanty and tent through one village than another wondering with each squealing two axles' turn as to why Father chose a cart for this final task than boat's gentle swift glide up river.

Four horses' steel horseshoed hooves clatter bass syncope to squeaks' aria annoying Qeyyapi's ears causing one thought to obscure all others. She opened her eyes to see Aotepi's eyes closed.

"Aotepi? Stop daydreaming about Prince Rhynn and tell me what you hear."

"I hear nothing. What do you hear?"

"That's just it, Aotepi! I hear nothing but cart's wheels rattling and horses' hooves clattering echoing in all otherwise quiet space. No sound of economy happens in shops and kiosk for no moneychangers' coins clink in jars and no voices raise in barter or banter. But yet everyone stands lining the street looking but not at us! I feel as if we are an invisible one-float parade. Look at the heads, Aotepi! All silent faces turn to the side as their eyes search up roadway as if looking for something to bloom on the horizon. Why are women holding bouquets and little girls hold baskets full of petals while men and boys wave flags on sticks? Even Mother and Father sit silent for their soft chatter has quit since I don't know when. They see it too."

An eagle soared high overhead in firmament so sheer as to appear

246

nearly white but for a guess of blue hue shading atmosphere's arced edge.

"Look, Qeyyapi! Did you see that?"

"Awesome! I've never seen such wings' span in all my life! How widely they spread casting shade on our eyes like an…"

"Umbrella! Oh, look! Here it flies back around circling above! Amazing!"

"But now it swoops away up the road! Wait! It glides back! Isn't it beautiful, Qeyyapi?

Then all ears heard the sound.

It began as a low dull rumble as distant thunder rolls but rose in crescendo as voices chanted a concerto across valley, heather plain, above river and waterfall over mountain's peaks.

The cart halted.

All eyes looked to the horizon seeing a vision unfolding on distant roadway emerging through vanishing point's gate to grow from tiny pin-dots to grand images of one hundred horsemen on horseback bearing high-flying flags waving in breezes above a carriage's crimson cloth-draped box being hand-pulled by the king's sentries striding on foot. A smaller carriage, though no less magnificent, followed the first carriage and in their wake followed the kingdom's chanting citizens in a long line that trails for miles.

"We are caught in a parade route!" Marcus Tsagalakis whispered to his wife as his daughters strained their necks for a better view of the oncoming spectacle. In less than a heartbeat Daphne's husband guided the cart off the street to stop beneath an oak tree's shady foliage. Aotepi looked around at the place they stopped and whispered to Qeyyapi that this oasis just has to be the place where all His Majesty's picnics must occur for the cart's wheels sinks in grass so silky of blade and color deeply verdant as to appear surreal.

A magnificent fountain spewed streams of glistening arcs in the air only to tumble into millions of bubbles in its majestic marble basin. No birds twitter above their heads and no insectflits above the fountain's mist. Butterflies in folded wings sat on leaves and dragonflies stilled their flight. Even grasshoppers patiently waited on bended knees.

"Isn't it all grand, Qeyyapi? We are here. Actually really, *really* here! And a parade! We are just in time!"

Qeyyapi's eyes did not look upon the lush scenery, butterflies or dragonflies' splendor, nor focus on fountain's theatre at all. Her longing gaze searched only the faces of the bystanders lining the street bearing flags on highest flagpoles.

Marcus leaned to his wife's ear, his tone low but distinct.

"A royal funeral cortege advances toward us, Daphne, beloved. See afar there? The flags bear the kingdom's symbol and the coffin's drape is embroidered with King Breretyn's coat of arms!"

Qeyyapi and Aotepi spun their heads about on their necks cleaving their gazes from handsome knights' faces and glorious flowers blossoming on tapered shrubs to seek explanation to their father's grim announcement.

~⁓

Lightfoot's head bobbed in rhythm to his fore hooves' steps tapping the highway's fine pavement wondering the whole while of the way at the unusual absence of his master's deep voice that accompanied their strolls in all years past. Even the presence of Pretzyl, though not unusual at all keeping pace at his side on any other day, today carried another in the royal saddle otherwise belonging to one prince known as Jaguar and Rhynn. And the body poised on Lightfoot's own back and these hands holding the reins commanding his bridle now seems as confident as those gone before for had not the prince learned horsemanship in King Breretyn's saddle?

Odd, but yet not odd at all the hands guiding my hooves now should feel exactly as those hands did then.

Lightfoot snorted softly as a fly's whirring wings tickled his ear.

Pretzyl whinnied. A lizard caught sunning itself on roadway's hot gravel darted away into shadowy ditch.

Ravenz stroked the steed's neck. "Tiz only a little reptile warming its belly, Pretzyl, is all."

The village's mercantile cobblestones gleam in late morning sunlight as ocean's salty air soothed Rhynn's scorched cheeks. The sovereign crown failed to offer adequate shade and his scalp itched in protest of pompous dress and unaccustomed attire. His brow aches.

Forgive me, Father, but I am to be a plain king of the valley, the river, heather plain and mountain. I cannot bear the weight of high heavy gem-encrusted golden crown maddening my neck's muscles and causing pain to flame in my brain. Tiz a distraction and hazard, is all, to my governance and rule. I am to be as I always remember you pushing up shirtsleeves casting aside silk jacket and cravat offering aid to a subject unknowing of his benefactor's true person. You and I are the same that way, Poppi, our rule is best served in anonymity's disguise joining in our kingdom's work as any free man in his labor while learning his grievances and play sharing his joys. It is the signet ring I bear on my sovereign finger that tells me apart from all others, as your signet ring happily betrayed you once, to a damsel's brick-maker father.

An eagle dived low over the roadway then soared up to the heavens shielded a moment from sight by a cloud's translucent veil.

Ah, Eagle, don't vanish from my view! Glide around the cloud and fly over me, magnificent sky-king! Come! Fly back!

Ravenz searched the sky for the eagle's grand form hovering

above with wings seemingly spanned beyond the ends of their tips so great is their protecting-reach over all below.

And the eagle did appear unto Ravenz' wishing-prayer circling two times over the heads of the royals; one a young king, the other a prince, identical twin sons of King Breretyn and Her Majesty, Latezia, the queen.

The bird landed itself in the roadway midway 'tween oncoming funeral cortege and flag-waving flower-bearing citizens lining long mercantile street. And it quivered not at many horses' thundering hooves, carriages' turning wheels or an advancing army's trampling feet but curled its steel talons about two warm cobblestones. Eagle's head turned not to face two royal heads-of-state leading the desolate parade but instead focused its two blazing white eyes on four luminous eyes in identical twin faces sitting in a cart hidden in shadow beneath an oak's far reaching branches.

Lightfoot and Pretzyl halted their hooves' fall at the sight of the eagle poised so regally thus stopping all turning wheels and every trampling foot. Voices chanting drifted away to silence as every eye turned to the cart on the lawn.

Marcus Tsagalakis could only whisper to his wife's ear,

"We are too late."

The identical royal faces of Ravenz, the prince and Rhynn, Jaguar and King turned to follow the eagle's gaze just as Aotepi raised her hand to her eyes shielding her vision against blinding white sunlight streaming through a crack in the branches. In that instant a beam caught an ancient sapphire's million faucets throwing a dazzle of stars into the street.

Rhynn did see two stars softly twinkling in eyes blue as cabochon sapphires sparkle in just the right ray.

"Aotepi!"

Aotepi gasped.

"You are mistaken, Father! We are just in time!"

Ravenz turned in his saddle to gaze upon two eyes serenely glowing into his as opals gleam in a full moon's high beam.

"Qeyyapi! It is *you*! You did happen before me that night in summertime past! You really happened before me in palace's fountain mist!"

Qeyyapi stared.

"There are *two* of them, Aotepi, *identical*, the same as one to the other is the same! I just *knew* it! My midsummer's night dream did not lie and neither do my eyes deceive!"

Daphne fainted.

So what are you waiting for, firstborn son and my throne's heir, good Rhynn? Are those not the starry eyes of a maiden named Aotepi? I spy my beloved mother's sapphire ring still adorning her pretty young finger you placed there all these long months passed! Run, humble young king! Waste not one moment more going one mile further in this crazy dismal cortege!

Ravenz and Rhynn dropped the reins of their mounts and cast off gold crowns glinting with gems and capes of ermine and sable into a heap on the street's cobbled pavement then sped to a cart shaded beneath an oak's branches.

Latezia! Throw off your widow's black mourning veil and raise your face to gaze upon yonder cart! It's that olive woman! She's fainted again! Her husband is in such a dither as she's fallen over his feet! You know what to do! Comfort him, Love! Hey, wait! That is my olive crate waiting in the back of his cart! It does have my name printed in block lettering across its side there! We are all just in time! It's a perfectly fantastic day for a picnic and what with all these exotic Tsagalakis olives and everyone gathering here in Kings Park...well...what else is it

251

that everyone just stands around waiting for?!

An on-shore breeze lofted the eagle from its grip on street's cobblestones unto soaring in clouds over the cheering multitude amassing in Kings Park partaking in the afternoon's wedding celebrations. Musicians quit blowing horns' *Taps*, The Bugler's Cryto harps' plucking and flutes' tooting *Canon in D*. Flags wave. Women carrying bouquets lead a father guiding his daughters-goddess-brides by their hands to a waiting king and prince waiting before the majestic bronze *King Breretyn* fountain-statue. Sheer mist anoints two unions. Young girls toss petals from their hand-baskets into the air causing a vast fragrant cascade-blessing above newlywed royals, floating over royal queen mother and olive queen mother-in-law and settling on all others.

One royal head bowed to his father's bronze statue. One royal head lifted his gaze to lock on the eagle's golden-eyed stare until its circling ended in a descending arc beyond the ocean's crest only to soar again and drift on gentle airwaves' stream above Ravenz' head then land in an oak tree's highest branch above an abandoned cart.

EPILOGUE

A *Summer Time*

"I want to sleep with Gramma Teeza! You promised last night that tonight is my turn to sleep in her big umbrella bed!"

"No one, not even a pretty little princess is sleeping in Queen Grandma's big high-poster-canopy bed until she is thoroughly bathed! And that goes for the rest of you, too, brothers included! Come! Bubbles are rising! Steam is escaping! Last one in the froth eats frogs' toes for breakfast!"

Shrieks and hollers rang over the slap-slap-slap of siblings' child-arches smacking marble tile racing to Kings Tub-Room soon to be muffled by water splashing and, "I can hold my nose under water for ten minutes!" to "Mummmmeeee! I've got soap in my eyeeeee!"

Latezia laughed out loud in the vacated bedchamber listening to her own sound in the wake of Queen Aotepi's babies' voices' ring as wind-chime tones echoing against stone walls.

"It is grand to hear you laugh so heartily, Your Majesty, Latezia!" Qiaona released a hairpin from its duty securing the implement between her teeth.

A ringlet fell to Latezia's shoulder just as it has done a million times a million nights before since she sat before a high mirror as a tiny girl just witnessing the event for the very first time.

Years and years and years ago but is it ever really so long when looking down or up Euclid's plane? What is this thing called time that races onward relentlessly ticking off hours and days and years but yet halts in a magical way as evidenced by the things time leaves standing in its wake? In a measure of time Breretyn's villages have turned into cities. Smooth paved streets lay as tar ribbons before tall buildings scraping the sky. Rooftops pierce the clouds. Nights have turned into near-white as any day's light for generators power currents through wires illuminating glass bulbs haloing the night sky. Candles' glow is reserved for romance... and cakes.

Trolley cars rattle along steel rails moving dwellers faster than a wish can be made.

Let's do lunch at The Plaza! But I'll be late for my two o'clock! Just take the trolley! It stops right in front!

Buses' brakes screech and exhale. Cars' horns honk. Trucks loading and unloading boxes at white-painted curbs block streets' traffic. Sirens wail. And a train's whistle blows long over all.

When did this all happen, Breretyn? I just blinked my eyes and then it was already done!

"May I turn down the duvet and plump the pillows, Your Majesty?" Qiaona bowed with a hint of a curtsey. Even after all these years her respect for Latezia's position still marveled the dowager queen.

"Oh, gracious no! Queen Aotepi's little ones have so much fun doing that! They love to pretend what we know is already real. It is such fun to hear them make up fantastical stories spoken in royal tones as if they are the king and the queen sleeping in high canopy-tent! They are King Rhynn's babies after all, and as such are already princesses and princes."

"Tomorrow is the grand opening of Ravenzpass Seaway, Your Majesty. Are you still planning an open boat ride down river or have your plans changed? The carriage is being readied."

"Of course, I plan on sitting in Rhynn's little rowboat! He's taking the oars, I'll have you know! Imagine, King Rhynn rowing Mummy down river to meet Ravenz and Qeyyapi sailing up on

Bako's big ship! It will be such fun seeing the looks on everyone's faces!"

"So, it is to be your sun bonnet, then and your hair in ribbons and ringlets?"

But Latezia stood and turned away to the window overlooking the courtyard and fountain's basin shivering with ripples under spouts' endless streams glistening in lampposts' beams. A moth darted about in the highest lantern's glow bumping its nose against the glass causing tachycardia in its fluttering wings vanishing it into darkness if only for a gasp at composure before emerging just as suddenly to resume its earnest mission. The royal statues encircling tranquil reflection pool stood resolute in soft gray tones as in shades happening between wakefulness and sleep.

Just stay where you stand at windowsill there, Latezia! Night's orb is being fashionably late, not an uncommon phenomenon for shy moon hesitates behind proud cloud, is all! Keep your eyes on mine and you'll see in a moment my face seeking yours in chamber's window! Blow me a kiss, my love, blow me a kiss...I cannot bear a single night's hour passing without even one kiss!

"Daddy! Daddy! Mummy says I can sleep with Gramma Teeza in her big magic tent-bed tonight! See! I washed the jam out 'tween all my toes! I scrubbed my heels, too!"

Latezia turned away her gaze from the courtyard's Reflection Pool of Ancestors to see... *a king standing in bedchamber's doorway...arms grasping a small girl-child to his shoulder... royal nose buried against little round belly and body swaying as a cradle gently rocks.*

Latezia's palms clutched the sill.

Breretyn! You were down there just then but stand here cuddling faire golden child!

A signet ring encircling sovereign finger mesmerized Latezia's gaze but it gleams differently somehow.

Breretyn? Your ring…it glows…but more like rising sun's brilliant promise and afternoon's shimmering beam unto evening repose.

"Well! Well, then! Blow me a kiss, princess, if this is to be your nighttime wish! Daddy can't sleep without your goodnight butterfly kiss!"

Of course your eyes twinkle gemstone-green and your hair shines wavy-auburn as a colt's coat shines at high noon. Your voice and manner mirrors your father, His Majesty, King Breretyn, so perfectly do you bring my Breretyn back to me.

~⁓

"Sweetie? Ravenz, hon-darling what's this?"

Ravenz looked to his wife's reflection aside his own pausing a moment before answering pondering just how simply magical mirrors can be and how profoundly poetic mirrors are in their simple silver-glass-flatness-way of reflecting all life's manner in perfect-exactness without trickery or veil, only duplicating the scene again back and forth and back as the eye sees.

Qeyyapi held a golden disc before candlelight's soft glow. King Neptyln's coin gleams and sparkles as her fingertips twirl it about. Wide opal eyes study its engraved face and backside.

"This is the prettiest coin I have laid eyes on for I've never seen a full face engraved upon any coin's front side. And what means these words inscribed on the back? All coins exchanging in the markets and shops show kings' profile on topside and kingdoms' symbol and mint-year on the back."

Ravenz lay down the hairbrush and crossed Bako's Persian rug wedding-gift feeling thick silky fine yarn between his toes.

Ah Bako, if rugs could talk…this thoughtful gift brought from afar over high sea is but a beautiful silent flat treasure-trove betraying nothing but embracing memories beyond count and vast weight.

"That coin, good and lovely wife, is my grandfather, King Neptlyn's coin. He had it especially engraved from one single nugget scooped from river's sediment-clogged crevices. It was given as an investiture gift to my father, King Breretyn. The inscription on the back reads; Reign humbly. Rule justly. Live wholly. It is King Neptlyn's likeness you see engraved on the front.

"My father kept this coin close to his person hidden in a secret pocket until one day while riding through mercantile street an accident occurred nearly claiming the life of a damsel beneath his mount's rearing hooves. An artist in the midst of painting a portrait dropped his brush and leapt off his stool to pull the wounded girl from beneath my father's frenzied horse.

"Prince Breretyn pressed the coin into the artist's hand commanding him to keep it to his person always as it had been given to him. When the artist protested he accepted no alternative simply stating, 'You must take it. It is…karma!' The prince told him that an occasion would arise when he would be just as grateful for an unselfish brave act carried out on his behalf and then must pass on the coin in gratitude.

"And this is how the coin came into my hand. I saved it from the snatch of a thief's greedy fingers making off with it in haste running up roadway past where I lay resting. I just answered the artist's plea for help, is all. But he ran after me and pressed the coin to my palm saying I must take it. 'It is…karma!' were his words to me and he told me the story of the startled horse. The damsel's life he saved that day in the street is my mother's, Queen Latezia, the brickmaker's daughter."

Qeyyapi remained silent only staring instead at Ravenz' hands as he held the coin in moon's light beaming through the porthole. She could tell even from mattress and pillow where she lay that his eyes dwelt on the face of his grandsire.

"Did you know him, Ravenz?"

"No. My father became king before he married my mother."

"Do you believe in karma, Ravenz?"

"Absolutely!"

"How so, beautiful husband? How does one really come to see and know this thing called *karma*?"

"It is quite simple, really. Karma just happens without any announcement or plan, like breathing after a sneeze or laughing, or like a thought that jumps into the mind, settles in for a brief ponder then evaporates at the first interruption. One doesn't know karma has happened until the time comes that an act committed affects other acts or persons thus causing one to fall into a meditation and then it dawns on the soul that karma happened."

"Have you experienced karma first hand?"

The coin warmed in Ravenz' hand as an element does when sitting in direct sunlight in summertime's noon heat. King Neptlyn's gold eyes glow platinum-white and the lips nearly parted unto voice.

"Three times"

Ravenz set the coin back into the cherry wood box and closed the lid. He blew out the flame watching the smoke curl in random swirls before vanishing from all sight. Only the scent of wick's char and melted wax lingers in the chamber's air.

"It happened first in the hour of our birth that Rhynn, being the first of us born, robust and perfectly healthy, was placed in the arms of our chloroformed mother who lay sleeping in anesthesia's stupor. The midwife waited for the afterbirth to expel, and it did but with me along with it drowning as oxygen smothered out of my lungs leaving me blue-black and near death. Perhaps I was already dead.But instead of hauling me away in a bowl buried in our placenta-jacket the midwife rushed to my aid resuscitating my heart to beating and oxygen flowing into my lungs. I squalled with her air in my lungs demanding food. She nursed me at her bosom. Because of her I live."

"But you call your mother, Queen Latezia and Her Majesty. Why?"

"Because that is who she is and I respect her station, is all."

"But you were raised in Falls House by four women."

"Rich people tend to hire stuff out, Qeyyapi, like wet nurses, nannies, governesses, tutors and all. I'm sure it was the same for Rhynn though he's never spoken of his caregivers and tutors. His upbringing must have been vastly complex and far-reaching for the preparation of ruling a kingdom seems overwhelmingly burdensome. But I was raised a kingdom's free child as much in the palace as in the valley and love both houses and all caring persons equally. But the best of it all were my nights in Mountainwing's suites when I would slide from my bed and stealth through hallways down stairwells across foyers to slip in Queen Latezia and King Breretyn's bedchamber.

"I would stand on skin-rugs in moonlight's glow streaming through windows illuminating the room and listen to their majesties' breathing in slumber as their heads dreamed on plump pillows in high canopy-bed. I even climbed the stepstool and watched my mother's queenly face, so serene did she lay there just sleeping. Then I would rush back to my bed and fall into my own dreams only to waken to chasing games down corridor through stairwell up hallway through passageway as Queen Latezia called after me chanting little nursery rhyme lines around and around in the courtyard over cobblestone pavement through hedge mazes around flower gardens catching me up in her arms."

Qeyyapi slipped from the mattress to stand at the porthole looking out to where dock's lights glimmer like flames' flickering casting reflections across the channel's glassy surface. Streets' luminescent lanterns light up like stars for miles lining avenues and boulevards, parks and cityscape's skyscrapers and high-rising penthouses. And lamps in hillside windows shine forth beckoning welcome comfort at day's end.

And how I sat at this little round window yearning for just this scene every day Bako's ship bobbed over the sea one more day closer…one more night closer…one more nautical mile after mile closer longing to behold the face of the one identical to the face loving Aotepi…and know…

"Come to our cabin's cozy bed, beautiful wife so I can say goodnight to your perfect moonbeam-eyes up close. You sit so far away there even in this cramped space. Tomorrow we sleep in the castle once Bako sails this ship up canal through channel and glides into lock to all the noisy pomp and fanfare bestowing on my seaway's Grand Opening."

Moonlight filtering through nightgown's sheer cloth quietly betrays the silhouette of a child's growing presence in Qeyyapi's womb.

"Wait there, Qeyyapi! I'm coming to *you* for the sight of you standing there in ultimate feminine state is a vision of artwork I simply can't see in any other light."

Qeyyapi turned, but not into a vacant space to cross rug-warm plank floor but into the arms of her husband, Ravenz and prince. His hands slid down her arms catching at her hips, fingertips coming to rest at the small of her back. An ear presses against her belly as her palm strokes the crown of her husband's royal head.

"Our daughter sleeps, Qeyyapi!"

"Why do you think the child is a girl, Ravenz? It very well could be your third son."

"You look different this time, Qeyyapi, not like the other times at all. You look...*rounder*...most lush everywhere you couldn't possibly be any *more* lush...twice as lush as you normally are. I have been meaning to speak to Physician Lizbett about this but I think twin sisters are slumbering in quiet waters there. We need to prepare ourselves for a multiple birth."

"I already know it, Ravenz. I hear tiny hearts' beating and little souls singing in my dreaming ears as my head sleeps on these pillows. My body's walls echo a tender symphony as one-trillion cells' multiply and divide in great Replication's business. A mother always knows the spirits dwelling in her belly, my beloved."

A Christmas Night

Bright spiral-striped-knitted overstuffed stockings hang from the mantle. Nubby nut-filled toes graze the hearth. Teddy bears and dolls sit on red and gold fringed rugs among painted wood rocking horses. A train's chugging engine pulls tiny toy cars around in circles on little steel tracks. Smoke puffs from its chimney and its headlight really glows.

Biscuits piled on silver trays like high haystacks sit beside crystal punchbowls bearing cinnamon-clove laced apple cider. Musicians in harlequin-sequined bell-trimmed jackets blow fifes and tap drums. Little lips toot shiny brass horns. Wintering orphans and royal cousins and all the court's children prance in a long line lead by none other than their masked Royal Majesties, King Rhynn and Prince Ravenz. Snow Fairy Queen Aotepi and Snowflake Princess Qeyyapi dance alongside animal-clad glitter-masked giggling child-gnomes.

"Follow the Jaguar King and Prince Raven Bird! Keep your eyes on them! We are heading down hallway through corridor across foyer into great Champagne Hall where the whole kingdom waits to see every Christmastime child glow!"

Snow falls softly against the windowpane turning otherwise black winter night into feathery-white. Holly berries shine crimson through boughs of green needle garlands gracing armoires and mirror's top. A gilded basket hosting pine cones rests by the hearth as a smoldering log crackles and hisses spitting cinders in the air behind brass appliqué fire-screen.

Latezia reached for Parqai's old snow globe turning it over in her hands. Glittering speckles float through invisible liquid to settle over tiny porcelain rooftop and spruce tree. The scroll in the music box turnscausing tinkling and chiming as its notches roll across fringed metal peg.

"It is still enchanting even after all these years, Your Majesty. The ancient carol never tires." Qiaona lifted a crystal vessel's spherical dipper watching precious perfume's tiny drop run to its tip.

"This fragrance tonight, or does another entice?"

Latezia reached for the stopper in Qiaona's fingertips holding the crystal wand beneath her nose.

Wedding bells ringing...Winter Solstice masked ball...Muskrat King-scamp and a teasing Snowflake Queen... 'Melt, little snowball between my warm paws...'

"This is the one, *especially* this one tonight, Qiaona! It is Winter Solstice, after all!"

Latezia closed her eyes to the soft tickle of the crystal wand brushing a trail of attar essence across her shoulders stopping briefly at nape of her neck.

"Shall I tie your mask's ribbons now, Your Majesty?"

"Tie them tightly so the mask won't fall over my nose when I spin away dancing beneath Champagne Hall's chandeliers! I will be the mystery beauty causing a guessing-game flutter among all court's dazzling guests! Oh, what fun I'll have! Such Christmas frolic waits this magical night! Run along, Qiaona! Dress yourself now! Don't be late! Champagne's impatient fizz'only wish is to tickle your nose!"

Qiaona curtsied then lifted her gaze from her bow to meet Latezia's powder-blue eyes.

"Good Christmas night, Your Majesty, Queen Latezia."

Latezia rose from the vanity and watched Qiaona slowly bow herself across the room.

"Dear sweet loyal Qiaona... long you have been with me waiting on me and loving me as a sister, listening to me as a saint silently listens still hearing my heart's words even when my lips remain closed."

The door closed with a hush shutting out all charade and holiday flourish happening in castle's halls enclosing Latezia unto utter silence within.

Latezia turned to the window, palms pressed against the frozen pane and eyes peering through feathery crystal frost-scape searching marble vagabond-traveler-king's jade-green gaze.

"Finally! We are alone, Breretyn, my husband and king! I thought she'd never leave! Tiz Christmas night, for Heaven's sake and our eternal togetherness-hour is nigh!"

"Ah, my beauty! My glorious snowflake queen! Float down to me here, damsel bride! We will swim once again in the fountain's basin beneath streams' silver mist as we did once...*the first time!*"

"Oh! Yes, yes, husband-king, I remember that well! But it is snowing tonight, Your Majesty! And I'm in my wedding gown still! What will everyone think?"

"Who cares what anyone thinks!

Tiz Christmastide, and I am king after all, most radiant bride!

Float, Latezia! Fly away from that dark silent room!

All enchantment happening in the castle this hour

Belongs to our sons and heirs,

Jaguar, King Rhynn

and

Ravenz Prince!

Come, tiz just a simple thing to do!

Float to me,

Damsel Latezia!"

"Oh, my! Great Heavens!

Is this *Heaven*, Breretyn, husband-king?"

"Ah, it is far more than mere Heaven, faire Snowflake-Queen! Look around! Look above!"

"I do see all now, Breretyn, your majesty, Muskrat-King!

The castle at Christmastime luminesces in snowfall's time...so white,

Our dancing Jaguar loving Aotepi

and Rhynn loving Qeyyapi

adoring their children,

And all in our kingdom

Dazzle at winter's eve play!"

"Tiz true, Latezia...my Latezia Beloved"

An eagle soars through firmament's halogen clouds above lazy river and thunderous waterfall to dive low circling over rippling lagoon before swooping above noisy highway to drift about a castle's tall turrets and cityscapes' rooftops up mountain's ridges to peak's rocky ledge. The sky king settles himself on granite, talons curling about a brave branch called from its seed's deep slumber unto daylight by way of Sun's patient urging.

Blazing white eyes blink shut in daylight's brilliance but upon opening come to focus their fovea on the face of a child whose small finger points to a statue of a gentlewoman sitting at the feet of a marble-king dressed in blacksmiths' garb clutching reins and gloves in one hand and the fingertips of this woman in the other. The king's gaze is on his queen's face as she peers up to his eyes. The sculptor carved a tear in the dress' hem and a flowing sash weaves about her ankles.Her free hand plays gently at the reflection pool's glassy surface as if to scoop water up in its palm. But it is the bangle dangling from the statue's wrist that has enraptured the child.

"What is the little animal's head I see there, Mamma? Look! Its eyes twinkle at me!"

"It's a jungle cat's face you see in Queen Latezia's bracelet! Legend has it that her husband, King Breretyn commissioned his court's artist, Parqai to carve it as a Christmas gift for this queen mother of his son, Rhynn, Jaguar and King."

"Hush, Mommy, look there!"

A small black shiny-feathered bird hopped along *Reflection Pool of Ancestors'* great stone rim stopping its journey before the child's curious gaze. Green eyes peer at mother and daughter a moment before opening its beak to drop a seed at the queen-statue's daintily-carved feet.

"Ah, it is your lucky day, Victoria for now you too, see the raven!" whispered the mother.

The fowl winked one eye at little Victoria then lifted its wings into short flight to perch a moment on Queen Latezia's smooth marble shoulder.

"The second part of this grand legend has it Queen Latezia gave birth to twin heirs in the palace one long-ago day! But the whole kingdom did not see the babies as two for they were born identical to one another in every way possible. All in King Breretyn's court and in the kingdom's villages saw little Prince Rhynn as possessing a fanciful mind for he seemed to be always at play with imaginary friends! But the queen-mother and king-father knew the truth at the heart of this tale, that the king's heirs were indeed *two* babies joyfully called Jaguar and Ravenz!

"And when they grew to be men the noble brothers, one and the other together ruled over Kings' Palace and all Peoples' Kingdom. 'Your Majesty, King Rhynn!' Subjects bow low at the waist. 'But, I am Ravenz,' and 'Hey, look! It's Prince Ravenz working about in our midst!' 'Alas, I'm simply Jaguar, King Rhynn at your service,' to the astonishment of all. And that is how the years passed for Ravenz, Jaguar and King."

Eagle sleeps